WINTER WARRIOR

To Charlotte,

WINTER WARRIOR

by

Bob Knapp

God Bless You,
Bob

A Blue Stone Media Publication

Published by Blue Stone Media

Cover by Alan Amrhine

ALSO BY BOB KNAPP:

THE DEVIL'S PALM

This novel is dedicated to my father, William G. Trimble, who led me to love the fine city of Enid and the great state of Oklahoma.

Chapter 1

Will Rogers Coleman awoke, or more accurately, opened his eyes. He had been lying awake, dreading this day as he dreaded every day. As far back into his sixteen years as he could remember, every day had been bad.

Opening his eyes didn't do much good. The room was pitch black. In another hour the first rays of sun would push their way through the sooty windows, signaling another dog day. Monday, February 4, 1935. How long had he lived here—about two weeks?

Hard, dull pain crept from his foot, clutched his shin, wrapped around his knee, then grabbed at his thigh. Not satisfied, the pain slithered along his back and neck, then squeezed his head in a slowly tightening vise.

He closed his eyes again, praying to finally reach his only remaining hope, a sleep wherein he no longer knew he existed-even if it was but for an instant.

It was hopeless.

With a steely grasp, he grabbed the back of his legs and pulled himself upright. He shivered as the tattered blankets fell away from his body. He yanked them off his legs. Then, with hands and arms doing most of the work, he lifted his legs, one at a time, from the bed. Once his feet found the icy floor, he bent forward, allowing his weight to settle onto them.

Searing pain shot up and down his body. In spite of the cold, sweat broke out on his face, trickled down his back and wet his palms. He thought of his pain as of two kinds, but fraternal twins. One the dull ache that bedeviled him at night, the other the searing agony by day. But those twins had been the easy part of his life.

Using the bed as support, he made his way to its foot. There, he found the chair into which he had cut an oval hole. His father had shown him how to use the tools and told him he was quite good, gifted, a natural carpenter. That was a father from another age; he wished he had him back. Beneath the hole sat his chamber pot.

It was routine. Next, he groped for clothes hung on nails in the wall. The struggle into his clothes shot waves of pain through his body—the hot twin again. He reached into his front pants pocket and touched the Prince Albert tobacco box containing a tattered newspaper picture of Fay Wray, the movie star, eliciting for him a vision of a dark-haired girl sitting in his English class. His pain faded.

He slid his crutches under his arms and grabbed the chamber pot by its handle, squeezing it and the handle of a crutch in one hand. The pot bumped against the crutch as he walked.

Involuntary tremors went up and down his body. Was it fear of the new day, or was it the hard cold of the room against the dampness of his body? He shrugged, setting off another spasm of pain.

His doorway curtains parted and revealed his mother carrying the kitchen lantern. Its mellow glow hinted at the attractiveness that had been hers. A teasing warmth drifted into his room from the kitchen.

She reached for the pot. "I'll carry that," she whispered. "It's snowing." She pulled her long black tresses back behind her head. Flickers of lamp light revealed streaks of gray at her temples.

Will muffled his voice. "No, Mom, don't."

The lid clattered as she tugged on the chamber pot handle. "Let go. You'll wake your pop."

"No." Will's iron grip held. He swung himself past his mother into the kitchen, the curtain brushing against his shoulder. The relative warmth of the kitchen enveloped him. He longed to rest there, but after emptying his pot in the outhouse he had to bring in more firewood before leaving for school. Without the kitchen cook-stove's fire, wind from the Oklahoma prairie would strip the heat from their little three-room house.

On the far side of the kitchen his parents' bedroom curtains parted and his father emerged, glowering, his black eyes piercing the gloom.

"There you went and done it," his mother whispered to Will.

"Done what?" His father, framed by the doorway, let his eyes dart over the room and then over them, measuring them. Simultaneously, he pressed his hand to his forehead, ran his palm back over his head and squeezed his neck.

Even in the dim light it was obvious that Charlie Coleman had slept in his clothes. They carried the rank stench of whisky and vomit; the stains on his shirt and pants verified their source. He answered his own question. "You're doing the boy's chores again, aren't you?"

"No, she's not, Dad. See, I'm carrying my can. And I'll be getting in the firewood."

"Just go back to bed, Charlie," his mother said. The quiver in her voice betrayed her attempt at bravery. "You're still tired. I'll bring you a cup of coffee as soon's it's done."

His father's chin jutted forward. "No woman's gonna tell me what to do." His nostrils flared in his prominent, hawk-like nose. A deep red crept over the bronze, pox-scarred complexion. He looked every bit the Choctaw.

He crossed to them in two quick strides. Will recoiled, stumbled and caught himself with the table.

Velma Coleman stepped between her husband and her son. Her eyes, large with fear, met her husband's. She gently pushed Will toward his bedroom. "Go into your room and finish getting dressed, Will."

Will trembled. He knew his father far too well. "I already finished."

"Velma, leave the boy be. He needs to see this." After a glance at Will, he coiled his right hand back, the muscles and veins in his arm standing out. His mother put up her arm and ducked. Will's father caught her arm with his left hand. His open hand struck her hard across her face. He twisted her arm behind her, then forced her body into his as he pushed up the arm.

Velma's face contorted with pain. "Charlie, don't." She pushed up on her toes, trying to relieve the stress on her shoulder.

Still forcing her into him with one arm, his father struck her again. "I'm not fooling with you, woman. You got your own work to do. Feeling sorry for him isn't loving him. How's the boy going to learn to take care of himself if you do everything for him?"

Will shrank at his father's onslaught. His fear thrust aside his wish for his father to beat him instead. He stood trembling, hating himself, knowing he ought to bring his crutch crashing down on his father's head. Instead, he gaped, paralyzed.

"Who can't take care of himself?" his mother said through bloody teeth. "Too bad you don't work, you lazy drunk." She pushed hard against his chest with her free hand.

Tears rimmed Will's eyes. He realized what was coming. His father released his mother and threw his ham-sized fist at her head. She ducked to the side and the blow landed on her neck. He swung with his other fist, catching her on the temple as she went down. She crumpled to the floor and didn't move.

His father smirked at him. "The lesson's over. Go ahead. Carry out your pot." His father grabbed a pitcher of water from the counter and slowly poured it over his mother's head and upper body. "Get up!" he said.

Will thought she wasn't going to move. His heart pounded in his chest and his face contorted as he held back tears. Finally, slowly, she pushed herself upright and leaned on one arm against the floor. Her hair, soaking wet, clung to her face and neck. Gritting her teeth, she struggled to her feet and glared at her husband. She wrapped her arms around herself and shivered. "What a sad day that was when I even laid eyes on you, Charlie Coleman."

"Go mop up your filthy kitchen. And see you don't do his chores for him—he'll never be a man." Will's father grabbed her arm to shove it, but she jerked her arm free of his touch.

"Don't ever forget, he's a Choctaw," his father said.

She tilted her head up. "And a Chickasaw."

"You half-breed!"

Will stood there, trembling, watching through tear blurred eyes as his mother painfully moved to retrieve the stringed mop from the corner.

Charlie feinted as if to strike his son. "What you staring at? Get busy."

Will jerked back, then made his way toward the door, past his father, struggling with the chamber pot.

"Hissss!" his father hissed into his ear and shoved him.

Will struggled to keep from falling, his legs and arms flailing in awkward spasms, trying to keep the pot from spilling as he and the crutches clattered to the floor. The pot clanged, then spilt its contents across the worn linoleum.

"You clumsy fool, add cleaning that up to your chores this morning," his father said, and gave the bucket a kick. It spun and rolled on its side. The stink struck Will full in the face.

"You still got plenty of time to get to school." His father glared until Will moved, then reentered his bedroom.

From his knees, Will sopped up the mess and wrung the rag over his pot as quickly as he could. In this position the pain up his legs and back was nearly unbearable. He saw his mother slowly mop the water from the floor where she had been drenched.

Will paused for a moment and listened. Soft sobs from his father drifted through the curtains of his parents' bedroom. Will went back to work. He had so much believed that after they arrived in Enid, things would be better.

* * *

Sleet, whipped by a nasty wind, stung Will's face and hands as he piled wood onto the carrier he had made. It was simply a sheet of canvas with a handle on each side. Will paused to face the eastern horizon.

Usually, by this time, a light grey sky, tinted with orange, blanketed the ebony eastern expanse. Then Uba Pisku, Our Father, the sun, would shoot out his golden arms, grasp the earth, and hoist himself up to sit and float in a clear blue lake to the other side of the world. Will saw that there would be no such journey today.

Nevertheless, Will began his ritual. His hand went to his breast and clasped his great-great grandfather's green jade amulet hanging about his neck, its triangular smooth shape familiar to his hand. His face pointed upward while his fingers ran unawares over the slithering silver snake clinging to its surface. Then he made his plea:

Uba Pisku, god of the sun, hear my plea. For my mother's sake, my dear mother, make my father stop hurting her. And I don't want to be a cripple. Take away my pain—it never gives up. And I want to . . . to run. But most of all, grant this one wish . . .

Will hung his head and sighed. Seconds ticked by. He could not, he did not have the faith to ask for this. Not even Pisku could grant it. He raised his head and finished the prayer: *Make this day one of fond remembrance. All is well. All is well. All is well.*

A pang of guilt struck him. His mother, Velma Coleman, would have cringed had she seen him pray to a pagan god. When they lived in Haskell County, she had taken Will to the Methodist meetings held in a school house.

He sighed and pulled the canvas carrier around the wood stacked in its middle, then with one hand grasped the two handles together along with the handle of his crutch and carried the wood into the house. His mother was drying and warming herself at the stove. He felt her eyes cling to him as he worked. He piled the wood next to the stove, opened the draft on the stovepipe, then fed a couple of lengths of wood into the firebox. He kissed his mother on the cheek. There was no use hurrying now; the other kids would be ahead of him in their trek to school.

* * *

The sleet, already several inches deep, looked like a blanket of snow. Will swung his body between his crutches. His feet left pairs of footprints several feet ahead of the previous pair. He paused and looked back down his quarter-mile long driveway at his tracks and imagined that the prints were the work of a giant rabbit, hopping to the warmth of a winter burrow. He glanced up the path to his doorway. His mother stood at the open door, watching him.

Relentless wind attacked Will's face and penetrated his old, wool coat. He shuddered. Sleet clung to the rags with which he had wrapped his shoes to keep cold out of the holes in the toes and soles. He had switched his rubber crutch tips for the pointed steel ones he had made for use on the compacted dirt roads in Enid's suburbs. The tips dug into the icy sleet.

The fields around his house had been painted bright white. He reached Walnut, the first street with a row of bungalows on each side. Their lawns and their roofs and those beyond were breath-taking in their whiteness. Everything looked clean and new. The air, though sharp, refreshed him. Perhaps the world was not such a bad place after all. Even his pain seemed washed away by the biting air and clean earth. Hadn't he handled the pain so far? He could face anything else that came his way!

He slipped into a rhythm that ate up long stretches of his two-and-a-half-mile jaunt. The exertion warmed him, and, after glancing back toward his house, he paused to roll up the sides of the watch cap his mother had insisted he wear.

He noticed that the small city tract surrounded by tall evergreen bushes at the corner of Grant and Randolph streets was now only two blocks away. He drew close enough to see that sleet had made its evergreen trees deceptively lovely. The wind tore at the trees, but did not dislodge the sleet from their lacy leaves.

Of all days, why could he not have gotten an early start? His heart hammered in his chest and throat. He paused to tighten his army-green backpack and wished he could be at home. Perhaps, considering the weather, they would not be there. He saw no movement. The only sound he heard was the rattle of sleet, the swoosh beneath his feet, and the creak of his crutches as he swung along.

Chapter 2

Will smelled tobacco smoke. But there were no voices, no footsteps, no rustle of clothing or shuffle of book bags. Still, he was certain they were watching him.

He quickened his pace. Maybe they were too busy smoking. Or they really weren't there. Maybe, because of the weather, they would leave him alone.

He was adjacent to the lot now. If he could make it the hundred feet to the corner, to Randolph, the main street into town from that neighborhood, they would not bother him. A passing motorist might see them attacking a . . . a . . . a . . .cripple.

He could barely think the word. In the presence of his father he had once said, "but I'm a cripple," and his father had lashed out, turned him over his knee. He was six years old and had spilled his milk.

His mother had started to clean it up. "Don't you dare," his father said. "He can clean up his own messes. He's old enough."

"But I'm only a cripple," Will had said.

That's when his father grabbed Will by the arm, pulled his suspenders off his shoulders and yanked down his pants. "Don't ever say that again," his father roared. He turned Will over his knee and paddled him with his hand. "Don't you cry," he shouted, then beat him until he did. "Never use that word again!"

His mother had stood there, sobbing, while her hands wrung her apron.

That was the first real physical punishment his father had meted out to him. Those were the Haskell County days, the days when they still had their Jersey cow.

Will's eyes eased shut for a moment and he saw himself sipping a glass of milk. He could almost feel the cool rich taste.

But that's what people called him. He had even heard his teachers, when they thought he couldn't hear them, refer to him as "the cripple." That's why girls weren't interested in him, why he couldn't talk to the girl in English class, or why he could never have a girlfriend.

From the corners of his eyes, Will scanned the evergreens at the top of the short embankment for a glimpse of a jacket, a face, movement, anything. Nothing.

A snowball whizzed by his nose. Another crashed into his head, catching him in mid-swing. One slammed into his arm, then another struck his head and tilted his knit cap onto his forehead.

Will shuffled his feet and crutches to maintain his balance. Loud guffaws came from behind the bushes. Through ice crystals clinging to his brows and eyelashes he saw arms winding up and slinging their missiles. He swung himself forward again, and another fusillade of snowballs sailed from behind the bushes, hitting him hard. A ball, its center a core of ice, struck him full in the face, like a boxer's fist. He planted his crutches in the white crust ahead of him to keep from falling.

His father's voice rang in his head. *Choctaw braves don't cry.*

He felt a trickle, wet and warm, run from his nose and across his upper lip. He wiped it with the back of his hand. He held it up to his face and examined it. There was a red smear. He sniffed hard to stop the flow of blood.

A boy appeared from between the tall evergreen bushes at the far end of the lot and bounded down the bank to the street corner. Looking up and down Randolph Avenue, he declared, "All clear," and then glanced back up Grant Street, behind Will. The boy remained at his post as two boys burst from behind the evergreens and down the embankment. One on each side, they grabbed Will by the arms and dragged him toward the lot. Will clung to his crutches while his feet plowed a furrow in the sleet behind him.

They struggled to get him up the slippery slope. A broad-shouldered boy pushed his way through the branches. "You ninnies," he said, and grabbed Will by the front of his jacket and yanked him up the bank and through the boughs. It was Sam.

Sam, who was in three of his classes, also wore bib overalls like his. But Sam's looked new. Sam had been the first student to ask him about himself when Will entered Enid High School.

The rows of evergreens encircling the lot knocked down the wind, giving the plot an eerie calm. A half-circle of sneering faces under newsboy hats faced Will. The smell of tobacco permeated the air.

"Stand here," Sam said. He supported Will while Will squared his crutches. Will looked at each of the boys. All, like himself, except for one, LeRoy, were sophomores at Enid High School, and younger than Will. He recognized them from his Algebra I class. Only one, Wade, didn't dwarf him.

They tightened their circle. Wade, the same boy who had scouted the corner for passers-by, took a drag from a cigarette held between thumb and forefinger, then removed his cigarette from between his lips and flicked the ash from its end with his remaining two fingers. Two other boys followed suit. The smoke rose above their heads and joined the vapor from their breaths.

Will watched them with fascination. His father never made such a display.

A boy cursed as he puffed on his smoke. "It's wet." He pinched the ends of the cigarette and put it into his jacket pocket. "I'll let it dry." There were sniggers.

LeRoy Mattison, a junior, walked from the dark shadows formed by two large trees into the circle. The circle parted to allow him to stand next to Will. LeRoy glared at the circle. The grins collapsed. Somebody coughed. Falling sleet bounced off their leather boots, making ticking sounds.

LeRoy liked letting people know that he had been thrown out of private school—the thrown-out part, especially. He was a head taller than everyone else. His woolen suit and short felt hat set him apart as someone whose father was making lots of money in spite of the hard times. He was the only one who sometimes got better grades than Will. LeRoy should have been in Trigonometry, but was in Algebra I with the rest of them. Math was not LeRoy's strong suit. And, for some strange reason, he was also retaking sophomore English.

LeRoy turned to face Will and asked, "How about a smoke?" then nodded to the boy at his right, Emery, who had red skin like Will's.

Emery, emotionless, reached beneath his jacket into a shirt pocket and pulled out a sheaf of paper, three inches square, Will guessed. He watched intently as Emery held the paper between three fingers to form a channel down its center, then tapped a row of dried brown flakes from a small package into the channel. Deftly, he rolled the paper around the tobacco to form a small cylinder—a cigarette, then ran his tongue along one edge of the paper to seal it. He tapped one end of the cigarette into the palm of his hand, put the cigarette between his lips and struck a wooden match against the flint on the side of the matchbox. The match flared. The smell of sulphur struck Will's nostrils. Emery quickly cupped the match to protect the flame and held it to the end of the cigarette. A blast of wind made it up and over the trees and snuffed out the match.

"Here, try this." LeRoy's hand, holding a silver cigarette lighter, made its way to the end of the cigarette. His thumb twirled the flint wheel twice and the lighter flared. Emery worked his cheeks, then removed the cigarette and expelled a stream of smoke from his mouth. LeRoy snapped the lighter lid closed, then palmed the lighter so that everyone could see the fancy engraved "M" in its side.

"Have a smoke," LeRoy said, his own cigarette wagging up and down between his lips as he spoke. He took the cigarette from Emery and held it out to Will. "Welcome to Enid High. If you stay away from my girl, you'll do fine." A crooked grin crossed his face. "Like I need to tell you that."

Will stared wide-eyed at LeRoy. Someone guffawed.

LeRoy put the cigarette to Will's lips.

Will rolled his lips tight.

"Come on, you'll like it. Nothing like you ever had." He pushed the cigarette against Will's lips, waiting, staring back at Will, a half grin on his face.

Will relaxed his lips and held the cigarette. Finally, maybe, he would be accepted. He hadn't received this much attention in the three weeks he had been attending Enid High.

"At-a-boy," LeRoy said.

The boys snickered as Will puffed on the smoke.

"No, no, don't blow on it, draw it in, like this." LeRoy demonstrated, then removed his cigarette and pursed his lips to aim a stream of smoke skyward. "You do it."

Will's hand trembled as he held the cigarette to his lips and sucked on it. He suddenly coughed; his body convulsed. Pain racked his legs. The cigarette shot from his mouth and fell into the deepening sleet.

"Hey, those things cost about two cents apiece," Emery said. He groped for the smoke in the sleet at Will's feet. He cursed as the cigarette came apart and spread the tobacco, its flakes stark against the white blanket.

"Emery, don't let him get away with it," somebody said.

Emery rose, glaring. "Now you've done it." He thrust the heels of his hands hard against Will's shoulders, driving him back. "You white double-crossing snake!"

Will tried to remain upright, but tumbled awkwardly to the ground. Will knew what Emery meant. Emery was a Comanche; Will was a Choctaw, considered one of the Five Civilized Tribes—and traitors.

The boys laughed as Will struggled, using his crutches to pull himself up. He clenched his teeth as his legs shook with pain.

"I want two cents for the gasper." Emery paused, waiting for Will to act. Will's silence infuriated Emery. "I said, I want my money."

Will had never so much as held two cents of his own in his entire life. Two cents were a fortune. He was astounded that he was asked for it. He looked blankly at Emery.

This time Emery shoved Will ruthlessly, driving him onto his back, causing his head to strike hard as he fell full length onto the cold ground.

A black shadow slipped over Will's eyes, leaving him in darkness. When he was able to see, Emery was bent over him, glaring.

"You're going to pay me back," Emery said with such ferocity that spittle sprayed across Will's face. Will saw a circle of faces around Emery, staring down at him.

Someone kicked him in the thigh. "Yeah, give Emery a snipe or his money."

"Can't you see he doesn't have any money?"

"Emery, I'll give you your two cents," LeRoy said.

"Okay then, Will, what's the idea getting those A's in algebra class?"

"Yeah. We can't have that."

Hands reached down and brought him to his feet. He tottered. They held him upright.

"No moron Injun is smart enough to get an A," someone snarled.

"Especially a crippled Injun."

They bounced him back and forth between them until he crumpled onto the slush by their feet. The wet seeped through his clothing. He shivered.

Someone kicked his crutches out of reach. He crawled toward them. The pain in his legs and back collapsed him face down into the sleet. In spite of the pain, he got back to his hands and knees again, inching toward the crutches. He refused to cower at their feet.

"Look at the snake. You're right, Emery. A crippled snake."

Hands, impatient for him to get up, yanked him to his feet.

A boy gripped his jacket at the throat, holding him. "Tell us about the math, snake. You cheatin'?"

Will pressed his lips together. Everything was a blur; it was happening so fast.

Choctaw braves don't cry. "A's 'cause I'm smart. Get off me!" He tried to concentrate on the eyes of the bully opposite him. He couldn't recognize anyone anymore.

Another boy squeezed his face in his hand. "You better fail today's exam." He shoved Will's face hard.

Math came easy to Will. If he missed something, he figured it out on his own.

"Yeah!" they all cried. One boy clutched Will's jacket sleeve and yanked upward as they yet again pushed Will to the ground. It made a ripping sound as the sleeve was torn at the shoulder.

They laughed.

"That's enough!" He recognized LeRoy's voice. "But remember what I told ya about my girl."

Big Sam grabbed him by the coat and pulled him to his feet, then handed him his crutches.

A horn oogahed on Grant Street from on the other side of the evergreens, bringing their attention to the chugs of a waiting Studebaker.

"We get a ride today. It's LeRoy's dad. Let's go." They scampered around, gathered their book bags and ran for the car.

"Don't forget the exam," Emery warned Will. Then, while holding his hat to keep it from being pulled from his head by the branches, disappeared between the evergreens.

Will bit his lower lip.

Choctaw braves don't cry.

Warm drops ran from the corners of his eyes across cold cheeks. He hated himself.

Chapter 3

His shivering would not stop.

Will went to the back of the lot where the embankment leading down to the street was the lowest, barely a foot-and-a-half high. Putting two crutches in one hand, he grasped the end of an evergreen branch and attempted to step backwards down the sleet-covered bank. He fell anyway, but not hard. Already cold and wet, he scarcely cared. He used his crutches to get back up onto his feet, shrugged his shoulders to adjust his backpack, and tugged at the torn sleeve in an attempt to pull it up to its place at the shoulder.

In spite of the day's brightness, gloom encircled him. The wind, whistling down the long, straight road, beat at Will's back and peppered him with sleet. Icy fingers found their way around his backpack and through his jacket, seeking his very bones.

He had to move, or soon he would be unable to.

He made his way the remaining fifty feet to Randolph Avenue and headed east toward school. Randolph had a sidewalk, but it was not visible beneath the mounting sleet. More than once, Will slipped and caught himself, racking his joints with pain. The pointed tips of his crutches worked well on the dirt roads of his neighborhood, but tended to slip on the cold concrete beneath the layer of white.

Will concentrated on each swing of his legs and the placement of his crutches. Shorter strides kept his center of gravity over the crutches and he slipped less. The occasional passing car, leaving long furrows in the icy white of the street, barely nicked his consciousness.

Everything was a blur of white and ice and cold. The sleet rattled on his backpack. His feet felt like blocks of ice, but that pain was nothing compared to the hurt inside. His mind replayed the boys leaving him behind. They had to know how tough it was for him to walk in this weather. The vision of them running gleefully for the car struck at his heart. He didn't know which was greater— his desire to hurt them, or his fear that the abuse and ostracism would escalate if he got revenge. Besides, he really had no desire to hurt anyone. What he really wanted were friends—and a certain girl. And how could he get back at them? Even if he were whole and the strongest of the bunch, together they would overwhelm him. Why did they hate him so much? Sam didn't seem quite so bad. Will was unsure of LeRoy. He ran the gang. And LeRoy was her boyfriend—Irene, the girl in his math and English classes.

His mind said, "Hurry, hurry," but each time the crutches poked through the sleet, he tested their grip on the unseen ground.

He had always been first to school so that he could be seated in the classroom when the other students arrived, talking and laughing. Then he didn't have to feel their eyes on him as he made his way down the long row of wooden desks, or have to put up with feet thrust into his path and then jerked back at the last second, or hear the whispered, "Injun boy," as he passed by.

Ordinarily, his worn-out clothes brought snickers. They joked about his holey shoes, threadbare shirts, faded bib overalls and even the green army surplus backpack. Nobody had a backpack; they carried their books under one arm or lugged a book bag as a display of their manhood.

And now he was wet, muddy and disheveled. He would be forced to get a late pass from the office, then face the scorn of his teacher for interrupting. At least his torn coat would be in his locker and they couldn't razz him about it.

Klachink-klachink-klachink. Will looked up. A car with chains on its rear wheels passed—a rare sight. Even under these slippery conditions, chains were hardly needed on the flat terrain of Enid's streets. He stopped and watched in fascination, temporarily forgetting his pain and misery.

When he turned to resume his struggle, he realized where he had stopped and was stunned, nearly disoriented. His heart thumped in his chest and the blood pounded in his ears. How had he gotten here?

Usually he prepared himself, even crossed the street to keep from staring and to keep from being seen, maybe to prevent himself from going to her door.

But here he was. The next house, it was hers.

It was very much like all of the other houses on the street--small, one and a-half-stories, gable end facing the front, and a wide porch on the right side. The house rested on a modest front lawn split by a concrete walkway. Long curtains graced long windows reaching nearly to their floors. Each front door had a round doorbell button next to it. All of the houses were well kept.

But her house always seemed to jump out at him. Its white was whiter, its curtains more graceful, its lawn neater, its porch more inviting. He was unable to explain why—they just were.

It had been his first day at Enid High when he saw her walk into their English class. Maybe it was her thick rich hair that got his attention. It was almost as black as his own, but had soft waves that flowed over her shoulders, and shimmered when she moved. Her eyes, which were large and a deep brown, had scanned the room. They did not glint with recognition of anyone yet there, and she chose the second desk from the front that, fortunately, was in the row next to his. Anytime he looked up, he could see her. She smoothed her skirt beneath her and slipped gracefully into the seat.

When she turned her head, he caught a glimpse of her face and the deep complexion that reminded him of the dark honey his mother had brought with them from Haskell County located at the southeastern tip of Oklahoma. The honey had been rich and sweet and comforting; it had reminded him of a life that he almost loved.

From that first day, after his eyes had feasted on her—on Irene—his eyes' appetite for more was never satisfied. Sometimes, when Mrs. Johnson, their English teacher, was writing on the blackboard, Irene would turn and look at LeRoy, who sat behind him. Now, when Will caught himself leaning so that he could gaze past the five wooden desks and their occupants, he would jerk himself upright lest she catch him staring.

One time, so he had thought, Irene had turned around and had looked directly into his eyes and smiled. He had been sure she was not looking at LeRoy. Will had looked away. The heat rose up his neck, flushed his face and burned his ears. Had she felt his eyes upon her? Would she think of him as some kind of oddball? A peeping Tom? But she had smiled. Was she laughing at him? Maybe she liked him.

His mother had told him he was handsome—and he had seen girls look at him before. But he had thought they stared because his crutches made him a curiosity. He knew everybody thought he was a freak. Maybe that wasn't the reason girls looked.

But what else would a mother tell her son?

He hunched behind the person in front of him, pretending to write, but still cast glances in Irene's direction. Not until the teacher called on him was he aware that the lesson had passed him by. He mumbled an answer; the class laughed. He would have preferred to shrink into his seat, but he willed himself to sit tall while the teacher admonished him for not paying attention.

From then on, he had been more diligent, although he still had to remind himself of why he was there.

Unlike most of the white crystalline landscape surrounding him, the sleet around her house lay undisturbed—not even the footprints of a rabbit had marred its surface. This told him Irene was still in the house and, if she was going to school, must soon leave. His heart increased its pounding. Usually, he was nearly inside the school by this time. Now he might unexpectedly meet her.

He panicked, but what he dreaded was also his greatest hope. His crutches suddenly felt slippery in his hands. He realized he had been standing rock still, staring at her house.

Embarrassment prickled his scalp and then flooded his body. What if she had looked out of a window and she had seen him? He sprang forward, forgetting about the unsure footing. He had to get away. If she ever got close, he knew she would not be able to bear him.

He reached the walkway that divided her lawn, or rather where he knew it lay, when her front door flew open. "Will, wait," Irene called, her voice strangely muffled by the blanket of sleet and the close, moist air.

He stopped. His throat went dry. He didn't know she even knew his name. He tried to scurry away, but his body would not respond.

Her dark eyes met his; he hadn't realized how beautiful they really were. Maybe it was the blue wool coat and the blue scarf flung round her collar that brought out her eyes. Her lips framed a broad smile. The pounding in his ears drowned out the sound, but he saw her lips form the words, "Wait for me."

Will watched her place each booted foot—carefully, lightly—on each of the icy steps. The boots were a shiny black with black laces. He looked down at his own shoes and reflexively curled his big toes down so that they would not stick out. His eyes darted around, looking for some escape, but once she stepped off the last step, she practically pranced to the street, holding her book bag.

She came right up to him, beaming. "Oh, isn't this wonderful?" She looked into his face, then waved her arm in a wide gesture. "It's so beautiful, and exciting. I just love it."

Will barely nodded his head and managed a weak, "Hello, Irene," through his constricted throat. His tongue felt large and awkward. He had never said her name out loud before. It sounded good coming from between his lips. It emboldened him a bit. He wanted to say a lot more, but instead hoped she would not notice his clothes. He wished with all his might that he did not need crutches. Then he would . . . there was so much that would be different.

"I'm sorry," she said, suddenly serious. "I guess this weather is difficult for you, with your crutches and all."

He flinched at the mention of his crutches. "Actually, it hardly makes any difference. I'm used to it." But it was never easy. "You better hurry ahead, or you'll be late. Don't wait for me."

"Momma said I could ride the bus today, because of the weather. The bus will be along soon." Her eyes held his, smiling again. "Ride with me."

Will's eyes pleaded for understanding. He couldn't tell her the truth, that he had no money, that he was too poor. Or especially that he didn't want to ride with her, a lie. What could be better than sitting next to her on the bus, cozy and warm? But his clothes were ragged, wet, dirty, even torn. Sit next to her? With her beautiful hair and face and clothes? Her fragrance alone made him feel weak. He could imagine how he must smell to her. She would be so repulsed; she would never even look at him again.

"I like walking," he said. It was true, in a way.

"I've got enough for two fares." She paused, then continued when he didn't respond. "And it'll be warmer after school. I can walk home, then. Momma doesn't have to know."

"I couldn't take your other fare." He meant it. Not hers.

"Come on. The stop is on that corner across the street." Her hair swept her shoulders as she turned to look the short distance down the block.

She turned back, then reached toward his arm. He flinched. If he could have done it quickly enough, he would have stepped back to protect her from himself.

But she grabbed the top of his coat sleeve. "What happened to your coat?" She tugged it up to meet his jacket's shoulder. "I guess you have a hard time staying upright in this snow." She gave the sleeve another tug. "There, that's better."

She had actually touched him! His sleeve, his threadbare, wet coat. He stood stock still, savoring the lingering sensation, reliving the image of her gloved hand on his arm. He shivered, but not from the cold.

With a single glance he noted she had full lips that surrounded even white teeth, all framed by smooth cheeks that glowed red from the cold. Her smile was beautiful. His eyes went back to her hair, the same hair he stared at every day, but was now so close. He wanted to finger it. Instead, he gripped his crutches and looked down at their shoes, shoes that nearly touched each other. But so different.

He looked back up, smiling. He felt lighter. The gloom lifted; the day brightened. "Thanks," was all he managed, meaning the tug she had given his sleeve. He wanted to thank her for more, even more than the offer to pay his fare. He wanted to tell her about the feelings her nearness brought him. His arms ached to reach out; his throat tightened. In spite of his desires, his arms would not move. No words came.

But then an icy tingle shot down his spine, a cold dread deep from within. It ran to his core and formed a knot—a suspicion—her motivation was solely charitable. She felt sorry for him; she was kindhearted. He was no more than a stray kitten lost in a storm.

No. That's not it. He pushed the fear down. He told himself she really liked him. His heart still beat hard, but it had lost its zing.

"Here comes the bus." She turned to run, but stopped to look back. "Hurry. No, don't hurry; I'll tell the driver to wait."

Will shook his head. "No, don't wait for me." He watched her cross the street, and then swung his legs between his crutches to continue on his way. He looked up in time to see a boy he had seen before, with books tucked under one arm, run out of the house near the bus stop. The boy smiled and grabbed Irene's book bag. She leaned past the boy and waved at Will before the bus hid them from view.

The bus waited, but Will didn't cross the street. His eyes searched the windows of the bus. He thought someone waved. Someone with a blue coat. He allowed himself to dream. A smile affixed itself to his face. Then the bus was gone.

Will hummed aloud as he swung along in rhythm to the tune:

Good night Irene, good night Irene,
I'll see you in my dreams.

Within what seemed a short time he arrived in front of a large brick building. Eight steps, covered with ice, led to its main entrance. Someone had spread cinders on the ice. Over the doorway were the words, "ENID HIGH SCHOOL."

Will smiled.

Chapter 4

Relief washed over him. The hissing from the steam radiator at the entrance whispered a promise to strip the cold from his clothes and caress his skin. And he was safe here, not like at home. He pulled himself and his crutches the remainder of the way through the doors. They rattled shut behind him. He sniffed the distinctive school smell, then sighed and paused to savor the warmth.

He surmounted the sixteen marble steps leading up to the main corridor. The sound of his crutches tapping the polished marble floor rolled down the hall, alternating with the shuffle of his feet, feet like blocks of ice that could hardly feel the floor.

"Office," announced the sign hanging over the door down the hall to the left. Usually it went unnoticed, but now it jumped out at him, arousing a dread that had been planted through his observation that wayward students were sent there. Tardy pupils always entered class with head hanging and eased an office late slip onto the teacher's desk.

Will bumped his way through the office door to the counter. The prim secretary, busy at her oak desk, asked pleasantly, "May I help you?" but when she looked up and saw Will's wet attire, she recoiled. She managed to force a smile.

"I'm late," Will said.

She glanced at the big round clock high on the wall across from her. "First period is nearly over. Now you must see Dr. Grover before I give you a late pass." A genuine smile crossed her face, one that reinforced Will's unease. "Write your full name and class, along with the time that you came in, on that chart behind you."

Will found a piece of chalk on the ledge and wrote, his hand stiff with cold, on the small blackboard attached to the wall next to the entrance. He stood there and waited.

"And it's 9:10, not 8:50. Use the eraser and fix it, Mr. Coleman."

"Sorry," Will muttered, and wrote "9:10."

"You can have a seat on that bench along the wall. Dr. Grover will call for you."

On the far side, behind the secretary, was a door with a translucent window on which was printed, "Dr. Hiram Grover, Principal." Will was startled by the paddle, hanging from a nail in the door frame, in which were burned the words in fancy print, "Board of Education." He saw the darkened form of a head moving behind the door's glass. The door opened and the head became LeRoy.

LeRoy! LeRoy, one of the top students in the Junior class misbehaved in school? LeRoy, to whom Irene's heart belonged? Will realized he was smiling when the secretary announced Will's presence to the man behind LeRoy. "Dr. Grover," she called him.

Dr. Grover's eyes, black and bulging, lit upon him. He made no change in his expression.

Undoubtedly, every student that Dr. Grover had ever disciplined wore tattered, worn, wet clothing and was cold to the bone—except LeRoy.

Will didn't flinch.

"Wait, LeRoy," Grover said.

LeRoy, now at the door to the hallway, stopped. He carried a small stack of papers.

"While I have a talk with . . .," Grover looked at the blackboard, "Mr. Coleman." His eyes went back to Will's face.

Will stared back.

Dr. Grover pointed to his open door and nodded in that direction. "Mr. Coleman." He followed Will into the room.

"Have a seat," Grover said. Sleet from his open window rattled on his steam radiator, then sizzled. Grover closed the door, then the window, and then sat behind his desk. The room was at least ten degrees cooler than the outer office. He leaned forward across his desk and looked squarely into Will's face.

"Mr. Coleman, you're new here, aren't you?" Dr. Grover didn't wait for an answer. "Enid High School is one of the best in Oklahoma. No, the best. And that is because of its students. It's simple—we listen to our instructors, cooperate with fellow students, do our homework and . . ." Dr. Grover rose slightly from his chair to push his face even closer to Will's, "and arrive on time." He then sat back in his chair, and with a slow turn of his head, focused his eyes on the wall opposite the window.

Will waited. Then, carefully, he glanced back and forth between the wall and Dr. Grover, finally allowing his own eyes to find and settle on a paddle hanging there. It was a duplicate of the one on the doorframe outside Dr. Grover's office.

Finally, when Dr. Grover spoke, Will found him staring at him again. "Very, very seldom do our students need any disciplining from me. It's better for everyone if we never have to meet."

Will shivered. He wondered if he had ever stopped shivering, or was it because of Dr. Grover?

Dr. Grover's eyes seemed to move with deliberate purpose. They never left Will's face while his hands gathered paper and pen. The pen dipped into the inkwell, and only then did his eyes move to the paper. He scratched out a brief note, folded it, placed it in an envelope, then addressed it with a single line that started with Mister, licked the flap with his tongue and sealed it. Between the envelope being upside down and Grover's handwriting, Will could not read the name.

Without saying another word, Grover rose and went out the door, not looking back at Will. "LeRoy," he called, "get Mr. Coleman a late pass, then take him and this envelope down to Mr. Wyzowaty. Then deliver those papers."

Will painfully followed LeRoy down the hall. His feet, now thawing, felt as if gripped by a giant vise while being shot with sharp, hot darts.

LeRoy, never looking behind him, said, "Dr. Grover is a little strange. Don't let him bother you."

At the far end of the hall they faced a forbidding, heavy metal door with a large lever for a handle. The door's crude appearance contrasted with the warm oak and marble of its surroundings. Printed in large black letters on its gray paint was simply, "No Admittance."

Will, ready to turn back, looked at LeRoy. Shocked that he would dare enter, he watched as LeRoy set the papers, envelope and late pass on the floor and grasped the lever. Then, with two hands, he put his weight onto the lever and pushed the door sideways. It rumbled as it slid open. Will could see that the door was hung on the inside from large grooved wheels that ran on an overhead track.

A volcanic smell and wave of heat met them. Will heard a distant roar. An overhead light barely revealed a passage and the concrete steps leading downward. "The boiler room," LeRoy said, motioning down the steps with his head. "Go ahead." He nodded again and handed Will the envelope. "For Mr. Whiz—Mr. Wyzowaty."

Will hesitated. "Don't forget to bring the papers."

"I'm not coming."

Will, uneasy, turned his head to look at LeRoy.

LeRoy leaned in the opposite direction against the big handle. "Go ahead. It's okay. I'm busy— gotta deliver the papers."

The door rolled behind Will, then clanged into place, cutting off the light from the hallway. The roar and the heat and the stench became stronger. Will paused while his eyes adjusted to the dim light, then placed the tips of his crutches on the first step below him and lowered his feet.

He stopped and twisted to look back at the heavy metal door, then stared at the letter and late pass.

He wondered what the letter said. He felt like he was entering a dungeon. Maybe he was to be locked up. Or Dr. Grover had put Mr. Whiz in charge of paddling, or even some kind of torture. Would anybody know if he turned around and went to class? He could write the time on the late pass himself.

He sighed and with his crutches reached down to the next step.

The walls on each side of the stairway and the sloping ceiling blocked his view of the room below. He worked slowly downward until he got to a landing that faced a wall. A dingy room opened to his left.

The roar, stronger now, was joined by hissing steam. Heat assaulted him. Soot and coal dust coated what had been white asbestos covered pipes. Light from several bare bulbs hanging from the ceiling did little to ease the gloom.

In front of him stood what looked like two throbbing monsters, each squatting on top of a short powerful leg. Into each opened a large funnel that looked every bit like a mouth stretched wide to be fed. Where the funnel met the leg, a blue-orange glow spilled from the joint, like a baby drooling its food.

Evidently, the beast had a voracious appetite; a man was working relentlessly to feed it, throwing shovelful after shovelful of black coal into is maw. The beast's white arms, which stuck out all over the place, clanged and clunked as steam, its life blood, rumbled through them, ready to squeeze the man should he slacken his pace, not allowing him a second to notice his visitor.

Stuck into the side of the leg was a large pipe with a bowl at its end. The beast sucked air through this pipe. The bowl was a huge electric fan that helped the animal get enough air. Will realized that this was the source of much of the roar. He felt intimidated, yet excited.

To Will's right was a ceiling-less room—a little room within a larger room—its wall a continuation of the landing wall he had faced. Near the outer corner was a door with a clear window in its upper half upon which had been stenciled with black paint, "Sigmund Wyzowaty, Custodian." Around the corner, the wall had embedded mesh windows in its upper half that looked out on the boilers. Much brighter light, from bulbs hung low into the room, shone through the windows onto the concrete floor.

With his entire body aching from its rapid thawing, Will waited and watched.

Perhaps the man had satisfied the monster's appetite, for he finally turned and peered over spectacles resting at the end of his nose. "Hello there, son. I didn't see you standing there." He removed his glasses with one hand while pulling a large blue handkerchief from his rear pocket with the other. He mopped his face.

"You must be Will. I've seen you around the building. Heard a lot of good things about you." He didn't try to explain how he knew him, and

Will didn't ask; he was the only cripple in the school. Will's hands shook as he held out the envelope.

The man took it. "You hurting?"

Will shrugged.

The man replaced his glasses, looked at the envelope, removed his striped cotton hat and ran the handkerchief over his nearly bald head. He walked back over to a boiler and hung his handkerchief on a valve handle. "That'll be dry in a couple of minutes." He refocused on the envelope. "Yep—Mr. Wyzowaty—that's me. Jack of all trades, master of none."

A pipe clanged and Will jumped. Wyzowaty appeared not to notice, but said, "It's only a big teapot." He tore open the envelope and read its contents. "Just what I figured." He glanced at Will's feet. "Go on in there and have a seat." He pointed inside the inner room at a wooden chair with a cane seat.

"Yes, sir." Will did as he was told while Wyzowaty disappeared into the back of the larger room. Will's eyes automatically went to the door frame. He shuddered; there hung a paddle, a duplicate of Dr. Grover's. Was one on every door frame in the school? He hadn't noticed them before. He wondered if the note told Wyzowaty to discipline him for his tardiness. The punishment shouldn't be too bad; the custodian seemed nice enough.

To distract himself, he allowed his eyes to wander about the room, which was neatly organized. A fair-sized wooden desk with a lamp hanging over it dominated the center rear of the room. "In" and "Out" boxes stacked with papers stood on the desk corners like soldiers on guard. Pens, like miniature rifles, and an ink pot—a cauldron of boiling oil—waited between them. A round oak-framed clock hung on the opposite wall. On the adjacent wall was a framed certificate. From his seat Will could read its largest print, "Oklahoma Agricultural and Mechanical College" and "Certificate of Custodial Operations." A large floor fan aimed air toward the ceiling. Bookshelves filled with books and technical manuals, an army green four-drawer file cabinet, three chairs—counting the one behind the desk, and a large RC Cola wall calendar completed the furnishings. Will realized there was something missing in the room—coal dust.

There was more clanging, but with a different tenor, like galvanized buckets. The outside room brightened a bit, a door banged shut, a pause, the door banged again. He heard water running into a bucket.

Was the water meant for him? Was Wyzowaty the school's torturer? What kind of punish . . .

Will gathered his crutches and pulled himself up. He had to get out!

"Whoa, young man." Wyzowaty, with a slight curl on his lips, was in the doorway lugging a large bucket of water. Ice floated on the water. "I didn't take that long, did I?" He nodded at the chairs behind Will. "Sit back down there and take it easy."

Will continued to face him, wanting to flee. His eyes pleaded. He had more than enough pain in his life.

"Please, Mister, let me go." He attempted to control his trembling. His father had given him another charge—*A Choctaw shows no fear.*

Wyzowaty looked puzzled. "Already. Why?"

Will tried to slip by him. *He expects me to enjoy whatever horrors he's planned!* "I have to go to class."

Wyzowaty stood firmly in the doorway. "There's plenty of time before your next class." His gaze strayed to the folded letter on his desk. "We've got to follow Dr. Grover's orders."

Will shuffled back to his seat. He eyed Wyzowaty as he knelt in front of him, then unlaced and gently removed Will's shoes and socks, all the while shaking his head and saying, "Tsk, tsk, tsk. My, my, my. My your foot's cold! It hurts, doesn't it, son?"

Will stared at the bucket of ice water. "What's that? I'm already cold," he said, although he was feeling warmer.

Wyzowaty didn't answer. He lifted Will's foot while pulling the bucket over in front of him. Will stiffened. Wyzowaty gently put Will's aching foot into the bucket. He looked up expectantly into Will's face.

Will's eyes opened wide with surprise. "It feels warm!"

"I'll be right back."

Will heard the clanging of a bucket again, then the running of water. Wyzowaty hurried into the room carrying a steaming bucket and set the bucket next to Will. A ragged towel was slung over his shoulder.

"Hey! There's room for both feet in that bucket," Wyzowaty said. "As soon as your feet feel cold, add a little of this warm water to it. You'll thaw them out gradually, and they won't hurt so much.

"Now I've got to finish feeding my babies. They eat an awful lot. Usually I'm done long afore now, but the sidewalks needed cinders spread on them this morning."

Wyzowaty seemed reluctant to move. He took a deep breath and sighed. He spoke in a soft voice. "I don't know if I can keep this up. I'm a hair older than I was ten minutes ago, and I can tell." Looking bent and tired, he tottered out of the room, but quickly reappeared with the towel wadded in his hand and threw it at Will.

Through the windows, Will watched Wyzowaty attack the coal he had wheeled over in a four-wheeled cart. Will poured hot water into his bucket and looked back at Wyzowaty. Will felt strangely disturbed. Why had he been so suspicious? The man looked over his shoulder once and gave Will a thumbs up sign. Will lifted his feet from the bucket and dried them. To hide the toe holes in his socks, he stuffed the holes between his toes. He grimaced with pain as he pushed his feet into his shoes.

Will stood behind the custodian, still intent on his work, throwing shovelful after shovelful of coal into the top of a large open hopper, wide at the top and narrow below where it entered the monster's mouth. The air pipe roared, blowing small nuggets of coal into the firebox while feeding it a large volume of air.

Where the pipe joined the firebox, Will saw a glowing bed of red coals and ash. Barely visible above this blanket of heat danced tiny blue flames. Sulphurous vapors, seeming to have come from hell, assaulted his nostrils.

Wyzowaty stopped and leaned his shovel against his side so he could mop his face and head. He turned toward Will and smiled broadly. "You like sneaking up on people, don't you?"

It was the second time Wyzowaty hadn't known he was behind him. Anyone else would have said, "You Injuns are all alike, always sneaking up on people."

"You feeling better now? You ought to get on to class."

Will shook his head. "Thank you, Mr. Wyzowaty. I . . ." He snatched Wyzowaty's shovel. "Let me try it." Clutching shovel and crutches, Will stepped in front of Wyzowaty and, leaning on his crutches, heaved a few shovelfuls of coal, albeit awkwardly. The crutch handles bit into his underarms. He shoveled a small pile of coal onto the floor in front of him, then dropped the crutches, knelt on the pile, and shoveled furiously. A smile spread across his face.

"Stop, stop," Wyzowaty said. "You're a . . ., a . . ., you, you'll . . . be late to class." He stared at Will tossing one shovelful of coal after another with relative ease.

"I've got fifteen minutes before third period. You need a break, Mr. Wyzowaty." *I'm not a cripple. You'll see.* He paused to shed his coat and hand it to Wyzowaty, then resumed his attack on the black rocks, intent on filling the hopper before he ran out of time.

"Okay, then." Wyzowaty finally turned toward his office.

When the hopper was piled full, Will rose. Perspiration dripped from his nose. With his crutches, he swung himself into Wyzowaty's office. Wyzowaty sat behind his desk.

"Mr. Wyzowaty, thanks. Boy, I'm not cold now. I feel pretty good. May I come and do this tomorrow?" He picked up the old towel. "May I use this?"

"Most students call me Mister Whiz. Sure—I mean about the towel." Wyzowaty looked at Will, blinking his eyes.

Will dunked one half of the towel in the bucket of cold water, wrung it out, and wiped perspiration from his body. "May I come, Mr. Whiz?" Will then dried himself with the dry end of the towel. His pants' knees were smudged with coal dust. He thought of Irene and wiped with the towel until the pants were clean.

"Well . . ."

"I can be here by seven o'clock."

Wyzowaty stood up, but still did not speak. He ran the back of a finger under his spectacles to wipe the corner of his eye.

"I can do it. You saw me. I want to help. It's fun."

Will stood, waiting.

"But making these old teapots boil—over the long haul, it's tough."

"I'm tough."

"Yeah, but . . ." Wyzowaty cleared his throat. He sneaked a look at Will's shoes. "I was thinking, maybe it could be your job—on a trial basis." Now his eyes darted, looking nowhere. "It maybe could pay a little."

Will's grin spread across his face. "Wow! That's swell."

"Six cents an hour."

Chapter 5

Six cents an hour. Wow! One hour per day, five days a week. Thirty cents. Will thought about all he could do with that. He could buy a chicken from the Randolph Street Market. Or some onions and potatoes.

He reached the top of the boiler room steps and slid the heavy metal door open. He realized that he hadn't been aware of climbing the steps.

And he'd like to have some fruit. Some apples. His mouth watered. The last apple he ate was in July, when he helped Mr. Wheatley, the farmer next door back in Haskell County, pick early cooking apples.

How many times had he seen his mom mending her dress? How much would a new one cost? His father's trousers, the seat so thin you could almost see through it. He laughed aloud. He bet trousers cost about a dollar.

Irene. His heart thumped. He had a vision of dark hair framing beautiful eyes. And the way she danced out to him in front of her house! Her voice calling, "Will, wait for me," echoed in his head. She had looked into his eyes and offered, "Ride with me."

Valentine's day was coming. What could he do? Dare he give her a Valentine present? He had a job now; he could buy her something. Boys gave girls chocolates. He would give her a box of chocolates, one with a big red heart with lace around it. He'd save up.

It was wonderful to have a job, and what a great one. He was helping to run the whole school. Mr. Whiz . . . Will laughed to himself . . . what a . . . Will stopped walking. He was at his Algebra class doorway, early for once, hardly knowing how he had gotten there.

Had he closed the boiler room door? He'd lose his job before he got started.

He had to quit his daydreaming. They had a test today. Everybody complained about how tough Miss Whitaker's tests were, although they sounded like they were bragging. "My brother, over at Phillips College. He had Miss Whitaker in 1925. He says their math exams are easier than that pill Whitaker's."

"Good morning, Miss Whitaker," Will said, louder than he would have liked, while squeezing himself and his crutches against the doorjamb to let her pass from the room. She seemed to have ignored him, but Will knew she would have reprimanded him had he not greeted her.

The smell of lilacs lingered in the doorway. He watched Miss Whitaker enter Mr. Brown's room across the hall, "for professional consultation," she often explained to the class.

Mr. Brown was the Mathematics Department head and taught calculus. Also, of which the students had become very much aware, Mr. Brown was a widower—which she had not explained.

Will stared at the blackboard surrounded by its oak framework and the dust-covered chalk ledge. The board was blank except for a notation in the upper left corner—"Examination: Adding and Subtracting Polynomials of Multiple Variables."

He didn't understand why most of his class, which consisted of fifteen boys and three girls, was upset about this test. Everyone knew that math came easily to males—the test should be easy for them, but not to females. (It didn't occur to him that Miss Whitaker was an exception to that rule.) Besides, the problems were more than simple, even if the vocabulary was not.

Students began filtering in, a few chatting with each other, some alone. They moved quickly to their seats, looked at the blackboard, and flipped open their books to cram for the test.

There was a ruckus in the hall, the crash of books falling to the floor, curses. Wade, his skin red with excitement in comparison to the white shirt framing his face, banged into the doorframe. He twisted his body to dodge a fist. There was a thud as the fist found its mark anyway—his shoulder. Wade dashed to his seat across the aisle from Will, laughing. Sam, Big Sam in starched pressed bib overalls, stood in the doorway, glaring, and pointed his finger at Wade. Wade grinned, his brown eyes dancing. Sam disappeared into the hall, then reappeared with books and papers askew between his bear-paw hands. "I'll get you," he said quietly, but was unable to suppress his grin. He jammed his body into his seat behind Will, his legs straddling the iron scroll desk with its wooden top and seat.

The boys' eyes found the cryptic blackboard note. Their faces turned sullen. Wade looked at Will from the corners of his eyes and gave a quick nod toward the blackboard. "Hey, Injun boy, don't forget," he said from the side of his mouth.

A knot formed in the pit of Will's stomach. He stared back at Wade, but was thumped on his back by Sam's open hand. Even if he wanted to help them cheat on the test, which he didn't, he had no idea how to do it.

Without warning, Emery, his open jacket flapping, raced into the room, down the aisle, banged his books onto his desk and threw himself into his seat behind Wade. The smell of Lucky Strikes trailed behind him.

The sniggers and catcalls directed at Emery had barely begun when they were squelched, followed by the clattering of seats and shuffling of feet as students rose to attention. Miss Whitaker was in the doorway, frowning. Her eyes, magnified by her spectacles, swept the room and landed on Emery.

"We don't have time for your tom-foolery today, Mr. Carlisle. I hope you are ready for the examination."

"Yes, ma'am."

A cough came from the rear of the room. Whitaker's eyes flew in that direction. "Be seated," she said, and again came the clattering of seats.

A tall male dressed in a brown three-piece suit appeared in the doorway. LeRoy was often late, ostensibly on some errand for the office, or, as Will had begun to suspect, had delivered Irene to her class. Miss Whitaker checked the doorway, saw who had arrived, and nodded deferentially. She picked up a sheaf of papers from her desk. "Are there any questions before the examination begins?" She moved toward the first row, licked a finger, and began to pull a sheet from the stack. "Yes, Anna Marie."

Anna Marie was the only student Miss Whitaker didn't call by last name. Anna Marie, petite, delicate with transparent skin that revealed snaking blue blood vessels, wore either airy white or pale pink or blue dresses, whose skirts billowed around her to the floor. The skirts were for support, it looked like to Will.

All heads turned to watch Anna Marie slip to her feet next to her desk. "Miss Whitaker, would you please remind us—just to be sure—how to subtract multiple variables?" Anna Marie's long white lashes batted as she cast a glance at Sam. Was that why Sam's clothes were always starched and pressed?

"Certainly, dear." Miss Whitaker's lips smiled—even if her eyes didn't. "All our memories could use a little nudging."

Anna Marie's classmates responded with uncontrolled grins and sighs. There would be no examination today. Had anyone else asked, the response would have been, "If you studied properly, you will have no difficulty," and the tests would have been distributed.

Anna Marie gave a little curtsy and slipped back into her seat. She seemed as if she was from a long-ago age. Most of the students were content to leave her there, but accepted her rescues.

"Don't think we won't have the exam today," Miss Whitaker said, noting the grins. She turned to the blackboard and sketched out a problem, the white chalk clacked with each stroke— parentheses, letters, numbers, pluses, minuses and equal signs, all piling up in long rows.

"Now . . .," she said, but suddenly straightened and glared at some offense on the board, then recovered and asked, "Who can tell me why this answer is wrong?"

Miss Whitaker's eyes scoured her students' faces. Their eyes darted from her gaze. Seats creaked and feet shuffled beneath desks. Miss Whitaker didn't need a paddle. She looked in LeRoy's direction in his seat at the front, but he was very busy with some papers inside his desk. "Mr. Coleman," she said, stopping her search.

Giggles of relief.

"Injun boy," was murmured somewhere behind him.

"Gimp."

Will squirmed. The answer was obvious, easy. But why him?

"Mr. Coleman, if you please."

"There is an . . ."

"Please stand before you address the class, Mr. Coleman."

Will pushed himself up.

More giggles.

Emery, his fist to his lips, coughed, "Cripple."

Miss Whitaker glared, her eyes swiftly falling on successive students, daring them.

Silence.

"Well, Mr. Coleman? Speak up."

Will knew that his ears, in spite of his dark red pigmentation, were bright red. "There is an addition instead of a subtraction in the second line, Miss Whitaker."

She held out a meter stick to him. "Take this and show us."

Will gathered his crutches to go to the front.

Murmurs from behind him. "Injun pet."

"Pill's pet."

He took the pointer and touched the blackboard.

"You may return to your seat," Miss Whitaker said, then launched into a new explanation of the problem.

Glares and downturned lips faced Will as he swung down the aisle to return to his seat. He stared back, his own lips tight.

"Pass the test paper to the person behind you and place it face down on your desk until I tell you to begin," Miss Whitaker said. The purple printed sheets carrying the smell of ditto fluid made their way down the rows. Soon only the rasp of pencil points and the rub of erasers could be heard—except for the heavy tread of Miss Whitaker patrolling the aisles.

Miss Whitaker's footsteps approached Will from behind. Then, as she passed, her form filled the aisle in front of him. Sam's heavy hand rested on his shoulder. As Will turned his head,

Wade snatched Will's test and slid his own into its place.

Miss Whitaker, hearing the rustle, turned on her heel but found everyone with heads down, working furiously, except for Will, who stared at her.

"Is there a problem? Finished so soon, Will?"

Will shook his head, bent to Wade's paper, and pretended to write. His palms perspired and the heat rose in his neck and cheeks. Behind him, papers switched almost silently. Searing pain shot down his legs. He winced as it squeezed sweat from under his sideburns to trickle down his cheek. In agony, he trembled.

Again, Sam's hand on his shoulder, but heavier, squeezing, a shake, carrying a message. Wade grabbed to take back his test while Will's own slid onto his desk from Emery. Will slapped his hand on Wade's paper to hold it in place. Wade was too slow.

"What in thunder is going on?" Miss Whitaker said, turning toward the disturbance. She glared in their direction, but settled on Wade.

Caught, Wade spoke. "Will's trying to cheat. He took my paper."

"Is that true, Mr. Coleman?" From behind, Sam's heavy foot ground into Will's ankle beneath his seat.

Will stared up at Miss Whitaker, now towering over him and examining the two test papers on his desk.

"Yes, ma'am, I saw him," Emery said.

Whitaker glanced at Anna Marie. Anna Marie made the slightest of shrugs.

"That's right, Miss Whitaker. He kept turning around when you weren't looking, trying to see my paper," Sam said.

Miss Whitaker glowered at Sam. "Why would he do that? Since he's been here, he gets the best grades in the class."

Sam shrugged. "I dunno."

"You three. Give me your papers. And you, too, Will Coleman."

Miss Whitaker loomed over them, larger than ever, while she shuffled through their papers. "Well, I never! How dare you? Nobody cheats in my class. Why on earth, Mr. Coleman, would you help these lazy ragamuffins?"

Someone snickered. She seemed not to notice.

"That will be a zero for this examination." She looked at Will. "For all of you." She pinched Sam's ear and tugged on it, appearing to lift the huge boy from his seat. "You boys get yourselves right on down to Dr. Grover. He'll deal with you."

More snickering. This time she glared while her eyes searched the room. Students shrunk in their seats. "Who's finished with the exam? Anna Marie. Please take my note to Dr. Grover."

Will felt as if he would bust. He was angry and hurt. Everyone knew exactly what had happened, except Miss Whitaker. LeRoy, grinning, caught his eye and blew him a kiss behind Mrs. Whitaker's back. Will wanted to knock the smirk off of his face. He had forgotten about the pain in his legs until he rose from his desk.

Chapter 6

"Back again so soon." Dr. Grover sat at his desk, his bulging black eyes boring a hole through Will's chest into his heart, leaving Will standing, hanging from his crutches by his armpits, shivering. For sure, not from the cold this time.

Will wondered why Dr. Grover had saved him for last; the others were sent to class—deemed not guilty he supposed.

"I see you got dried out," Dr. Grover said.

Dr. Grover held a note written on graph paper. The boys' four exam papers lay spread out in front of him on the desk. "Let's see what Miss Whitaker has to say about you. Anna Marie brought the letter."

Will remembered Anna Marie floating past him in the hall on his way to the office. She had looked away, then caught up to the other three boys who had run ahead of him. Then they had put their heads together with Anna Marie's, and whispered while casting glances at him. If it weren't for Irene, he would have liked Anna Marie, but no longer.

In the office Will had sat on the bench next to Sam and Wade, who had already arrived. Emery slipped in a few minutes later. His clothing reeked with another layer of cigarette smoke, signaling that he had borne the cold to make a trip outside to the back corner of the building. Sam had been the first called into the principal's office.

Dr. Grover's eyes turned themselves, ever so slowly, to the blue graph paper in his hands. He read, then turned his eyes back to Will. "Cheating on an exam. That right?"

Dr. Grover must have read the note for every one of them. Why again? Will stared back, trembling, his lips pressed together. You can't trust a white man.

"Defiant, eh? Enid High students don't cheat, Will," he said, turning Will's paper toward him. "Or help other students cheat. Your exam had all correct answers but one. So did theirs. And the same wrong answer, by the way." His lips floated a smile.

Dr. Grover waited. Waited for Will's reaction. For his confession.

Will stared back, his jaw clamped shut. He hadn't done anything wrong.

Grover shook his head—just barely. "But theirs had erasures, and some of their answers' work was not consistent with . . ." His head wagged noticeably now. "Miss Whitaker said you're an excellent student." He let out a deep sigh. "Nothing to say, Will?"

Perspiration ran down Will's side. He'd get back at them; he didn't need Dr. Grover's help.

Again Dr. Grover's eyes and head moved in slow motion to finally allow his eyes to rest on the paddle. "Equal justice for all. Hand me the Board of Education, Will."

Will shuddered, then retrieved the paddle from the doorframe while Dr. Grover's eyes followed him.

"Lay it on my desk, please." Dr. Grover's black eyes bulged into a point as they stared at the paddle. "Will, were you cheating, or helping them cheat?" Grover's eyes didn't move, didn't blink.

Will froze. His mouth wouldn't open. He envisioned Miss Whitaker's broad back in the aisle in front of him, Wade snatching his exam, the paper passing behind him, Emery copying his answers, and Anna Marie shrugging—capping off their treachery. Everyone saw. He was sure their lies were recorded on Miss Whitaker's note.

That's what they were doing in the hallway, making sure they all had the story straight. Making sure no one ratted out. If he denied cheating, Dr. Grover would add lying to his crimes. Plus, it was his second time in one day in the principal's office. But they'd get their just desserts.

"Will?"

Will only stared.

Dr. Grover finally looked up. "Does this mean you were cheating? Did you help them?" He wagged his head. "I don't want to believe you did."

Dr. Grover let his fingertips glide over the Board of Education. Back and forth.

"There's the bell. Okay, Will. Report to your next class, but return to me after school for detention." His chest expanded as he took a deep breath, then slowly let it deflate along with his eyes.

At first Will was confused, then realized he had received a short reprieve. He shuddered as he thought about after school detention. Would any of the others be present? He was hardly aware of how he got into the hall. The noise and bustle in the hallway forced him to dodge his more sure-footed peers, preoccupying him and crowding out his fears. Swept along, he found himself at his destination, the gymnasium.

Boring. A lonely vigil. That was physical education. Most boys ran to the class and hurriedly put on their gym uniforms. Will didn't even own one. His exercise—observing the other boys play. He had to attend PE; he needed gym credits for graduation.

He watched the early arriving classmates chase down basketballs, take shots, dart around the court, hurrying their play before Coach Mattingly arrived. The double doors banged open again and again as boys rushed in to compete for basketballs.

Looming large, a ball bounced toward him. Will reached out, greedy for its feel, eager to throw it. It was snatched away. A lanky kid, perspiration already darkening the collar of his red and white Enid High School T-shirt, glanced at him. It was all there in his eyes—the gimp can't play; who cares? The boy laughed and disappeared with the ball. LeRoy Mattison. It was a mixed class—sophomores, juniors, seniors.

Will hated school. Hated physical education class. Hated the gym students. Hated Coach

Mattingly. Hated Miss Whitaker. Hated Dr. Grover. Hated LeRoy. Hated all the students. All the teachers. Hated his father for insisting that he graduate.

A whistle sounded.

Except for the squeak of a tennis shoe on the hardwood floor, the gymnasium stilled. Within seconds the boys gathered themselves into a straight line organized alphabetically by last name. They faced Coach with his ever-present clipboard and sounded off. Their voices traveled down the line by turn—Atkins, Bayer, Bradley, Campfield, Carlisle . . . Oddly, as always, "Coleman" sounded from another part of the gym.

There had been snickers on the first day. But not since. After having sat out that gym period, the boys' faces had been like stone during attendance check.

. . . Griffin, Jackson, Kibble, Mattison, Moynihan. Roll call—thirty seconds and done.

They formed into a large semi-circle facing Coach Mattingly, their backs to Will. Coach now crouched with one knee on the floor and talked, pointed and smacked his thigh. Rising, he strode to the blackboard next to his office door, hauling the circle with him. He drew, made X's and O's.

Sam turned and waved for Will to join them. Hope struck through Will's breast like lightning. At least one person was considerate. He started to move in their direction. No, not from Sam. It was a setup. He wasn't about to let that bunch of goons razz him.

Three long manila climbing ropes, hung from a beam, were suspended directly above Will's head. He looked at his class. Coach was directing it in a shooting drill. They would never notice him. He looked at the wall where a pulley rope was tied that held the climbing ropes out of the way when they were not being used. Will swung himself over to the wall, glanced at his class, and released the one-and-a-half inch ropes.

During the gymnastics unit, Will had watched his classmates, looking like inch worms, struggle to climb using their hands and feet. Most had managed to rise but a few feet from the floor. Only Emery had gone well above their heads.

Will grabbed a rope above head height and pulled. A thrill passed through his body as he lifted his feet off the floor. He attempted to pull up his legs to grip the rope with his feet as the others had, but his legs hung limply below him. With one hand he reached over the other and pulled again. Looking up at the beam (twenty-four feet high, Coach had said), Will climbed. A smile played at his lips. He was better than them; they were a bunch of cream puffs.

He paused and looked down. Almost the same excitement pounded through his head as when Irene, gorgeous Irene, had met him outside her house. If only Irene were here to see him.

He stared up at the beam as he climbed. It loomed larger and larger. With each pull his smile widened.

He imagined Irene was there, looking up, impressed with his power, fearing he would lose his grip, but cheering him on.

He slowed. His arms ached, but Will paid scant heed to their protest. With Irene looking on he had to reach the beam; he could not fail.

How many others could say they touched one of those great beams that supported the huge gym roof? He wondered if Coach kept a list. How many names on it? Not Sam's. Not Wade's. Not even Emery's.

He was there! Clutching the rope to him with one hand, he reached up and slapped the beam.

"Hoo, Hoo!" The yell of a Choctaw brave, announcing his homecoming after a successful foray, echoed through the gym.

Bodies halted. Only the bounce from an unattended ball answered the Choctaw's cry. Eyes darted to search the room for the origin of the strange call. They found the ropes hanging loosely to the floor and followed them to the roof where their eyes alighted upon Will.

The class stared. Jaws fell slack. With his dark hands blending with the rope and his legs dangling below him, Will appeared to float upright at the ceiling.

Will looked down on their heads. "Whoop!" he called.

Coach broke and ran to the storage room. He flung the doors open, sending them crashing against the wall. "Grab a mat. Grab a mat," he yelled. "Simmons, run, hold Coleman's rope. Somebody spot him." Boys started as from a trance and ran to help. They dragged the mats toward the ropes, leaning at hard angles to keep them moving.

Will laughed, then hand-over-hand glided to the floor as Wade arrived. Will stood, grinning, hanging onto the rope for support, watching the class struggle with the mats.

Their eyes wild, the boys glanced up and spotted Will. They ceased hauling the mats. Astounded, their eyes followed the rope back to the beam and back to Will. Murmurs of, "Did you see that!" passed through the group. "Way to go, Will!" Sam said.

Coach, his face red, strode through the gaggle of boys to Will's side. "Coleman, what do you think you're doing? You'll get yourself hurt, maybe killed." He yanked the rope from Will's hand. The smile slipped from Will's face. Without the aid of the rope, he tottered. A boy sprang forward with Will's crutches. Tired and grateful, Will leaned on them.

Coach glowered at Will. "Where were you during the lecture on safety?" Then his voice mellowed. "Class, what must we always do when rope climbing?"

Boys wiped smiles from their faces. "Place mats beneath the rope." "Have a spotter." "Somebody should stand on the extra rope several feet away to hold it still."

"And Will, what did you do—besides using the rope without my permission?" Coach's voice began to rise again. "You are a part of the class, attend to the instruction."

Will's head dropped. All he saw was the floor between his worn shoes. "Yes, sir."

"This is very serious. I should send you to Dr. Grover."

The class crowded around Will and Coach. Most members frowned; Wade, Emery and LeRoy wore a slight grin.

"Yes, sir."

Coach put his hand on Will's shoulder. "I hate to do it Will, but that was very dangerous. You have to understand . . ."

Will, in a voice so soft that all leaned forward straining their ears, said, "Please. I've already been there . . ." His voice dropped further still, "twice today."

A few boys snickered.

Coach looked around and caught Wade. Coach's eyes blazed.

The class quieted.

"Everybody gets to play, but I, I have to watch," Will said. Everybody has fun—except me." He looked into Coach's round mellow face. "I can do it, Coach. I can play. I'm tough."

Coach nodded, looked Will in the eye. "Okay, Coleman. We'll find out."

Chapter 7

Except for the slow ticking of the wall clock and an occasional drawer slamming shut in the principal's office, the school was silent. The windows across from Will gradually turned from clear bright, to a somber gray, then to black. Two white globes, hung by long chains from the twelve-foot-high ceiling, filled the room with light.

Beneath him the wooden office bench grew hard. The three boys next to him squirmed, serving a part of their sentence for cheating, guilty or not. They listened to students clamoring down the hall to exit the building. Then, in silence, they watched the office staff filter out.

Will worried. He hadn't shown up to shovel coal after school. He'd arrive at work extra early tomorrow morning and show Mr. Whiz that he was reliable. He smiled as he thought of Mr. Whiz and the six cents an hour.

But, after this, would Mr. Whiz say, "What job?"

He should be home doing his chores. And when he got home his father would . . . He didn't want to think about it. Would he have to go to bed before getting his homework done?

At least it would be too late for a gang to wait at the lot to throw ice balls at him . . . he hoped, although the three next to him could out distance him and wait. One good thing, Irene had not seen him sitting in detention.

He heard a door bang shut from far off, its sound echoing down the hall behind them. Was that Mr. Whiz leaving?

Finally, the windows in Dr. Hiram Grover's office slammed shut against the cold night air. The office door jerked open and Dr. Grover emerged. With his suit jacket in hand and shirt sleeves rolled up to below his elbow, he revealed thick, muscular forearms.

Will's eyes followed the principal as he carefully hung his jacket on a clothes pole, then turned and removed the Board of Education—the first paddle Will had seen—from its nail in the doorframe. The boys slumped and released a collective sigh.

Grover grabbed the secretary's oak chair with one hand and lifted it over the counter. He sat and faced the boys. His other hand, its grip on the paddle turning his knuckles white, rested on his leg. A dozen holes had been drilled in its business end for extra sting. Unlike the paddle in his office, this one's varnish had been worn off.

Dr. Grover's bulging eyes, looking sad, moved slowly to rest on each face. The corners of his mouth sagged. He pointed at Sam and beckoned him. "Stand up." Grover slapped the paddle in his palm.

Sam stiffened. Tears sprang to the corners of his eyes. His lip quivered as he fought to show his bravery.

Grover shook his head "no." He pointed at Emery. "Stand," and again slapped his palm with the paddle, again shook his head "no."

Will's pulse pounded in his ears. His palms sweated. *Who was first? I won't cry in front of them. Choctaw braves don't cry.*

Grover pointed at Will. Will pulled on his crutches to struggle to his feet.

"No."

Grover pointed at Wade. "No."

The principal looked down the row of standing boys. He frowned, pondering something. "Sit," he said. Will sat and felt the bench trembling beneath him.

Slap. Slap. Slap. The paddle slapping Grover's palm, in time with the ticking of the clock, filled the silence. Their eyes glanced away as his found theirs.

Finally, Grover spoke. Slap, slap, slap emphasized each word. "You . . . boys . . . cheated . . . on . . . an . . . exam." He looked into their eyes, challenging, waiting for disagreement.

He stared at Will. "Or assisted."

No one answered. What was Dr. Grover waiting for? Confession?

But I didn't cheat; I didn't help them cheat, Will thought. *This morning, did he want me to say I did? Or now? I won't.*

Grover slapped the paddle in his palm again.

He stared at Emery. "Mr. Carlisle . . ."

Emery recoiled.

". . . you will return to me after school in four days to retake an exam on adding and subtracting polynomials—a looong exam." And for each answer you get w-r-r-o-o-n-g . . ." Dr. Grover slapped the palm of his hand, hard, making a resounding "whomp." The boys jumped, then leaned back, their eyes wide. Grover displayed both palms—one a blood red, the other, white as a sheet of paper. "Mr. Simmons, Mr. Thompson, Mr. Coleman. The same for you. Count yourselves very fortunate. Good afternoon, gentlemen."

They sat staring, uncomprehending. Then the other three jumped to their feet and scrambled from the office. Will pulled himself up and balanced himself on his crutches, ready to follow.

"Mr. Coleman," Dr. Grover said. His black eyes had deflated a bit. Water rimmed their lower lids.

Will stopped.

"I know you got dragged into this. One day you'll understand. Go on home."

* * *

Will found himself on the sidewalk in front of the school. The air was cold and crisp. He looked through the bare limbs of the trees lining the roadway. White clouds scudded below the sliver of moon framed by myriad white stars. Leftovers from the morning's storm of sleet lay beside the walk. His body felt as if it had been washed clean by emotion, emotions waiting to wash yet again.

Strange, after all that had happened today, how looking up into the sky as he walked brought thoughts of Irene. Irene . . .

"Look, Irene, how the tree limbs form a frame. See the stars surrounding the moon—the queen and her court?" The sky's almost as beautiful as Irene is.

My hand reaches for hers; she reaches for mine. Our fingers entwine as we walk along. How soft and warm she is!

A great gust of wind blew down the street and shoved its icy fingers through Will's coat. He didn't notice.

We stop and turn toward each other. I bend toward her and my lips brush hers before she turns her head away. She laughs and skips ahead, pulling me along. She slows, then snuggles up closer. The blood throbs through my temples where my cap encircles my head.

Will's crutch slipped as it hit an icy spot. He stumbled but managed to regain his balance. He had to be careful. Freezing temperatures had arrived with the darkness, bringing the melt to a stop and holding it into slick black patches amid stretches of white sleet that had lain hidden from the sun.

What was he doing with crutches—the man who had climbed a rope to the ceiling? Suddenly, the crutches were strange in his hands—they weren't his. He twisted his mouth into a snarl and hurled them. The crutches skittered across the hard ground until they clattered up against a tree trunk. Freedom—he didn't need those things. A sense of relief flooded over him.

He took his next step, and the next, but with his weak knees, tottered until his center of gravity went much too far forward. His feet began running, his old shoes flopped, his arms flailed, and his head lurched back and forth as he tried to regain his balance. He sprawled face down on the ground. Searing torment made its way from his legs and up his back. Will groaned.

A Model T Ford chugged by, followed by a Model A. Neither car slowed. He had not been seen, and, for that, he was grateful. He felt foolish and admitted his delight in his self-sufficiency was premature. His only punishment was an abrasion on the heel of his hand where he had caught himself.

It seemed he had been walking for a long time, but looking around, he realized he had traveled less than a block. His tardy arrival home would undoubtedly be punished, and when his father learned the reasons, the consequences would be even greater.

Will gathered up his crutches, concentrated on avoiding ice, and propelled himself along. At Irene's house his heart skipped a beat, but he did not allow himself to dally and pine over her.

A twinge of anxiety shot through him as he skittered by the lot at the corner of Randolph. Protected from the sun by its circle of trees, its white blanket was still intact except where the boys had roughed it up in their tussle with him. But no whiff of cigarette smoke or movement caught Will's attention. He considered how he might get revenge the next day, but came up with no plan that would not interfere with his getting to his job on time.

Maybe revenge wasn't such a good idea, anyway. What he really wanted were some friends. What he *really* wanted was . . . impossible. His heart hurt. Oh, Irene!

The long driveway to his house loomed in front of him. Patches of white sleet covered the ground where it had been sufficiently shaded during the day. He was surprised—a car's tires had left tracks in the sleet on the driveway. He couldn't remember a time when a car drove up to their house—maybe a car never had until now.

At the house, the car, stark black in contrast to its white surroundings, waited. He hoped that its arrival had nothing to do with him, but was certain it did. His hands turned cold, yet his crutches became wet and slippery in his grip. If he had some place else to go, he would have gone there. He found himself alternately hurrying, then stopping, tempted to turn back. He squinted to make out the car.

A Studebaker. LeRoy's father's car. Why Mr. Mattison?

Will tried to think of some good reason. Maybe to offer his father a job? His heart pounded. So much good luck in one day! He swung quickly along, not feeling an ache.

Will stopped. No. His father would have to go to LeRoy's father's business to get a job. Something was wrong. Something about him. So much bad luck in one day!

At the door, Will hesitated. Inside a masculine voice responded to his father's. A shudder passed over Will. He started to knock, then feeling foolish—it was his own house—

pushed open the door and clambered across the sill.

After the clean night air, the house was pungent with wood smoke and fumes from the coal oil lamp burning on the kitchen table, its wick set extravagantly long to give extra light. Had there not been guests, the stifling air would have had him tearing off his coat even before pushing the door shut behind him.

His father stood near the door, his back to the light, his face inscrutable, a paper in his hands. But Will knew that his father, who was especially suspicious of visitors after dark, was smoldering. And his own absence undoubtedly had already made him edgy. His father's wrath would focus on him, would build while he waited for all to leave. Then his mother would be held accountable.

Opposite his father was a young man. Will's mouth fell slack. What was LeRoy Mattison doing here?

Looking sharp in his usual brown wool suit and tie, Roy stood with both hands holding his hat to his abdomen. The perfect gentleman. The light caught Roy in profile, grinning at Will.

Will's mother was farther back, nearer the lamp, and more easily seen. She held the bottom of her kitchen apron in her hands, continuously wringing it.

A fragrance, so familiar, so wonderful, wafted across the entrance and blotted from his mind the stink of burning wood and kerosene. Someone else was present. He sniffed, filled his nostrils, stimulated his memory, and thought of a girl. His eyes darted beyond his father, past LeRoy.

Then he saw her. Rather, inhaled her. Irene! Partially hidden by LeRoy, she blended into the shadows the others cast. But for the moment, she was the only one there.

He felt himself turn a brighter shade of red that, in the gloom, thankfully, she could not see. Shame overtook him—because of his house, his father, his mother, and himself. Shame for how he looked, for being a cripple, for coming home so late. Why had she come?

The soft glow of lamplight rimmed the hair caressing her face and shoulders. She pressed forward—nearer. "Hello, W—"

Roy stepped between them to shake hands, blocking his view of her, cutting her off. "Hi, Will," he said. "Glad you made it."

Will barely heard him.

He knew why she had come. Roy had dragged her there. Right into his house. LeRoy, strutting Roy. Royalty. Leader. Favored. Claiming her. To torture him. To humiliate him. To make himself look good. That was why. A new heat rose into Will's temples. His lips curled back from his teeth. He gripped his crutches as if they were encircling Roy's neck.

But her wide, smiling eyes, reflecting the warm glow of the lamp, sought his and took him away. Each time he saw her eyes, they were more beautiful.

They met his. Not Roy's. But his. They pulled him in and held him. His hands relaxed.

LeRoy patted Will's shoulder. "I thought I was going to have to leave before seeing you."

Will frowned. *About what?*

Irene managed to squeeze in front of Roy. "Half the school's talking about what you did, Will."

She said my name—again. Even with her coat on, she is lovely. Will tried to control his breathing. *Roy was lucky.*

But "What you did," she said! Does she think I'm a cheat? Involuntarily, Will shrank back, confused. *And LeRoy—trusted by the principal, by his father, by Irene—coming to see me. LeRoy—who hung around with younger boys and threw snowballs at a . . . a . . . cripple.* Will wished again that he hadn't yet come home.

"Principal Grover asked me to deliver a letter to your parents," Roy explained.

The letter! Irene knows. She does think I'm a cheat. Has my father already read the letter?

"He would have come himself, but had to hold a YMCA meeting and was running late," Roy said. "He said he called two of the four parents, but you don't have a telephone. Sam's parents don't, either. My dad's at the same meeting, so he asked me to deliver the letters."

His words floated over Will's head. *So that's why he didn't paddle us tonight. He didn't have time before the meeting. What's in the letter?*

"I better be going. I have to deliver Sam's letter."

"Will, why don't you come with us?" Irene said, practically bouncing. "Riding in a car is so much fun."

A band around Will's chest was released. Not because of the ride, which he'd love, but because Irene wanted him—anyway. But his tongue stuck to the roof of his mouth.

"Will." Will's father's voice was deep and harsh—clipped.

Will recoiled.

"You haven't done your chores."

Even though his father's face was in shadow, he knew his eyes were boring into him. The band cinched his chest again. Will glanced at his mother. Fear clothed her face. She looked away.

Roy dropped his smile. "Dad said I've got to get the car home soon." He looked at Irene from the corners of his eyes. "In fact, I must drop Irene off before getting to Sam's to save time. Otherwise, I'd love for you to come. Guess you have to get busy on your chores."

Roy took formal leave of Will's parents, tapped Will on his arm with a, "See ya, buddy. We better get a wiggle on," and escorted Irene to the door. Will, with his eyes fixed on Irene, moved aside to let them pass into the crisp night. Irene looked his way and smiled.

Will watched them walk to the Studebaker. At each step the crunch of ice beneath her boots begged, "Come. Come. Come with me." Will reluctantly closed the door and forced his mind to his father and the letter from Dr. Grover.

"Will!" his father said, startling him again.

There was a knock at the door before Will turned completely around. Still feeling the heat of his father's summons, he opened the door. Irene stood before him, grinning. Behind her the car's motor putt-putted, its exhaust pipe sending white vapor curling into the sky.

"I had to come back. I think you misunderstood what we said about school." She touched his arm. "You were awfully brave to climb that rope—and strong." The bright night sky lit the silver cross at her throat—the Choctaw symbol for "paths crossing." "See you tomorrow," she said, then was gone.

He grasped the amulet at his heart. Did it throb for Irene?

"Will! Get in here!"

Or because of his father?

Chapter 8

"Will, get in here!" Will's father repeated. He stood waiting, then turned back toward the stove where Will's mother had retreated. "Woman, you better stop this boy from mooning over that girl. She's trouble."

"It's natural he wants a girl, Charlie."

He glowered, deliberating. "Can't you find a Choctaw? There ought to be lots of our people, at least Indian people, in that school."

The heat rose in Will's cheeks along with his embarrassment. How had his father figured out that he liked Irene?

Will shrugged. "I don't like girls." He feared that his father noticed the quiver in his voice. It was true—he didn't like girls. He liked *a* girl—Irene.

"Don't you lie to me. I'm talking about that girl, and you know it.

"Now let's get to the letter." His father's eyes moved to the paper in his hand but went back quickly to Will's coat sleeve. "What happened to your coat? We try to send you to school clothed decently, and look at you. You're sixteen. A lot of sixteen-year-olds are out on their own. Can't trust you to even take care of your coat. I can't afford to buy you coats all the time."

"Charlie, why—"

"Shut up, woman." Will's father spoke through bared teeth. "I shouldn't have to do your job for you. Shut up or else. He turned to glare at Will. "Sew that coat up. Tonight."

"It wasn't my fault," Will said. Some boys grabbed—"

"Quiet. Back to the letter. It's from—Principal Grover. Cheating on an algebra exam, it says."

"But I didn't—"

"You gave them answers. Same thing. If the principal sends a letter, it must be serious."

"But, I—"

"Stop, interrupting. Woman, you better teach this boy some manners. Will, you and I'll take care of this cheating thing out at the woodpile, soon as we cut some wood. Now let's get to it."

Will struggled to hold his father's stare. The only sounds came from the hiss of the oil lamp and the pop of wood in the stove. His father turned toward the door.

"Dad, I got a job!" Will shouted the last word. The shout came unbidden.

His father turned back to glare at him.

"I got a job."

"Did you hear that, Charlie?" Will's mother said. "Will has a job."

"That's crazy. Who would hire him?"

"It's true. I do. Shoveling coal."

"Ha, ha, ha. You, shovel coal? That's the funniest thing I've ever heard. Nice try. You think you can make me forget that whipping. That lie'll add a little extra."

"No, it's true. Six cents an hour, an hour a day. I can buy us milk and eggs and bananas and . . ."

Will suddenly stopped. Irene. He wanted to get Irene a Valentine. He couldn't do both. He had to explain why he suddenly stopped.

"Okay. I was fibbing. Just a little." But he had to keep the job. "Only three cents an hour. But I'm gonna get a raise."

"Cheating and lying. Coming home late, worrying your mother. Anything else you want to tell me, boy?"

Will's mother said, "Next thing you know, he'll be taking after his old man, getting all whiskey'd up, getting in all hours of the morning." Fear and regret clouded her eyes at her own words. Sometimes she just had to let it out.

Will's father's visage blackened. He drew back his arm and unleashed a backhand across Will's mother's face. "That's enough out of you, Velma." The blow knocked her back against the table, shaking the lamp. Their shadows danced crazily on the walls.

His mother sniffed back a sob. "I, I'm sorry. It's just that, I, it's hard to put up with the drinking and . . ." Trembling, she retreated to the far side of the stove. "I worry about him." She hung her head, then looked directly at her husband. "And you."

His father sneered.

Why didn't she . . . couldn't she stop him? Will thought. He couldn't stand to see her hurt anymore. He had to do something.

"Yeah, Dad. I have something else to say." He shuffled over to where his father stood to thrust his chin up toward his father's face. "I was late getting to school. I was smoking with my friends." With that, Will, with his fingertips, pushed his father's arm. It was more proper that he get whipped than his mother.

Will's father's black eyes pierced the gloom. He thrust Will's hand aside. "Don't you touch me, boy! Velma, this boy's impertinence and back-talk has got to stop. Boy, what do you mean you were smoking?"

"Up on the lot across from Nichols' store. You can ask LeRoy."

Will felt past caring what his father did to him. He felt defiant. It felt good, better than he'd felt in some time.

"That LeRoy's a fine boy. Polite. Reserved. Especially for a white. Can't believe he'd smoke at his age. He's too intelligent for that. You'd do well to follow after him. Not after that girl." His father's eyes narrowed.

"And I didn't ask you where," his father said. "What were you doing smoking? You think you are a man? Where'd you get the money for that? Wasting your pay, already."

"One of the fellas gave me one."

"You smart aleck. You're building yourself up for quite a licking. Come on. We'd better get to cutting firewood. I'll keep my eye open for a piece that'll make a nice paddle."

* * *

The air, cold and crisp, felt good after the atmosphere of the house. Although the moon was barely waxing, the sky was white with stars, bright enough to cast sharp shadows.

Will, on his crutches, followed his father to the old barn. Its size suggested that it had once served a spread of nearly a thousand acres. Over the course of many generations its wood had been bleached white by the bright Oklahoma sun and its joints had rotted with age. Will liked to imagine that it, like all the trees, bowed north to face some powerful boreal god. Actually, they all had bent to flee the strong southern Texana Wind.

Will waited to the side as his father, standing with feet spread next to the barn, swung a heavy maul at a long vertical piece of the siding that formed the wall of the barn. The wood emitted a crack. His father swung again. The lumber jumped noticeably. His father gave one more hefty swing and the piece quivered.

"Grab a-hold," he said.

Together they pulled the board. The wood creaked and groaned, protesting its release of the nails that had held it comfortably in place for so many years. The siding suddenly released its grip and Will scrambled to keep his balance. The entire structure groaned and shuddered as it took a more northern slant.

"I think she's going pretty soon," his father said. "Should make it easier." He held the end of the loose board up for Will to grab. "Okay," he said, and nodded.

The ten-foot board was heavy. Will clutched it with one hand, avoiding the rusty nails, and, using one crutch to keep his balance, dragged the lumber toward the sawhorse while his father attacked the next piece of siding.

Physically, dragging the lumber was nearly impossible for Will because of the weakness of his legs. He had learned to plant himself and pull with one arm, then move ahead to pull again.

Sweat gathered beneath his shirt. He unbuttoned his coat. Tonight, he was glad for the cold air.

Back when they arrived in Enid, when his father first demanded that he help cut wood, he had thought it not possible for him, even unfair, considering his condition. Pain often shot down his legs as they worked. Now, when he washed from the kitchen basin in front of their old fading mirror, and no one was around, he admired the forming muscles in his arms and chest. Already, the work had its benefits. He still hated cutting wood, but it came more easily than when he had started.

Will pulled again. It reminded him of a motion he had made earlier in the day—climbing the rope! Will gritted his teeth and pulled with all his might. I'll climb that rope in record time. And Irene will be watching.

By the time Will got to the sawhorse, his father, with two boards across a shoulder, arrived. He slipped them off and let them clatter to the ground. He picked up the other end of Will's board and together they placed it in the sawhorse. From the side of their small outbuilding his father retrieved a long two-man saw with huge teeth, meant for sawing logs.

Will hung onto the handle at his end of the saw, letting his feet and crutches anchor him as a single pivot, and worked his arms back-and-forth in rhythm. Except for the steady rasp of the blade against wood that faded to his subconscious, there was silence. He imagined he was in a tug of war with his father, first winning as he pulled the blade toward him, then losing as his father pulled.

Will forgot that he had not yet eaten. He even forgot that he was about to be paddled.

The sawed-off end of the lumber fell to the ground.

"That's a good piece," his father said. He picked it up and splintered hunks from the side of one end. "It's started to rot. This'll make a good handle." He scraped the paddle handle across the saw blade to smooth it off and tested the remainder. "Still strong," he said. It lacked the sophistication of the "Board of Education," but was a lot larger.

"Let's finish up, and then we'll get to it," his father said.

Will pulled at his end, but his enthusiasm had fled. They worked on in silence. As they made their last cut, Will ventured, "Maybe we should cut some more. It might not be enough. It's awfully cold tonight."

His father answered by retrieving his new paddle that he had set aside. "Lean across the sawhorse."

Choctaw braves don't cry.

The clear air carried from a distance the distinctive chug of a Model T. Charlie Coleman, weighing the paddle in his hand, paused, then raised his arm. The chugging came closer, then changed to a lower pitch followed by a higher one as the low gear engaged and the engine caught up. The chugging drew near to the house.

Will's father clutched his homemade paddle and strode purposely to the front of the house. Will followed, swinging between his crutches as rapidly as he could. Two cars at their house in one night!

His father turned his head to call back to Will, "Don't think this will get you out of this."

The chugging stopped. Will rounded the side of the house.

Coach Mattingly climbed from his Tudor Model T.

* * *

The house smelled wonderfully of fatback and beans, one of Will's favorite meals. The table was set with their checked blue oilcloth. To Will, with Coach present, the dark cracks in the cups and dishes seemed monstrously wide. Thankfully, the dented aluminum coffee percolator on the stove had yet to draw attention to itself by percolating.

"Won't you stay and eat with us, Mr. Mattingly?" Will's mom asked. China clattered as she pulled a plate from the cupboard shelf. "I'll set another place."

To Will, Coach Mattingly looked awkward in a suit and tie and holding his fedora. He couldn't imagine him wearing anything besides khakis and a tee shirt, and a whistle hanging about his neck.

Coach stared at Will's mother's face, then dropped his eyes and fumbled with the hat's brim. Her dark complexion couldn't hide the bruises on her face and neck.

Will pushed his own thoughts about her aside. They hurt too much.

"Thank you, Mrs. Coleman. It smells wonderful, but I've already eaten," Coach said. He cast a longing glance at the pots heating on the stove. "I apologize for interrupting the start of your dinner."

Will's mother blushed. He thought she looked beautiful. "The men hadn't finished their chores outside yet, Mr. Mattingly."

Will's father clutched the paddle behind one leg. "How can we help you, Mr. Mattingly?"

Coach's eyes were drawn toward his father's hidden hand.

"We were cutting firewood," his father explained, and promptly tossed the paddle into the wood box next to the stove.

"Will, the stove could use more fuel," his mother said. "Please add a few sticks for us while we see what Mr. Mattingly wants."

Will swung over to the stove and tossed the paddle into the cook stove's fire box. He felt his father's stare on his back. Will rolled his lips together to keep from laughing. Perhaps Uba Pisku answered prayers after all.

"Will wants to participate in physical education," Coach Mattingly said, then looked first at Will's mother, then at his father. The slack in his parents' faces registered incomprehension. "Right now, he attends class and listens to instruction—that's all." The coach paused. "He must have physical education credits to receive a high school diploma."

His father's visage, already shaded in the poorly lit room, darkened, but otherwise remained passive as if he had not understood, like when a mind is preoccupied.

"Oh, is that all?" his mother said. "I thought maybe Will had been in some sort of trouble. You know he's a cr—" She looked at her husband then quickly glanced to the floor.

Will immediately spoke up. "I can do it. I know I can. Please."

Coach Mattingly smiled and nodded at Will. "He's a very determined young man. You know he rope climbed to the gym ceiling today?"

"No!" his mother said. "How could he? He's a—" She snapped her mouth shut.

"You were going to say, 'he's a cripple'—again," his father said. "Always excusing him. He can do a whole lot more than you think. Well, he's not taking advantage of me."

Coach didn't react to the outburst, although his ears were a little red. But he had just come in from the cold. He merely said, "No one else has done that since I've been at Enid High."

"Floor to I-beam, twenty-four feet," Will said. He wished he could climb right then. He swung himself back and forth a little on his crutches.

"But he does have some ah . . . obstacles," Coach said. "I'm willing to work with him, but under the circumstances I thought it best I check with you first." He looked at Will's father. "I've been doing some real thinking." Coach pressed his lips together and bowed his head. "A lot. I'd like to have him do some special exercises." He looked back up and studied Will's face. "Lunch is a whole period, and if he could come to the gym for part of it. Maybe after school, too?"

Will looked hopeful, but his father spoke first.

"He said he has a job, shoveling coal. At school." He frowned, his was voice flat. "He has chores to do at home. First thing you know, he'll be neglecting his responsibilities. And his schoolwork."

"Oh, Will, this sounds like too much for you," his mother said.

"I'm strong. I know I can do it. You'll see."

"By not doing your school work and neglecting to help here at home, that's how. I'm not having it! You're already in trouble with the principal." Will knew without looking that his father's face had turned a deeper red.

"Exercises? A job? Staying after school? Evidently, you haven't had enough to do." His father's voice came from the back of his throat as he spat out the words. "I'll exercise you right here at home.

"Pretending you can't do, evidently. I don't know what you pulled on Mr. Mattingly to get him to want to keep you after school. I apologize, Mr. Mattingly, for the trouble Will has caused you. He won't bother you again."

"Please, Mr. Coleman, understand that he has been no trouble. None." Sweat glistened on

Coach's brow. "These were my ideas. I'd like him to participate in physical education."

"I don't know how he fooled an educated man like you, Mr. Mattingly, but this will be the end of it. I assure you." He turned his black eyes to glare at Will. "You do whatever Mr. Mattingly tells you, but you better be home on time."

Will trembled. He didn't know what his father wanted. There was nothing he could do to please him. The wood in the stove popped, drawing Will's eyes to the red glow visible through the air intake. His father would make a new paddle.

* * *

The sound of Coach's Model T had barely faded when Will's father pushed Will outside and stalked to the woodpile. A silence born of anger deadened the air. The stars seemed to retreat and sink into a black void. Will trembled as his father tore into the pile, throwing down one piece of wood, white as bone, one after another.

His father finally stood with a wide piece in his hand. "Any piece'll do," he growled. "Boy, bend over the sawhorse."

Will shook so badly that he could barely shuffle to the horse.

"Bend over, I said!"

Even as he bent to lean on the saw horse, Will could hear his father's boots scrape the ground to seek purchase, the rustle of his coat as it was twisted for him to reach far back over his shoulder with his hands gripping each side of the lumber, and the whistle of the paddle as it zipped through the air.

The blow rocked Will and the saw horse forward. Will clamped his teeth together to keep from crying out.

"Don't you ever embarrass me like that again!" his father shouted. The sound of the paddle cutting through the air came again. The paddle landed with a mighty whomp!

"Please, Dad. No more!"

Again came the paddle. "This for cheating."

Again. "This for being late to school."

Whomp. "Don't ever come home late again."

They took Will's breath away. He could not cry out.

Again the paddle. "No more backtalk."

"Stop mooning over that paleface girl!"

That's worse than a licking. I must see her. Wham! A terrible blow.

Again, the whistle of lumber. "This for pushing me."

Will gasped for breath. Even that conflagration that shot up his legs and back could not match the ferocity of the pain.

The sound of pounding feet running toward them filled the pause between strokes. "No, Charlie, no!" It was his mother.

Whomp. His father put in another quick lick. "For the torn coat."

"No, Charlie!" Through Will's gasps he heard tussling behind him. He looked back and saw his mother grab his father's arm.

"Get off! Get away." His father pushed her off, knocking her to the ground.

Wham! It came again. "For burning up the paddle."

"Charlie, stop. Have you gone mad?"

"I'll show you." The wood whistled again, landing with such a blow as to knock Will and the sawhorse to the ground.

"Get off of me!" his father shouted at his mother.

Will pushed up on the sawhorse, wanting to assist her, but he couldn't even straighten up. He saw her wrap her arms about his father's arm and clutch it to her, forcing the board toward the ground.

"No, Charlie, no. No. No." Her sobs came in spasms.

His father turned and twisted to free his arm, but could not shake her loose.

He pummeled her head with his fist.

She did not let go. "Stop, stop," she cried.

Finally, his father dropped the paddle while his mother clung to him, sobbing. He stood there with his legs spread. Then as his mother loosened her grasp and slid in a heap to the ground, he walked to the house.

Dogs barked from somewhere distant.

Choctaw braves don't cry. Will put a trembling hand to his face. He had not cried.

"Supper is cold," his mother said. She rose, then collapsed to her knees, sobbing.

Will drug himself to his mother's side. "Mom, you okay?" A tear rolled off his cheek to join hers.

"This isn't the last of this!" his father shouted through the walls of the house.

Chapter 9

"Keep Out!" the sign said.

After the beating, pain had ravaged Will's body and had driven him to struggle out of bed two hours earlier than he had planned. He was gone long before his mother or father knew that he was up, long before the gang usually appeared at the corner, and long before a light shone from the window of Irene's bedroom.

He leaned on his crutches for relief from the throbbing ache and stared at the ugly double doors beneath the sign, the doors meant only for use by Mr. Wyzowaty, the custodian. Disobeying the sign at the rear of Enid High made him feel like he was breaking in, but filled him with pride—he was an employee.

Will stared at the perpetually burning light bulb that illuminated the shadowed landing at the bottom of the steps. Steep, rough concrete steps with concrete walls fell to the boiler room's doors. Progressively larger patches of sleet and ice lay in the corners of each succeeding step. In spite of the cold, perspiration, born of pain, poured from him as he lowered his crutches to the steps.

The doors were locked. Will pounded a door. He stuck his nose against a door's meshed glass window to peer inside, but only saw his reflection. Mr. Wyzowaty had not yet arrived.

As soon as he leaned back against the wall to wait, he winced as pain shot down his legs. He then thrust himself forward to brace himself with his crutches. The pain had to stop.

He closed his eyes. *Good night Irene, Good Night Irene, I'll see you in my dreams.* Her image came to him. Dark hair embraced the back of a neat white blouse. He imagined warm tan shoulders beneath the blouse. Irene turned. She looked back. Her brown eyes found his and held. He had to work—for Irene.

Will heard footsteps on the landing above him and turned to look. Bright sunlight enveloped the silhouette and spilled down the stairway and into his eyes.

"Ahh, Will!" Mr. Wyzowaty's voice rang. "We've got to get those teapots boiling."

Will stepped aside to allow Mr. Wyzowaty to unlock the lower door, then shuffled in behind him, head down.

Wyzowaty's eyes followed the boy as he dragged himself toward a pile of coal and a shovel. His voice dropped. "Ahh, Will. Maybe this job is too much for you."

"No! I'm fine. You'll see." He pulled off his flannel shirt and revealed a threadbare undershirt. He hung his shirt on a nearby valve, then thrust his crutches far ahead, planted them, and swung forward. "Unh," escaped Will's lips. His body convulsed.

Wyzowaty's face sagged. "I can see. You look worn out. You already missed yesterday afternoon. Maybe I should get someone else." He lifted Will's shirt from the valve to take it to his office.

"I can shovel." Will stopped in front of the coal cart, forced himself upright and threw a shovelful of coal onto the floor, then knelt upon it. He thrust the shovel into the coal cart's pile and clamped his teeth together. He tossed the coal into the hopper, then jerked with pain. He set his jaw and pushed the shovel back into the pile. Again, pain shot through him. Sweat drenched his undershirt. He lifted the shovel. The weight of the coal settled onto his back; suddenly it was like the wham from his father's paddle hit full force. Will fell forward onto the shovel.

Mr. Wyzowaty stood there, staring at him. "It's going to be cold today, Will. Real cold. My babies are mighty hungry. They can't wait to be fed. You need help today?"

"No. I'm fine. Just a little stiff."

"A lot of boys would like to do this. Maybe it's harder than you thought, Will. Maybe you've too much else to do."

I have to have this job! My father will say I lied about a job. He'll kill me! And I've got to get Irene a valentine.

"I needed to rest a second. That's all, Mr. Whiz. I'll get done before class. I know I'm a little slow today, but I can fill the hoppers faster than those babies can eat. You won't have to pay me extra if I take a little more time."

Will stabbed the pile, half-filled the shovel, and threw coal into the hopper. Pain danced up and down his back, but didn't knock him down. He'd win, half-shovelfuls at a time!

But the big boiler slurped the coal, draining the hopper as fast as he could fill it. He glanced over his shoulder. Thankfully, Mr. Whiz was busy washing out some mops.

Will tired. He repeatedly looked through the custodian's office window at the clock. Its hands raced. It was 8:05. Homeroom class was at 8:20. A vision of his name on the office late blackboard passed before his eyes. He jammed the shovel deep into the coal and heaved. Pain wracked his legs, his back, his neck. Everything went black. He teetered forward, caught himself on the shovel still planted in the coal. Uba Pisku. Help.

What is my father trying to do? Keep me from working, from having a girlfriend? He wishes I would die.

Yeah—wants to kill me.

I'll get him. Let him try. I'll get him first.

Consciousness returned as a haze. He looked up. Wyzowaty was staring at him.

Will shook with agony as he pulled on the shovel. The pain sapped his strength. He could not free the shovel from the coal. He clutched his crutches and struggled to his feet. He managed to drape his body over his crutches. This was worse than the beating. He hated himself.

Finally, Mr. Wyzowaty spoke. "You've coal dust all over you. There's a pan of water and a towel behind the screen." Mr. Wyzowaty took the shovel and shoveled coal. He never looked back.

* * *

The desk seat was hard and the pain brought sweat to his upper lip and temples. When the bell finally sounded ending homeroom, Will rose immediately.

"Since you are in such a big hurry to get to class, Will Coleman, you can spend some time learning how to be polite," Mrs. Smith, his homeroom teacher, said. She wore red lipstick and he liked to watch her lips. He wished he had her for Algebra.

"The bell is my signal, not yours. Wait until everyone else has left, then I'll dismiss you."

Leaving last was worth it; he watched her lips and she didn't make him sit back in his seat. Her lips reminded him of Irene's.

Will was almost late to U.S. History class. Mr. Bender was thin and pale with sharp, black features. "Hawk" they called him behind his back.

"Just stand in the back and don't cause any trouble," was all he said to Will's inquiry.

Will didn't bother to ask his Biology teacher, Mr. Goldstein, if he could stand. It was lab day. Most of the time Will stood, peering through a microscope, lost in what he saw.

But his next class was Algebra.

"After what you did in my class yesterday, now you want to stand up?" Miss Whitaker said. A smile passed over her face. "I suppose it has something to do with your meeting with Dr. Grover yesterday afternoon."

Around the room snickers burst from behind hands clamped over mouths.

Will clenched his fist around his pencil and thrust out his jaw. He was sick of the laughter. He could feel his anger building.

Except for the narrowing of her eyes, Miss Whitaker ignored the snickering. "It serves you right. You can just sit on it. You don't see the other three asking to stand up."

At that, Emery and Wade guffawed. Miss Whitaker responded with a half-hearted frown. If she hadn't been there, Will would have punched them; he knew he would. He felt resentment, and a confidence growing inside. Maybe from having climbed the rope.

When opportunity presented itself, Will sat on his hands for cushioning and shifted in his seat for relief, but not slyly enough.

"Will Coleman, please be still. What has gotten into you?" Miss Whitaker insisted.

"May I please go to the restroom, Miss Whitaker?"

"No, you may not."

Will had known she would not fall for that, but he was desperate. The hands on the clock crawled. He prayed for some distraction. Uba Pisku answered.

"What is A times A, Emery Carlisle?" Miss Whitaker asked.

Will bolted upright to rivet his attention on Emery. Emery needed to pass Dr. Grover's exam.

Emery stood, hemmed and hawed, then settled on "Two A's."

Will smiled. That was an easy Algebra I question.

Miss Whitaker gave Emery a withering look, picked up her grade book, searched through and marked it. "Is his answer correct, Mr. Simmons?"

"Sixty-four," Wade bluffed, answering as he rose.

Will grinned more.

Miss Whitaker held her pen over the page, giving Wade a second's reprieve.

"Oh, I thought you said eight times eight," Wade said.

Miss Whitaker wrote, then asked, "What do you say, Mr. Thompson? A times A?"

"I don't know, Miss Whitaker. I need help," Sam said after standing. He pretended his overalls strap button had a problem.

"That answer is quite correct, although not the answer I'm looking for." She did not mark her grade book. "Help us, Mr. Coleman."

Although Will struggled to rise, he gladly got to his feet. "A times A equals A squared."

Miss Whitaker echoed Will's response by writing it on the blackboard. "Simple enough, wasn't it?" She glared at Emery, Wade and Sam. "You boys certainly have a lot of work to do before retaking the exam. You better get some help.

"Mr. Coleman, since you like to help them so much, you can tutor them during your lunch hour. I'm sure you can find a corner table in the cafeteria where you won't be bothered." She stared at Will. "What do you have to say, Mr. Coleman?"

Will's face turned blood red. His stomach felt as if it had been jabbed. At least he had given a correct answer.

Half the day was left to heat the school and he planned on shoveling coal during lunch to show Mr. Whiz he was reliable. Besides, he wanted to say he couldn't help them. Those goofs had already gotten him into heaps of trouble.

"I have a job," Will said.

There was no snickering from the class now. Mrs. Whitaker had become too worked up to cross.

"How could you have a job?" Miss Whitaker asked. "You're in school all day. And besides . . ." She didn't finish what everyone was thinking. "I'm giving you a job—see that your accomplices pass the test."

"Yes, ma'am." What was he going to do? He had to keep his job. Or Irene would think, what, a cripple can't keep a job? He'd never have a chance with her.

"You boys can be seated."

Will sat back down and winced; he'd forgotten to ease into his seat. Maybe it would not be too late to save his job if he shoveled during Study Hall.

As Miss Whitaker turned to the blackboard, he felt a slight punch on his arm. He turned. Emery glared and bared his teeth.

Will scowled back. "I'll knock those buckteeth out," he whispered. Why was Emery so hateful?

Will tried to listen, but worried. *Mr. Whiz'll fire me before I get started. Valentine's Day will pass, and Irene will think I don't even care. And look at LeRoy—nifty in his suit, bending over his work, impressing Miss Whitaker, impressing the girls, impressing Irene. It's Irene he's after. And gym is next. I told Coach Mattingly, "I can play. I'm tough." And Coach replied, "Okay, Coleman. We'll find out." What's he got planned for me? And my father told Coach I'd do whatever he told me to do, including staying after school for special exercise—and I'm supposed to shovel coal after school, and then not be late getting home.*

The dismissal bell rang.

Coach greeted Will at the locker room door with an Enid High gym uniform and some sneakers in hand. "Put these on," Coach said. His face was stiff, lips tight. "They're left-behinds from last year. They're clean. The shoes are only for gym." The name, "Timothy Baker," was hand-lettered beneath the Enid High insignia on the shirt. The shirt and shorts were obviously too large. "Your locker is number 306." Coach pointed with his head. "In the third row." He left and went through the gym doors.

Emery burst into the row as Will removed his street clothes. LeRoy appeared at the end of the row and called Emery back, and, cupping his hand around Emery's ear, whispered into it.

Emery strode down the row and threw open his locker, three down from Will's. "Gonna show us up again today, huh, climber-boy?" He tore off his street clothes and pulled his Enid High T-shirt over his head. "Hope I get to guard you playing basketball. We'll see whose teeth are left on the floor."

"Just try it," Will said. He balanced himself against the locker, pulled off his flannel shirt and began removing his pants. What bad luck, Emery's locker near his.

"Whooo, will you look at this?" Emery called, pointing to Will's back. "Will Coleman, the Injun, turning into a jigaboo. A jigaboo!"

Feet shuffled and pounded the floor and lockers slammed as students scurried toward row three. "Look at that, a deep blue-black nigger. He's not an Indian."

The row quickly filled. Boys pushed and jumped in attempts to see over those in front of them.

"Who's that? I've never seen a Negro before," came from the back.

Boys jostled into Will from the press behind them. He nearly fell but caught himself with the locker door. Someone yanked his pants down.

"Oh! Look at that!"

"Get off me!" Will yanked his pants back up with one hand. He shook with pain. There was sudden silence from those up front, but students in the back continued to push.

"Wow. That must have been some beating."

"Can't you see he's hurting. Leave him alone."

The quiet spread to the back of the crowd.

"Hah. Hah. You don't mess with Dr. Grover, huh, Will?"

The pushing and shouting from the back started again.

Wham! Something crashing into a locker overwhelmed the sounds of voices and scuffling.

"Get out of my way." Now the noise from the back quieted. Wham! It happened again, followed by "Oof", the sound made when air is suddenly expelled from a body.

Heads turned and saw Sam forcing his way through the mob. "You, get out of my way!" Sam said. He lifted a boy up by his shirt and shorts and slammed him into the bank of lockers. Wham! Boys crowded one another to make room for Sam Thompson. Sam didn't stop shoving people until he was next to Will.

Sam faced the crowd. "What's wrong with you saps? Leave him alone." He lowered his voice. "Yeah, Will, you look like you're becoming a Negro." Sam looked around the crowd. "So what? It's not his fault."

Sam looked at the crowd. "I cheated, tried to copy his test. He only tried to finish the test—on his own. And we let Whitaker blame him." He took Will by the shoulder and gave him a friendly shake. "I'm sorry, Will."

The shaking sent pain down his back, but not very much pain.

"That's okay, Sam."

Sam turned behind him and reached past Will for Emery's arm and pulled him forward. "Tell him, Emery. Tell him you're sorry."

Emery didn't speak, but yanked himself free of Sam's grasp.

"I said, tell him!" Sam forced his way through what was left of an aisle until his body was against Emery's. Uneasiness registered on the onlookers' faces.

Sam grabbed Emery by the nape of the neck and an arm and forced him toward Will. "Tell him, Emery. Tell him you're sorry. Or I'll squeeze the blood out of you." Sam's big hand squeezed Emery's neck. Sam shoved him toward Will. "Say it!"

Emery, his face nearly purple, clawed at Sam's hand. "Okay, okay," he forced through his collapsed wind pipe. Sam loosened his grip. Emery looked at the floor and uttered a strangled, "I'm sorry."

Sam's heavy fingers tapped Emery on the back of the head, knocking him forward. "Like you mean it!"

"I'm sorry, Will."

Sam scowled at the sea of faces. "How about the rest of you? How would you like to be Will?"

"Sorry, Will," rose from their throats, but not from all of them. Some, as they shuffled from the aisle, gave him a friendly tap, offered a handshake or added a personal, "I'm sorry."

While Emery fooled with his locker, Will finished putting on his uniform. The locker room emptied. Will put his crutches under his arms to join the class.

"I'll get you," Emery said quietly, evenly, then ran off ahead of him to the gym. Will glimpsed LeRoy pat Emery on the back.

By the time Will arrived in the gym, the class had finished its free play and was sitting on the first-row bleacher seat, listening to Coach give instructions.

"Here he is now," Coach said. "Try to get here a little faster, Mr. Coleman. I was explaining that we'll make some adjustments to help you participate. No one has any problem with that, right gentlemen?" Coach let his eyes run down the row of faces in front of him. A few averted their gaze.

"First drill, two-hand chest pass—two on one, one ball. Coleman, against the wall so you won't need crutches. Tim Atkins, Emery Carlisle, join him. Coleman, you are the one, Atkins and Carlisle, you are the two. Keep the ball moving. Work those arms. The rest of you, count off in three's. Spread around the gym. You know the drill." Coach blew his whistle. "Okay, move. Get at it."

Will moved as quickly as he could on his crutches to the wall. He tried to use the wall for support as Coach had said. Pain struck as he leaned on his bruised back. Tim Atkins heaved the ball to him with two hands. Catching the ball drove Will against the wall. Pain shot down his back. Will emulated Atkin's throw and threw the ball to Emery. With the throw his back was again pressed to the wall.

Emery screwed up his face as he threw the ball as hard as he could to Will. Will's back struck the wall. It was like a blow from his father. Emery grinned.

Will braced himself with one hand against the wall and threw with the other to Atkins. The twisting of the throw tortured his bruised muscles. Pain ran up and down his back and legs, even between passes. His legs trembled under the full weight of his body.

He couldn't give up. He was a Choctaw, wasn't he? He caught and threw the ball with one hand, braced himself with the other.

Coach saw him.

"Hey, Coleman, this is a two-hand drill. Do it right!"

Coach looked at his stopwatch and blew his whistle. "Okay, everybody, switch. Carlisle, you're against the wall with Coleman." Coach blew his whistle and the passes started again.

Being in the two-position brought Will a little relief.

Emery dove for a ball thrown to Will, jammed his shoulder into Will's side, knocked him to the floor and fell on top of him. Will groaned in agony. He couldn't move.

"Why'd you do that Emery?" Atkins said. "Get off of him. Take my hand, Will. I'll help you up."

Emery grinned. "Sorry, Will." As Emery untangled himself he whispered in Will's ear, "Told you I'd get you, and I ain't finished."

"Coach, Will's not moving," Atkins called. "Hurry."

Balls stopped as everyone looked. Coach blew his whistle. "Switch. Keep it going." The balls started again as Coach ran to Will. "What happened?"

The balls slowed while boys watched between passes.

"I'm all right, Coach. Just give me a minute to get up. It was an accident." He glared at Emery. "Emery bumped into me."

"It was just an accident, Coach," Emery said.

Will pushed himself up with his arms and worked into a sitting position, then rested. Coach went behind Will to help, wrapped his arms around him and pulled, pulling his shirt partway up.

"No! No! My back! Bring me my crutches. I'll get up."

Coach released him.

Some boys had worked their way over to look. Sounds from a few balls slapping hands were still heard.

"Coach, look, his back. Pull up his shirt. Look."

Coach carefully pulled up the shirt. Startled, he drew back. "That couldn't have just happened. It's too black."

All the balls stopped.

"It was Dr. Grover's paddle—yesterday," someone volunteered.

"No, it wasn't," Coach Mattingly said. "I was at Will's house last night. He was okay, then."

"Let me alone. It's nobody else's business." Will slowly turned onto his hands and knees and crawled toward his crutches. Right then the pain was so horrible he didn't care about passing physical education, or even graduating from high school, or what his father wanted from him. How could he possibly shovel coal? But . . . Irene . . . He had to work.

The class stared in complete silence. No one even moved while Will made his way toward the doors leading to the locker room. LeRoy stepped forward to hold a door open for him. "The ladies will be impressed by what you did today, Lover Boy," LeRoy whispered.

* * *

Blacked out by his thoughts and the pain, the sounds from balls pounding the floor and Coach's whistle did not reach him. Will dressed as quickly as he could, though painfully, and swung slowly on his crutches, his teeth clenched, from the locker room. He carried his backpack with a hand clamped around its straps and a crutch handle to keep it off his back.

* * *

Will entered the cafeteria before his lunch period started. It was noisy with upperclassmen finishing their lunches. A few studied or wrote. Some cursory glances reached him as he worked his way to a table on the far side of the room. He sat and put his head on the table to wait the start of his own lunch period and the arrival of his three "accomplices," as Miss Whitaker had called them. With much of his weight on the table in front of him, he had less pain. It did not run amok up and down his back.

"Will, wake up."

He had actually fallen asleep. He looked around, hoping that Irene had not seen him sleeping on the table. Where was she sitting? He looked up. Sam towered above him.

Sam squeezed himself into the seat across from him, then emptied his lunch bag on the table—two sandwiches wrapped in wax paper, a half dozen cookies packaged the same way, a banana, an orange and a box of Raisinets candy. He fished two half pint bottles of milk from his pocket that he had bought in the milk line.

"You already ate?" Sam asked. He opened the sandwiches and stacked one on top of the other, then chomped down on both of them at once. He shook the milk containers to disperse the cream, popped the cardboard lids from their tops, slid a straw into one, then guzzled all its milk in one draught.

Will eyed Sam's food. Real fruit, even a banana. "I'm not hungry." He was starving. He had managed to slip a corn biscuit into his pocket on the way out of the house that morning and had eaten it on his way to school. Had he made breakfast he would have awakened his parents.

"Where are Wade and Emery?" Will asked.

"They said they needed a ciggy. We can't wait for them before we start the lesson."

Will tried to divert his eyes from the remainder of Sam's food.

Sam started on the cookies. "Want one?"

Will snatched one of the two remaining. It was chocolate chip. "Thanks." He felt guilty taking someone's food.

He broke it in two. He wanted to make it last, but crammed a half into his mouth and swallowed it nearly as quickly as Sam had his.

The second half of the cookie Will held in his hand, turned it slowly, examined its texture, counted the chocolate bits. Saliva flowed. He pressed the cookie to his mouth and noted the crumbly feel on his lips, making certain to catch any crumb that broke off. He licked his lips. He sniffed the cookie and took a nibble. The crumbs dissolved on his tongue. He pressed them to the roof of his mouth. Chocolate melted and spread, flowing between his teeth and gums. He chewed, then swallowed only when he could no longer hold it in his mouth. He took another nibble and closed his eyes. He could not remember the last time he had a chocolate chip cookie.

"Will, you better hurry up with that cookie. I want to pass that exam."

Will opened his eyes. Sam was on the box of Raisinets. He tilted his head back and poured them into his mouth from the box. He then scooped the trash from the table, took it to the trash can and sat back down. "I'm ready," Sam said.

Will sat the remainder of his cookie to the side and opened his math notebook. "These are all of the work papers and homework related to the test," Will said. "We'll start with the first one and find out what you know. Then work on what you need."

The boys leaned toward each other, intent on the papers in front of them. There were explanations and questions. Pencils worked. Will forgot his pain. He smiled and laughed for the first time in weeks.

"Sam, you catch on fast," Will said. "Why'd you fail the test?" He nibbled at his cookie and replaced the rest on the table.

"It's hard to sit and listen to Whitaker. And I hate homework." He leaned back and eyed Will. "Maybe you could come over my house sometimes and we could work together—you could help me. You make it fun."

It was Will's turn to stare. He had not been invited to join with a peer to do anything since his grade school days. His face and neck grew warm. He thought about his father, his job, getting home, his chores. What about Irene? And his clothes; Sam's always looked new and starched and ironed. Will's mouth opened, but no sound came out.

Sam frowned. "It's okay, if you don't want to."

"No, I—"

The odor of cigarette smoke broke into Will's deliberations. Emery and Wade! Will turned and saw them staring from the end of the table.

"We're here for our mathematics lessons, Professor," Emery said.

"How is he going to teach you anything—with only five minutes left?" Sam said.

"That's not our problem." Emery pointed his finger at Will. "Remember, Whitaker told you it's your responsibility to see that we passed."

Emery edged closer to the table where Will sat. "This your cookie?"

Emery didn't wait for an answer. His balled-up hand slammed down on the remainder of Will's cookie, smashing it into bits.

"This is what is going to happen to you, if we fail." He swept the crumbs onto the floor and stomped on them like he was putting out a cigarette.

Sam rose and reached across the table for Emery. Emery jumped back, out of range.

"I thought we were buddies," Emery said. He turned toward the cafeteria exit and called over his shoulder. "Go ahead. Hit me. I'll see you get expelled from school. Come on, Wade."

Sam started after the two as the bell rang signaling the end of the lunch period.

"Wait, Sam." Will reached for Sam. His fingers bit into Sam's arm. "I'll take care of them myself."

"You couldn't catch a dead horse," Emery called as he and Wade scooted for the door. Will saw them push past a girl with dark hair who stood in the doorway.

Irene!

She walked toward Will as he and Sam gathered their belongings.

Will's heart pounded as she drew close. His face was crimson. Was LeRoy watching?

"Will, I waited, hoping to see you on your way out, then I saw you over here."

He looked at her. "Hello," was all he could manage. He should at least say her name. "Hello, Irene."

Their eyes met. His heart missed a beat, then thudded. It felt like it was in his throat, choking him.

"I saved this for you." She held out an apple for him to take.

He pulled his eyes from hers to look at her hand. In it was the shiniest red apple he had ever seen.

Chapter 10

As hungry as he was, Will didn't think he would ever be able to eat the apple. He'd keep it forever. He shoved it into his backpack. It made a lump. Fixed in his vision was Irene's smile as she hurried off to class. She had even looked over her shoulder to smile again before she disappeared into the crowded hallway. Will scooted after her; tried to get her back in sight, but she was gone. He shrugged. In a few minutes he would see her in English class.

Someone came up quickly from behind Will and bumped him—hard—nearly knocking him off balance. He caught a glimpse of a tall, erect boy wearing a fine brown suit—LeRoy, scooting around a corner.

Students were quickly disappearing from the hall. It was time for the late bell. But ahead of Will, walking slowly toward his class's doorway, lingering even, were Irene and LeRoy, oblivious, looking at each other.

LeRoy released her hand, then gave her books to her from the pile under his other arm. She faced LeRoy, toward Will—he could see her face and the silver cross at her neck. She looked up into LeRoy's eyes and smiled that same smile that Will had thought was meant only for him. She continued to look into LeRoy's face, then disappeared into the room while LeRoy watched her.

LeRoy turned and saw him. He glared as his smile faded. He went down the hall, now hurrying.

Will was angry enough to spit. *She toys with me,* he thought. *She sees how she affects me. She does it for amusement. Irene and LeRoy laugh at me.*

Will passed through the doorway as the late bell rang. I'll never—

"You are to be in your seat when the tardy bell rings, Will Coleman," Mrs. Johnson said.

To avoid a scolding was reason enough to arrive early, but mostly he did not want to walk down the aisle in front of the class, down his aisle next to where Irene sat.

Will felt the eyes on him, eyes that thought about his worn clothes and the backpack, and now the lump in it—the dratted apple. And her beautiful eyes, laughing at him.

He couldn't help it. He cast a glance her way as he passed her seat. Her eyes caught his, her lips curved into a smile, just for him.

But that was the same smile she had for LeRoy. He must forget her.

Will shuffled into his seat and propped his crutches against his desk. Except for the noises the seat made as he sat, there was not a sound in the room. Everywhere he glanced, he saw that they watched him. Embarrassment overwhelmed the pain shooting through his back and legs.

That cross at her throat—Will saw it as the Choctaw symbol for "paths crossing"—their paths, his and hers.

But he knew better. She was performing her Christian duty— "Inasmuch as ye have done unto one of the least of these my brethren, ye have done unto me." When Will's family lived in Haskell County, his mother had dragged him to church every Sunday. That's what Irene wants to do. Will wondered if she took LeRoy to church. He must forget her.

"Will Coleman, what has gotten into you?" Will became aware that Mrs. Johnson was talking to him. "Please answer the question."

Some students snickered as Will pushed himself to his feet. "Would you repeat that, Mrs. Johnson?"

Heat rose in his neck and burned his ears. She went on to another student.

He'd have none of it. He'd not be a missionary project. Not even for Irene. He'd eat the apple at his first chance. He wished he could bite it right then.

He wasn't her equal. She was meant for someone like LeRoy, who dressed nicely and had money, and was respected by the principal. If that was what was important to her, let LeRoy have her. He'd forget about her.

Will thrust his hand into his bag at his feet, yanked out the apple and ducked behind the student in front of him. He bit hard, angrily, into the apple. *That's the end of Irene.* The snap of a crisp, juicy apple being bitten resonated through the room. Heads turned toward the sound; he dared not chew. Will closed his mouth around the bite as the tart sweetness engulfed his taste buds and saliva flowed. He slipped his hand holding the apple into his desk.

Mrs. Johnson looked his way. "Is that you, Mr. Coleman?"

With head down, Will deliberately dipped his pen into the inkwell and copied the home assignment from the blackboard, "Using your essay, write a poem that expresses its central—" it said. Pressure in his mouth from the bite of apple and saliva mounted. He chewed once, dipped his pen again, chewed once more and swallowed. It went down his gullet like a rock.

"Just doing my work, Mrs. Johnson."

"Then who's eating? I smell apple," Mrs. Johnson said.

The apple was fantastic—like Irene. *Stop thinking about her!* He wanted to bite it again—badly—but kept working, his one hand inside the desk, holding the apple.

"Please recite the lines from Tennyson that you memorized," Mrs. Johnson said.

Will wasn't even going to look at Irene any more. He'd ask to have his seat changed so he couldn't see her. Hand inside the desk, he hefted the apple. He'd eat it, but only because he was hungry.

Will looked up. Mrs. Johnson was staring at him. "Are you going to answer, Mr. Coleman?"

"Pardon me, Mrs. Johnson." Will dropped the apple in his desk and clambered to his feet.

"The verses you memorized—or didn't you do it?"

Will turned a darker shade of red, but recovered. "It's from the second verse of 'The Charge of the Light Brigade.' " He took a deep breath and exhaled. He dared not look at the class. Even so, he knew that Irene had turned around and was watching him. " *'Theirs not to make reply/ Theirs not to reason why/ Theirs but to do and die.'* "

"What does that mean to you, Will?"

Wasn't it enough that he recited the verse? Will's head was pounding. He bent and reached into his desk and withdrew the apple. He didn't care what Irene thought, or anybody else. "This!" he said, and took a huge bite from the apple, making it snap. He crunched the apple as the teacher's jaw dropped. "It means, if I don't want to end up dead like the six hundred horsemen of the Light Brigade, I shouldn't let people push me around." He took another bite of the apple, even though the first had not been swallowed.

"Oh," Mrs. Johnson said. She regarded Will with a careful eye. "I'm gratified you found Tennyson so meaningful."

Will expected to hear next, "Go see Dr. Grover," but instead Mrs. Johnson smiled. "You certainly demonstrated the depth of feeling that the poem elicits from you, Mr. Coleman. You brought the poem to life for all of us."

The class was dead silent as Will lowered himself into his seat. Somebody snickered. He found Mrs. Johnson regarding him with wide, staring eyes. His heart pounded while he wondered what she meant. She wouldn't fail him for that, would she? Would his classmates have respect for him now, or call him "apple polisher?"

Students recited verses from Tennyson as Will wrapped the remains of his apple in notebook paper and stuffed it back into his backpack. The shuffling of books awakened him to the realization that they were shifting into another activity. He brought his attention back to Mrs. Johnson.

"Turn to page 191, where you will find another Tennyson poem, 'Duet.' I need someone who has some passion to read it aloud—two someone's, actually." She gazed about the room, but seemed to have already settled upon her choice. "Like Will. Will, come to the front. And Irene."

Irene! Will's heart pounded. Again, the blood rose in his face. One embarrassment after another. He wanted to turn and look at LeRoy. What was LeRoy thinking?

Mrs. Johnson was extracting a first payment. Pain had returned to Will's back; at least he could get out of his seat.

"Irene, read the heading and the lines numbered one. Will, read number two's."

Will's eyes went to the pendant at Irene's neck—two paths crossing. Someone had said certain people are meant for each other. Irene's eyes searched deeply. He looked back. Her smooth, lovely cheeks reddened.

He could not escape her; his anger fled. His breath came fast and shallow. Thankfully, he had crutches for support or else he surely would have collapsed.

The class waited.

"You may begin," Mrs. Johnson said.

"*'Duet,' by Alfred, Lord Tennyson.*" Irene's breast rose as she breathed deeply, then continued, "*'Is it the wind of the dawn that I hear in the pine overhead?'* "

Will answered. "*'No; but the voice of the deep as it hollows the cliffs of the land.'* "

Will's voice sounded deep, masculine. He scarcely noticed.

"*'Is there a voice coming up with the voice of the deep from the strand, Once coming up with a Song in the flush of the glimmering red?'* " she responded.

"*Glimmering red.*" His eyes met her lips. Full. Red. Glimmering red. Her black hair framed her lovely face. Irene was beautiful. *If only my lips could but touch hers.*

She waited, searching his face, noting his attention to her. Color again brushed her cheeks.

Will caught her gaze. The class was but a distant mist. Now he read to her, his voice hushed. "*'Love that is born of the deep coming up with the sun from the sea.'* "

"*Love,*" it said. His eyes were drawn back to Irene. Her book trembled. His heart wanted to escape its bounds.

"*'Love that can shape or can shatter a life'* "— she stopped and looked at him in mid-sentence, then finished—"*'till the life shall have fled?'* "

None breathed. Only the steam radiators "ssshed" under the windows, but no one noticed. The clock's second hand slipped from second to second—none cared.

Will looked at her eyes. She caught him staring. He looked quickly at his page. His finger, quavering, sought his place and found it.

"'Nay, let us welcome him, Love that can lift up a life from the dead.'"

Her voice, sweet, breathed the next line.

"'Keep him away from the lone little isle. Let us be, let us be,'" she read.

"Keep him away, let us be," reminded him of LeRoy. Who would she keep away? Will glanced at her. Was she thinking of LeRoy? She had clasped her book to her bosom—breathing, watching, waiting for him.

"'Nay, let him make it his own, let him reign in it —he, it is he, Love that is born of the deep coming up with the sun from the sea,'" he read.

Their eyes met as they finished. She breathed heavily. How he yearned to, to touch . . . to hold her hand.

Had Will looked, he would have seen LeRoy staring at him with murderous eyes.

Chapter 11

Will nodded at the boiler room door. "It's scary looking, isn't it?" He leaned, wincing in pain, onto the handle of the steel-clad door, barely inching it open. Sam, stretching behind him, put his big hand on the handle and pushed. The heavy metal door rumbled open on its track. The boys peered into the dimly lit opening, and then stepped inside onto the landing. Sam pushed the door shut behind them.

"Whew! What's that smell?" Sam asked. "And the heat?"

"Yeah, like the depths of hell. That smell is sulphur, from burning coal." Will glanced back at Sam to see if his words had the desired effect. Big Sam had paled. Will lowered himself onto the first step and asked, "You sure you want to help?" He hid his grin and stepped down another step.

"Sure. Sure. I owe you." Sam remained on the landing. "I wouldn't be able to pass that math exam if it weren't for you. So, you've already paid me." He took a deep breath, then coughed. "You went down here by yourself?"

"Yeah, but Mr. Whiz is a swell fellow. You'll like him. Come on."

"But the door said, 'No Admittance.'"

"That's for the other students. Remember, I work here and you're with me."

Will swung down the steps with Sam behind him. The roar from the furnaces, funneled up the narrow stairway, became deafening.

Will watched Sam, his mouth hanging open, look around. "These are Mr. Whiz's babies," Will shouted and nodded at the bellowing furnaces. Will's chest expanded. "They have a big appetite and eat all the time."

A pipe overhead clanged and Sam jumped. Will grinned. "It's nothing, Sam. A little water is fighting with the steam in the pipes." Will turned and swung himself toward the interior room with the windows. Sam was at his heels. They peered through the windows at Mr. Wyzowaty, sitting at his desk, writing. "You know Mr. Whiz, right?"

"Sure, everybody knows Mr. Whiz."

Will knocked, and then opened the door with "Sigmund Wyzowaty, Custodian," stenciled on its glass pane. The noise level dropped as they stepped inside. Mr. Wyzowaty looked up. "You couldn't creep up on me this time, Injun boy," Wyzowaty said, and broke into a broad smile. "Come on in. Who's this fellow? I've seen him around. Couldn't' have missed him, could I?" He winked and offered his hand to Sam. They shook hands.

"Sam Thompson. He's in some of my classes." Will dropped his eyes. Maybe Mr. Whiz would think that he couldn't handle the job. "Sam's going to help me shovel coal."

"That's great. The more the better. I'm busy. Can you show Sam what to do?"

Will looked back up. "Sure, Mr. Whiz. Come on, Sam."

Sam remained anchored, staring at the wall with Mr. Wyzowaty's diploma and certificates on it.

Mr. Wyzowaty noticed his gaze and laughed. "Yep, it takes quite a bit of education to mop a floor." He returned to his bookkeeping, leaving Sam to stare while Will waited.

Mr. Wyzowaty surrendered to Sam's gaze. "Sam, I have to keep those teapots from blowing up. Plus keep the building going. Make repairs of all sorts—electrical, plumbing, structural, the roof, appliances, *and* do the cleaning. Anything they want done. Add a wall, take down a wall, paint. Plus manage my budget—pay for the utilities, order supplies, and keep payroll—at least, used to. It's more than a janitorial service." Wyzowaty looked down and shook his head. "I had to lay off my permanent help because of this, ah, dang depression. I can hardly keep up with all the work. Can't." He swept his hand toward the wall. "Not a few of those jobs takes some education." He laughed again. "I pinned those up on the wall in case Dr. Grover gets a notion to fire me. They're like insurance policies."

Will and Sam laughed along with Mr. Wyzowaty. "Wow, Mr. Whiz," Sam said. "I didn't know you had so much to do."

"Me either," Will said. *Mr. Whiz has one of the hardest jobs in the world. Cowabunga. I'm his assistant!* "Let me show you what to do, Sam." He opened the door and strode on his crutches into the main boiler room. The noise and smell assaulted them anew.

Will noticed perspiration forming on Sam's brow and running down his cheeks. "First we'll take off our shirts—it's too hot. We can wash up when we're done."

Sam stopped in the midst of unbuttoning his shirt and stared at Will's back. "Your back's an awful mess—looks worse now than I remembered in gym. What happened?"

Will hesitated. He felt ashamed, even if it wasn't his fault. What good would it do to tell Sam about his father? Will kept his eyes glued to his feet while he refastened the overalls over his shoulders.

"That's okay, if you don't want to tell me," Sam said. He allowed his overall top to hang about his waist, leaving his upper body bare.

Will looked up. Sam's arms were immense. He had never seen anyone so big. "It's all right. I was on a ladder, trying to push a corner roofing shingle into place. The ladder was too short. It was standing too much up and down, you know, vertically. So, it went over backwards and I hit the ground hard. I just missed a rock. Tore up my back something terrible."

Sam stopped and stared at Will. "Nice try. But you expect me to believe that?" He smiled while his eyes danced. "You, up on a ladder, repairing a roof?" He burst out laughing.

"I climbed the rope at school, didn't I?"

"Yeah, but carrying the ladder, putting it up and doing that on crutches."

"It was the snowball fight, knocking me on the ground. I didn't want you to feel badly, so I told you the ladder thing."

Sam's lips turned in and down. His brow wrinkled across his broad forehead. "I'm sorry, Will, if we did that."

It was difficult for Will to look at Sam's usually smiling face.

"But it looks worse than anything we could have done," Sam said. "The black and blue goes all the way across. I . . . I don't know what to say."

Will feared Sam might cry. "Sam, it really wasn't your fault. I was afraid to admit, it was my father. He gave me a little whipping. Please don't tell anybody. If he found out . . ."

"Oh," Sam said. His expression didn't change except the corners of his mouth and eyes turned up a little. "I didn't realize. I won't tell. I've had a few lickings myself."

Will sighed. What bothered him most came tumbling out. "But he really didn't have good reasons. He even whacked me for talking with Irene; really, for walking by her house on the way to school."

"Wow! That's pretty stiff punishment. My dad would never hit me for that."

"He told me never to see her again. How am I going to do that? She sits in front of me in English class."

"If I were you, I'd stay away from her. Besides, LeRoy is dizzy over her. He thinks she's his filly. She likes him, too."

"Yeah, Don't I know it! But sometimes I think she likes me. I just can't figure her out."

"Hey, don't worry about her. She's only a dame. There're lots of them out there. And you're smart, and not bad looking, either. Somebody else will come along."

So, Will thought, *maybe girls do find me attractive.* He smiled. "Ah, so you're the real Miss 'Dorothy Dix Talks.'"

Sam balled up his fist and took a half-swing at Will, landing it on his upper arm. "That's me, Dotty Dix, adviser to the lovelorn," Sam said in a falsetto and with a wide grin replacing his frown.

Although meant as a tap, Will felt the power behind Sam's fist. His arm ached to the bone. He would hate to have Sam angry with him. "I'm not lovelorn. I just don't want anybody else." His return compliment was a hard right to Sam's arm.

"Hey, fella, that hurt. Don't you know your own strength?" Sam allowed the shovel to clatter to the floor and grabbed Will's arm. "Wanna see how it really feels?" He raised his fist, but Will nodded toward Mr. Wyzowaty's door where Mr. Wyzowaty stood, staring at them. "I'm not paying you boys for horseplay," he said, and then walked back to his desk.

Will felt red creep up his neck and cheeks. Sam dropped Will's arm and picked up the shovel to heave coal in earnest. The furnaces, reigning over a sudden hush, were louder than ever.

"Sorry," Will shouted toward Sam's ear.

Will saw Sam's mouth form the reply, "Sorry," while Sam kept the shovel moving. Except for the sweat pouring out of him, it appeared that a shovelful of coal weighed nothing to Sam. He felt closer to Sam than almost anybody, except maybe his mother—and Irene.

"Where do you put the shovel?" Sam asked.

Will could hardly believe that Sam had finished so quickly—he wasn't through talking to him about Irene and LeRoy. But the hoppers were piled high and Sam had refilled the cart.

It was true, Will Coleman would never have Irene as a girlfriend. He shook his head. But allowing LeRoy to have her—he couldn't. LeRoy was nothing but scum.

"Where do you put the shovel?" Sam repeated.

Will pointed to the wall where the tools stood and showed Sam the wash pan and the towels. Sam talked, but Will replied stiffly, trying to hold up his end of the conversation. It wasn't Sam's fault life was a bunch of hooey.

After cleaning up, they waved goodbye to Mr. Wyzowaty and left by the outside boiler room door. Mr. Wyzowaty locked it behind them. Cold from the outside stairway and the silence of the outdoors fell upon them. Will felt as if he had lost his hearing.

"Thanks, Sam," Will yelled.

"It was fun, and I'll help as long as you need me," Sam yelled back. "And we don't have to yell anymore."

They both laughed at their howler. They walked north on Monroe Street toward Randolph Avenue and their homes. Will laughed to himself. Sam could substitute for Irene, but they wouldn't hold hands!

A stiff breeze—the Texana—struck their backs as they left the shelter of the school building. The sun, low and to the west, cast long shadows. Will chilled whenever he swung through the shade. He wondered what Sam thought about Irene and LeRoy and himself.

"LeRoy's okay," Will said.

Sam started. "What did you say?"

"LeRoy's okay."

"Yeah, I heard that. I wasn't thinking about him," Sam said. "You don't really mean that."

"He's good looking, especially with all those swell clothes. And vinegar'd be honey in his mouth, especially around teachers—and Irene."

"And other girls. So, you really giving up on her, since ol' Roy's so nice and athletic? And there's so many other fish in the sea? And the fish think you're such good-looking bait."

"Humph! You convinced me—I'm so good looking, I'll never give up! I'll catch the best fish. Irene. Besides, he's not good enough for her. He's—"

"And you are?" Sam grimaced. "That didn't come out right. I was joking." He smiled. "No, you'd be great for her."

Maybe Sam was right the first time. Lots of truth in a joke. I'm just torturing myself thinking about her. Such sweet torture.

"I know LeRoy's mean. If he ever hurts her, I'll kill him." Will envisioned his hands around LeRoy's neck. "I bet when they get married, he'll beat her like my father beats my—" Will felt his face warm. He had said too much.

"You think LeRoy has her all wrapped up. They're getting married, then?"

"No. It's . . ." Will shrugged. "I don't know what to do. She's not going to really, *really like* somebody like me."

"Listen Will. You're a lot smarter and a lot nicer than LeRoy. Better looking. Actually, a lot better looking. He just has swanky clothes and drives his father's expensive automobile. He's a lady's man, wants to be an egg, too. If Irene can't figure that out for herself, or if she's a gold-digger, then she deserves the nincompoop. Stop the worrying, it'll work out. Like I said, there're a lot of dames around, some swell ones, too."

Will's eyes spat fire. "She's no gold-digger!" Irene had practically ignored his tattered clothes. Sam nodded in assent and Will calmed a little. He swung along thoughtfully.

"But these are the real problem—these dang crutches! You didn't account for that." Will slung one crutch far up the walk, watched it, and then threw the other. The crutches skittered over the cold hard pavement, one end burying itself in a leftover pile of sleet.

Sam stopped and smirked at Will. "Woof-woof!"

"Hah!" Will said, and lurched up the sidewalk, fell and struggled to get himself up. Will looked at Sam. "You're going to just watch me?"

"Yeah. Suppose I wasn't here?"

When Will finally arrived at his crutches, Sam joined him, then started laughing and brushing the dirt from Will's clothes. Will dusted off his hands, examined them for scratches, and laughed with him.

"I think LeRoy would like to beat me up," Will said. "He gets the other guys to pick on me."

"See? That proves Irene likes you. What other reason could it be? He knows it."

"But he's bigger than I am. And I heard he's a really good pitcher, an athlete. And Emery's told me a number of times that he wants to beat me up, too. Suppose they gang up on me?"

"Woof-woof!"

He felt like punching Sam on the nose—if he could reach it. "What's that supposed to mean?"

Sam looked him in the eye. "You afraid of them?"

Will spat.

"Use a crutch on them," Sam said.

"That wouldn't be fair."

"Ganging up on you is fair? They must be afraid of you if they have to gang up on you and you being a—I'm sorry, it almost sort of slipped out. Anyway, you can bet those palookas aren't going to do anything as long as I'm around. I'll knock the pea-waddin' outta them."

When they reached Randolph Avenue Sam said, "I forgot. I promised my mom I'd stop at Buttery Grocery on the square. See you tomorrow." He waved and headed east. Will turned toward home and faced the last of the day's sunlight and Uba Pisku.

Sam's sudden absence struck Will. This had been the first time anyone had walked home with him from Enid High. Maybe someday soon it would be Irene.

An ache grew inside him. He envisioned Irene standing with him at the front of their English class. *"Love that is born of the deep coming up with the sun from the sea,"* he recalled. Unconsciously he stopped walking to watch her lips answer, *"Love that can shape or can shatter a life . . ."*

Oh, surely, she was meant for him! He resumed walking, picturing himself strolling with her, carrying her books and holding her hand—and there were no crutches. He walked smoothly, yet slowly, not wanting their walk to end. They reached her house and she invited him inside . . .

Owww. The pain from the backpack pressing on his sore posterior penetrated his daydreaming. He stopped, took off the backpack and held it in his hand with his crutch and began walking. The bag swinging and striking the crutch made it difficult to move smoothly and caused pain of its own. Every few minutes Will stopped and alternated the hand holding the bag.

Somehow, he would get rid of the crutches. He must. Coach said he could help him. He'd do whatever coach said. Didn't his father tell him to do just that? But his father also said to be home on time.

What if I'm not and he hurts my mother again to punish me? Pain flared down Will's back. He shifted his bag and cursed to himself. *I wouldn't let LeRoy hurt Irene. And I'll be danged if I ever let my father beat me or my mother again.*

Will paused to wipe the palms of his hands on his coat. His thoughts had been bothering him more than he had realized.

He was three quarters of the way home. It had taken him much longer than usual to come this far. The sun, having dropped below the horizon and now only visible through the spaces between the houses and trees, bled red across the earth's rim in the west. Light quickly faded from the sky. The air chilled and a breeze moaned in the bare maples lining the street.

Will tried to still his soul as he approached Irene's house, but it was not possible.

The city bus roared next to him, and then screeched to a halt. A man bounded lightly from the bus to the curb, just a step in front of Will. The bus's engine roared and inched it away, then belched diesel fumes which, strangely, Will savored. A strong wind gust battered Will and the man, and scattered the exhaust. The man clutched at his fedora. Will shuddered.

The man appeared familiar. Even though he wore an overcoat, his bearing and form reminded Will of someone. Will tried to keep pace in order not to lose what little he could see of the man in the fading light.

He was not greatly surprised when the man strode onto Irene's walkway and, taking advantage of that quarter turn, twisted to look fully into Will's face.

Will slowed. Though hard to discern in the half-light, the man appeared to have dark features like Irene's—dark skin color, dark full eyebrows and lashes, big black eyes. Will thought the resemblance strong. The man was returning home from work. *Irene's father!*

The man took another step, but suddenly reared about and spoke. "Your father ever work in a mine, a coal mine?"

The question brought Will to a halt at the intersection of the two walks.

"I—I think so." Will felt the heat in his neck. He had been barely more than an infant when his father worked a mine in Haskell County.

"Coleman. Charlie Coleman, isn't it? So, he's come up to Enid. You must be, ah, . . . Will." Even in the half-dark Will could see the spark in his eyes, the curling down of his lips—the latter not at all like Irene's. "You stay away from Irene—from my whole family."

Will's jaw dropped. Before he could respond, the man strode up the walk to his house and closed the door behind him without looking back. Will felt like he had been slapped across the face. His blood boiled and he stared at the closed front door.

Chapter 12

The silver cross at Irene's throat, the Choctaw sign for "paths crossing," burned in Will's mind. He snorted. Rocky twisting paths covered with thorns and lined with pitfalls, that's what they were. Maybe Mr. North had been telling Irene to stay away from him. But it wasn't Mr. North's business. He didn't even know Will.

Who cared what anyone's father thought? Only one person could stop him—Irene. Or could being a . . . a . . . a cripple? He hated himself. His father hated cripples—hated him. He hated his father.

Will stepped inside his house, threw his crutches against the wall and watched as they clattered to the floor. He reached for a chair to hold himself up.

Were all fathers cruel? He couldn't believe Mr. Whiz or Coach or even Dr. Grover would be so unfair. His father and Mr. North knew each other a long time ago, and now, these many years later, neither one wanted Irene and him together. Evidently, the reason surpassed crutches. Or maybe it was Mr. North's reasons.

Will didn't care what Mr. North's reasons were or what his father's reasons were. Nobody was going to stop him.

His parent's bedroom curtains parted and his father, his clothes disheveled and smelly, stalked out. "What's all that racket?"

Even though the light was dim, his father squinted. He saw Will grasping a chair, then his eyes found the crutches askew on the floor next to the wall. "Velma, this boy is . . ." He trailed off, realizing Will's mother was not in the house. "What's the matter with you, boy?" His lips pulled back and he spoke through his teeth. "You didn't get enough, yesterday, did you? You heard me say that wasn't the last of it."

Will was too angry to be frightened. "So, what difference does it make? You always are beating somebody." He glared at his father. "I saw Mr. North!"

"What? You're just trying to change the subject. And keep your voice down."

"No. I saw Mr. North," he shouted. "Irene's father."

"What'd I say? Don't you yell at me." His father's jaw jutted and his fists clenched.

Will stood defiant, his eyes blazing.

After a few deep breaths, his father unclenched his hands. "Ira North? Iradele North. And I told you to stay away from that girl. What were you doing around there?"

"Walking home. Dad, you were a miner, weren't you?"

Charlie Coleman scowled at his son. "What did that liar tell you?" He crossed the short distance to shake Will by the shoulder. The chair rattled against the floor. "What'd he tell you?"

"Nothing. He just asked if you were a miner. Down in Haskell County, when I was little, right? He seemed to know who I was."

His father grew pensive. "We both worked for the San Bois Mining Company," he finally said.

The back door opened, letting in light, followed by a cold draft. His mother entered, carrying water, a pail in each hand, her thin shoulders sagging from the load. The door slammed shut. She shrank beneath his father's glare. With obvious intent she dampened her movements.

"There was a big explosion. Seventy-two miners were buried alive."

Will waited. The oven door creaked. His mother took baked potatoes out of the oven with a pot holder.

"Is that all?" Will said.

"Is that all! Seventy-two men were killed! What is the matter with you?"

"I mean, that's awful, but what has that to do with Mr. North not wanting me to see Irene?"

"So, he doesn't want you to see her, either." Half his face turned up in a smile. "Then stay away from her."

"But why?"

His father grew thoughtful and scowled. "That's between North and me. Just stay away.

"Woman, hurry up and get supper on. Will and I have something to do."

* * *

The old wheelbarrow, running on its spoked steel wheel, bounced along the frozen path. Will sat in its bed, his legs hanging over the front, his crutches and backpack on one side of him, a shovel and an eight-pound-maul on the other, while his father, whistling, pushed the barrow. The jarring sent sharp pain through Will's bruised bottom and rattled his teeth. The cold from the metal went through him and he shivered in the sharp night air. He raised himself on his hands to lessen the impact.

They were striking out into flat, open countryside lying between the little housing development near where they lived and an area north of Enid's center. The huge grain elevators toward which they were headed hadn't appeared any closer since they first came into view. He could not yet see any of the track or trains that serviced the elevators, although he had often heard the trains' whistles, especially at night while lying in bed.

"Dad, stop, stop. Let me walk. It's fun, but it hurts."

Will expected an argument, but his father pushed up the handles so Will could get his feet on the ground and his crutches under him.

"Thanks, Dad. Why we going to the elevators?"

"Hopefully, to get groceries."

"They have a store?"

His father sniggered. "From the trains there. You'll see."

They went on a few more yards with the wheelbarrow bouncing hard and the tools rattling loudly in its bottom. His father stopped and attacked the frozen ground with his shovel. Finally, he loosened enough dirt to shovel into the bed. "Without you in it, it was too noisy," he said. Most days, he probably would have made Will get back into the wheelbarrow. Will thought him in an unusually good humor.

A thought, a dreadful thought, still in pieces, not fully born, made its way to the forefront of Will's mind. He stopped and watched his father walking ahead, shrinking with distance. His father looked back. "Come on Will. What you waiting for?" he called in a forced whisper.

The grain elevators, though still at a distance, loomed huge and white in the milky-white starlight, miniaturizing the trees and houses around them. A small, dark wood lay in their path.

"Come on, Will!"

The shovel and the maul!

In Haskell County he had seen a calf slaughtered. They had cracked its skull with a maul, like the one bouncing in the wheelbarrow. The calf collapsed to the ground. *"It didn't feel a thing,"* the butcher had said to reassure Will.

Dad's mood—so unlike him, so pleasant.

"This isn't the last of this!" came unbidden to Will's mind—his father's yell after the paddling. He had reminded Will only minutes ago.

The seventy-two buried miners. Buried! Alive! A shovel was riding in the wheelbarrow. His father was a miner—an expert with a shovel. Will trembled.

His father turned around, pushed his whisper back to Will. "Will, what are you doing?"

"I want to go back home . . ." He had to give a reason . . . "to get my homework done."

"You'll have time for that. Come on."

"No. It's too much."

His father waited, unrelenting.

Will swung up to him and looked into his face, his eyes wide with fright. "Dad," he suddenly said, inspired with a distraction, "what does Irene have to do with the mine explosion?"

His father walked on, not answering, his eyes down, unfocussed, not seeing. "Well, it . . . it's a long story. It's North." He stopped, then started walking. "You wouldn't understand. But, well . . ." He stopped again, seeming ready to talk, but said, "Nothing. It's better if you don't know."

"But . . ."

"Just shut up." He headed off at a great clip with the wheelbarrow, his strides hard, angry, leaving him behind.

Will dallied, watching him. *Why is he so mad?*

His father passed into the gloom made by the clump of trees and waited. No one at any distance would be able to see them in that grove. Compared to its surroundings, it was pitch black. The blood pounded through the arteries in Will's neck and beat in his ears; he felt limp. He couldn't see if his father held the maul. His father fished for something in his jacket and removed it. It glinted—a jackknife! He looked back at Will, hesitated, put it to his lips and then reared back, producing the silhouette of a man taking a snort. He coughed while trying to smother the sound, then wiped his lips with the back of his hand.

Will stood stock still. *I knew he wouldn't kill me.* He smiled at his own stupidity.

Suddenly his father strode to Will and thrust his face next to Will's.

Will recoiled.

"Okay, I'm gonna tell you the whole thing. Better from me than Ira North," he rasped from a whiskey caressed throat. "Here, sit in the wheelbarrow." He wheeled the barrow near to the tree's trunk, then leaned against the tree. He took another pull from the bottle and then held it in his hand, swirling the liquid.

To insulate himself from the cold dirt and the metal of the barrow, Will threw his book bag on top of them, and then hefted himself into the wheelbarrow.

"I just told you about the 1923 mine explosion—killing seventy-two miners at the Number 6 Mine."

Will didn't budge.

"Mattison, the father of that hotshot boy— what's his name— that came to the house?"

"LeRoy." Will felt his pulse quicken. LeRoy! Irene!

"His father is a big shot at the San Bois mines. Hah! He was superintendent of the Number 6 and some of their other mines. It's no accident that he's here in Enid—to get him away to help quiet the scandal. And they sent North up here, too, to their bank, the Enid San Bois Bank, so they'll keep an eye on each other.

"No wonder North isn't too happy I'm here—afraid I'll spread word around about who he is. And what really happened. But who's going to listen to me, a drunk?"

"I understand about Mr. Mattison. But what does Mr. North have to do with it?"

"Mr. North was the Number 6's manager, chief of the whole mine. I . . . I . . . was foreman of the shift that got killed." He looked away and took another nip. "Just listen. Don't interrupt and you'll understand.

"They were all about efficiency—profit. Never mind the miners' working conditions and safety."

"After the explosion, the mine closed. Mattison disappeared. After we moved here, I learned he had been transferred to the San Bois Mines Enid corporate office—a promotion, I suppose. But I just told you the real reason." His father looked at him from the corners of his eyes. "Not all the time I spend in a saloon is wasted.

"Your Mr. Iradele North, manager for the Number 6 Mine, my mine, blamed that tragedy on Charlie Coleman, me, foreman of the crew that had been wiped out. And . . . and . . . your Uncle Lee, your Mom's brother, was down there." Will's father suppressed a sob.

Choctaw braves don't cry. Will frowned. *All those times he hollered at me.*

"You can imagine how your mother feels. She talked me into helping him get that job. Now he's dead, and everybody says the whole thing's my fault."

"I don't, Dad."

"Just be quiet 'til I finish." His father took another swig from his bottle. "You see, I'd been warning North about the improper ventilation, lack of stoppings and other safety stuff—even little things, like using the new miner's lamps. They just looked at me. I knew what they were thinking—too expensive, all unnecessary.

"Mattison's policy, of course. He wanted his mines to be the leading money-makers—had his eyes on a vice-presidency." Will's father stared out into the night. "And shut down the mine? So they could shore it up and ventilate properly? Not a chance. Keep production going. Greed before deed, I called it.

"That day, I ordered all the men out. The canaries had died—they're susceptible to the gas, you know, even though we can't smell it. Well, North ordered us all back in, saying nothing happened. I was in his office, yelling at him, 'Shut it down!' He said, 'Did the little birdie die?' I couldn't believe it. That's when I grabbed him by the throat and pushed him over in his chair. He fired me, right then. He only cared about the haul—three hundred and forty-eight tons per day—or else.

"I slammed his door so hard the glass, the 'Iradele North, Manager, San Bois Mine Number 6' door pane, broke to pieces. I headed back to the mine to get the men out.

"I was on my way down when the explosion came. Fifty more feet, and I would have been there.

"I wish I would have been. Why were those seventy-two taken? Why Lee? Why not me?"

Will's father stopped. Looked away. Took a deep breath.

"And when it all blew up, they were only too happy to blame Charlie Coleman—he didn't report unsafe conditions—he let the men go in there—he didn't get the men out. He's a damn Indian savage!"

Will felt his ears burning.

"They say they fired me *after* it happened. They ruined my reputation. I couldn't get a job of no kind nowhere around there.

"And you want to hook up to the North family? Over my dead body!

"And your mother, even before the explosion, she'd said she was going to leave me, but I told her I would . . . I would . . ."

Will could see the hateful furrow of his father's brow, the narrowing of his eyes, the curl of his lips. Will believed him. He had seen more than he had ever wanted to see.

His father motioned Will out of the wheelbarrow, threw the mall and shovel into it, and marched off. "Let's go!" They passed from under the gloom of the trees. Will glimpsed the scowl fixed to his father's face.

His father suddenly stopped. Will nearly bumped into him.

His father cocked his head. "Listen."

Will heard only their breathing; watched the mist rising from their mouths.

"From now on, stay quiet. When we get to the train, I want you to walk in its shadow, toward the caboose at the left, where the conductor stays. If you see anyone coming, throw a stone as far as you can in my direction so it hits the train and warns me."

Will squinted in the direction of the elevators. He knew he could throw a stone a long distance, but he couldn't even see a train. "Suppose they stop me and ask what I'm doing?"

"That's why you have your backpack. Say you're going to study with a friend." He pointed with a long bony finger. "Keep going til you get to the first road that crosses the rail. I'll meet you there."

Will sighed. "What are the shovel and sledge hammer for?"

"You'll see. Now, come on." His lips flashed an evil grin.

'You'll see.' The maul had made a hollow thud as it smashed into the calf's head. Will's blood throbbed in his ears.

As they drew closer to the elevators, the long shadows running along their base took the form of railroad cars. They looked small, like toys.

He could make it look like I got hit by a railroad car, or even run over! He hates me. But why would he do that? He wouldn't. I can't keep thinking this. Think of Irene—beautiful Irene.

Nobody, not Dad, not LeRoy, not Mr. North, has given me good reason to stay away from her. I don't care what they think; Irene'll be my girl.

Valentine's Day is almost here. I've got to do something, get something for her.

His father reached the train well ahead of Will and waited in the deep shadow the train cast from the lights near the base of the elevator. When Will arrived, his father pointed and shook his finger toward the end of the train, the way in which Will was to go, then turned on his heel and strode in the opposite direction.

Will was awed. A railroad car was bigger than their house. Their wheels, from where he stood on the rail bed, reached waist high. But compared to the grain elevator, the boxcars were still like toys.

Will stumbled as he started down the railway. He quickly learned to set his feet and crutches securely among the stones of the sloping bed and remnants of ice before swinging between his crutches, and then raise them to clear the stones for the next stride. Further from the train offered easier going, but he had to stay in the train's shadow.

All was quiet except for the shuffle and crunch of his feet on the stone, the creak of his crutches and the occasional displaced stone. The air was cold, still, and smelled of creosote, grease, wood and steel. The odor of wood smoke drifted to his nostrils. He realized that it came from the stove in the caboose he could not yet see.

The maul and the shovel. After his father had finished, then would he . . .?

A clang from afar reverberated along the side of the train, startling Will, causing him to look back. Another clang resounded. It was the sledge hammer, smashing a lock. Now he had become a thief. He wished anew that he had not come. He strained his ears but heard no more. He bent awkwardly, then knelt on one knee and felt for a stone. He pulled one loose from the icy grip of refrozen sleet. He needed to be ready if the time came.

A faint light appeared far down near the end of the train. In a few moments he discerned that it was swinging, like someone was walking with a lantern, probably coming his way. An icy fear grabbed at his gut. He turned and threw the stone as hard as he could while aiming for the distant top of a railroad car. The stone disappeared in the blackness of the night. He heard a faint rattle. Surely, his father heard it.

That light ahead of him, though still at a distance, appeared a little larger, brighter. It definitely was swinging. He fingered the amulet at his breast, rubbed his finger over the snake on its surface. He would be shrewd, like the snake. He eyed the distant light.

"What you doing here?" suddenly came at his elbow from the dark of a railroad car.

Will jumped and almost lost his footing. His heart slammed against his chest.

A flashlight flicked on. Its beam hit him in the face, temporarily blinded him, and blackened the shadow further.

"I said, what you doing here?" The voice came from the black behind the flashlight. The swinging lamp had drawn close enough to make visible a ghostly upper body.

"I'm going to my friend's, to study." Will croaked. He thought of Sam. Yes, that was it. "To help him get ready for a math exam." He cleared his throat. He had to act normally. "Who are you?" Will asked.

The beam left Will's face and swept down Will's body to his feet. "Crutches, huh? You should be on the street. You have no business here. You're trespassing." The man patted Will's pockets.

"What's this? Take it out."

The man took Will's Prince Albert tin from him and shone his flashlight on it. "You smoke?"

"My pictures are in it."

"Humph. Pictures of naked girls, I suppose." He shook the can at his ear and then handed it back to Will.

The swinging lantern arrived and was held up to spread its light across their faces. Will blinked. He could see that the first man, the one with the flashlight, wore a suit. Light glinted from a badge on his lapel. The man with the lantern wore bib overalls, with stripes—Will saw when the light swung up.

"I was taking a shortcut." Will tried to control his breathing. "You a policeman?" he asked the man in the suit.

"Kinda like that. Pinkerton's. You hear any noises, like bangs?"

"No," Will said. His heart hammered—he had lied.

"Well, I did," the man with the lantern said, "all the way to the caboose." He held the light up close to Will's face. "That's why I came out. I was eating. You do something to my train?"

Will shook his head.

"He's a cripple, Clem," the Pinkerton man said.

"Cripples can pull a caper, too. Now get out of here before you get hurt. People like to rob trains, and wouldn't mind robbing a young man, maybe bashing in his head to do it."

A clang reverberated along the length of the train, like metal on metal.

"There! That's like the one I heard," Clem said.

It came again, and again.

The Pinkerton man drew a pistol and ran in the direction from which the sound came. The crunch of his feet running on the rocks faded away.

Will frowned. His father must not have heard the stone. He should have thrown a larger one.

"Get out of here before you get hurt—or arrested," Clem said, and turned in the direction the Pinkerton man had taken. He had paled into a vaporous torso when he called over his shoulder, "Keep going until you get to a cross street a little way past the caboose. Get moving!"

Will heard Clem's steps quicken before they disappeared. He wanted to follow, but had no choice but to leave.

After a few minutes, Will looked back, but could see no one. Then, out of the dark, he heard, "And nothing better happen to my caboose, or I'm comin' after ya."

He hurried as best he could. Waiting for freight trains at railroad crossings had tried his patience, but walking even half this train's length took forever.

Then, the sound faint, Will heard someone yelling. He stopped to listen, straining his ears.

Dad! The Pinkerton man had found him! He turned to go back. But it would be over; they'd be gone before he got there. Except for his shaking, he felt anchored to the ground.

He had no alternative but to hope his father was okay and to wait for him at the railroad crossing. He dragged his feet toward the caboose. Its window was dark.

The crossing sign came into view, made visible by a street lamp. He stood beneath the light. Away from the trains and the grain elevators, it was bright and seemed safe.

It was deathly quiet. Will shuddered. He didn't hear a car anywhere, or even a dog's bark. He watched the still cold air condense his breath while he imagined his father, hands tied behind his back, lying on the ground as Clem kicked him. Or being stuffed into the back of a paddy wagon. Maybe his father was in jail by now. *Hah! Served him right!*

At least he'd have a warm place to live, good food—and wouldn't have to cut wood.

Will grew stiff with cold. He felt his amulet at his breast. It provided him scant comfort.

He moved away from the lamppost. There was no use waiting.

Chapter 13

Will was desperate for sleep. By bedtime his father had not arrived home, and Will, though exhausted, lay awake, staring into the cold blackness of his room. He wondered how, only hours before, he had feared that his father intended to kill him. Now he lay worrying about him, visualizing him pursued and wounded, or even dead. He attempted to chase the evening's events from his mind by imagining the lovely face and exciting eyes of Irene.

Upon the morning's slow arrival, Will, as usual, went outside to bring in firewood for the stove. A foreboding lingered in his breast that had been sharpened by the night—his father had been killed. However, light from the brightening sky revealed an empty wheelbarrow lying on its side near the barn. Will sighed with relief. Evidently, his father had arrived home during the night. He hoped that his father's grocery shopping had paid off and he allowed his mouth to water over an imagined breakfast of ham and biscuits.

His wood carrier stacked to capacity, Will eagerly made his way to the back door, glad not only to get out of the cold, but to finally be able to fill the aching hollow of his gut. One hand clutched a crutch and the wood carrier's handle with its bundle of wood. With his other hand and a crutch under that arm, Will opened the door and backed his way into the house.

"Good morning," his mother said, in a voice that was anything but cheery. "Your father got home late and is asleep." She stirred a spoon in a battered pot sitting on a woodstove burner. She brushed some loose hairs back with her fingers to reset them under her tortoise hair comb and pulled a faded blue robe up around her neck before wrapping it more snuggly around her. Her gauntness spoke of missed meals, many, so that Will and his father could eat.

His father sleeping off his liquor was but a signal that the day would be routine for his mother, the routine of trying to keep him asleep to avoid arguments and fighting. Then his father caroused all night—usually at Al's Saloon, the closest one to home.

His father always managed to obtain liquor, always seemed to have some. He had bragged that he could convince any bartender that he was sober, even when he wasn't. Will suspected liquor absorbed most of the family's money.

His mother shivered and inched her way a bit closer to the stove so that her robe almost touched it. "Stoke up the fire a little, Will. The water better come to a boil soon, or I won't have time to make your breakfast."

A pan of boiling water on the stove—that meant hominy grits. Grits again meant that they had neared the last of their food; it meant his father had come home empty-handed. And Will would have nothing to take with him to school for lunch. What had happened at the box cars?

Perhaps Uba Pisku was teaching Will a lesson—there is no reward for thievery.

For supper, the best he could hope for was leftover grits cooled until firm, sliced and fried so that it could be served with syrup. The sweetness always made the meal tolerable, even enjoyable. Will frowned. The chances of syrup in the house were slim.

Will opened the damper a notch to give the fire more air, stirred the coals in the bottom of the stove to release their heat, and added some of the smaller pieces of firewood to the firebox. Within seconds flames leapt up, and light from slits in the upper portion of the stove danced across the room. He paused to watch, gaining comfort from the promised warmth—like how it might feel to cuddle with Irene. He stood staring at the fire in the stove.

"You had better finish getting ready for school," his mother said, awakening him from his reverie. She poured grits into the boiling water and added some fatback. The latter assured breakfast wouldn't taste entirely bad.

* * *

Will's school day had been routine, if not interminable. Of course, English class hadn't lasted long enough. Irene, even from afar, always made his heart pound. And his back felt remarkably well; he only had to contend with his usual pain. LeRoy had kept his eyes on him, and had whispered something to Emery, following which Emery's harassment intensified. After school Sam had joined Will and insisted on shoveling coal.

And now it was a supper of hominy grits. What was different was his father—he was clean and shaven—but he was not entirely different. His breath reeked of alcohol. The three of them stared in their bowls while they ate. The hoped-for syrup made no appearance.

Will desperately wanted to bring up their excursion of the previous evening, but did not want to disturb the peace. He had a million questions. He wondered if they would eat only grits until they were gone and then starve.

"Dad, what happened at the train?"

His father glowered, but made no other response. His scowl was the more terrible for having replaced a near smile. He suddenly brought his fist holding his spoon down hard on the table, making the dishes jump and clatter.

"Grits, five times in a row, can't you do any better than that, woman?" The facts were a slight exaggeration—three times was closer to the truth. His mother, not finished eating, did not answer, but immediately slid from her place and carried her bowl to the wash basin, putting distance between herself and her husband.

"Answer me!" his father said.

He pushed the table away and scraped his chair back from the table. Dishes and utensils rattled. His mother shrank back as his father approached her. Will grabbed for his crutches as fear for his mother melded into anger. He pulled himself to his feet and swung after his father. He had to do something. After all, he was a Choctaw.

"You know the answer the same as I do," she said. "Grits is all the food left—and it will soon be gone."

"You lie. Where's all the food we had last week?" His father's fists clenched and unclenched at his side.

All the food? What food? Will thought. It was almost funny.

His father drew back his arm, threatening to smack his mother across the face. From behind him, Will dropped his crutch and caught his father's wrist.

His father's eyes opened wide with surprise. "What?" he said, and twisted about, yanking his wrist to get it free. He shoved Will with his other hand, but could not loosen Will's grip.

Will, his face set like iron, glared, his grasp like a bulldog's. "Dad, stop. Stop! You're not going to hurt her. "Dad. Stop. Listen. Let me explain." *If you stopped boozing, we'd have food.* He couldn't say it.

"Let go of me, boy, or I'll beat you to a pulp." His father reared back and aimed a fist at Will's head. Will saw only black before he crashed against the table. He grabbed for the table, but the room went black as he slipped to the floor.

Will slowly regained consciousness. The kitchen was still hazy. He found himself looking up into his father's stare. Will reached for the chair, but his father kicked it, knocking it over and banging it against the table. Will struggled to his knees and reached for the table to pull himself up. His father kicked Will in the abdomen and swung his leg back to kick again, but lost his balance and staggered about, trying to remain upright.

Will hardly felt the kick. He pulled himself up, placed the chair on its legs, and sat down.

"Don't you ever touch me again!" his father roared, and slammed Will and the back of the chair against the table, but lost his balance and had to hang onto Will. The table emitted a "crack," but didn't collapse. He shoved against Will to get erect.

"You hear what I said to him, woman?" his father asked, and then attempted to launch himself across the table toward Will's mother, who cowered near the wash basin. The table legs screeched. She edged backwards, increasing the distance between them.

"He has no respect. You better teach him some manners." He went around the table after her, but she dodged and danced away. He dove after her again, completely lost his balance and struck his head against the iron enameled wash stand. He remained on hands and knees on the floor for a number of seconds, and then rose to his feet. A knot was already growing on his forehead. Eyes blazing, he stumbled after Will's mother making her way to Will's side. His father had no chance to catch her; she was still lithe and quick.

Will trembled. He was weak all over.

His mother picked up his crutches and grabbed his arm to help him up. He could feel her shaking. "Go on into your bedroom," she said.

He attempted to stand, but fell back into the chair.

"Leave him be, or I'll kill you!" his father yelled. He wrenched the crutches from her grasp and flung them next to Will. "Let him get himself up."

Will set his crutches upright and pulled on them until he was in a standing position. He braced himself with the crutches until strength returned. He felt the glare of his father's eyes.

"Now go on and git into your room."

Will slowly placed his crutches in front of him. As the kitchen returned to its familiar warm rosy light, Will looked back and saw his mother's eyes rimmed with tears. At his bedroom doorway he turned to glare at his father, but could not look him in the face. Again, he hated himself. He had failed his mother. He pushed the curtain aside to enter the blackness of his room and stood listening.

Will heard a chair scraping across the floor. "I'll kill you," he heard his father growl. "And then what will that mollycoddled son of yours do?" She answered him in tones so low Will could not hear. "He'd be better off dead, too, then to put up with you!" his father said.

Will peeked through the two halves of the curtain into the kitchen. He saw his mother backing away from his father, keeping a chair between herself and him. He stumbled around after her, threatening, but finally stomped to the back door. He did not step out into the night until he cursed them, and afterwards slammed the door behind him. Headed for a saloon, Will presumed.

Will heaved a big sigh and gingerly rubbed his jaw. The vision of his father attempting to grab and strike his mother, and saying over and over that he would kill her, would not leave. He had tried to stand up to his father, but what good did it do? A knot formed in his stomach; his trembling wouldn't stop. His father could get out of control and kill them both.

And LeRoy. Will suspected that he was like his father. LeRoy acted fine as long as adults were around or he was trying to impress someone, especially Irene. Otherwise, he was nasty. But he didn't have the courage his father did. He cajoled and bribed others so inclined to express his hate and violence. His experiences with the boys on the corner lot proved that. Or maybe LeRoy would become violent on his own when liquored up. Or when alone with a girl—like Irene. Will had to do something.

Will returned to the kitchen, went to the back door and opened it a crack. He breathed in the sharp air, clearing his head. A sliver of light from the doorway fell upon the ground. From the vantage point of this opening, Will watched his father push the wheelbarrow into the gloom of the old barn. Behind him, his mother placed her hand on his back to peer over his shoulder.

The Texana wind kicked up, seeking entrance into the house. It moaned, pierced crevices and whistled over edges and corners. Though the door was open but a crack, the wind made them shiver. It visibly pushed the already precariously leaning barn to a sharper angle.

The wind carried the rattle of the iron wheel of the wheelbarrow on loose boards back to them. Then there was silence and nothing to see but the star-filled sky. Bored with waiting, Will started to close the door. But his father emerged from the barn with the wheelbarrow, a box sitting in its tray. Will hesitated. His father stopped, pulled a bottle from his pocket and raised it to his lips for a draught. After returning the bottle, he glared at the door and then waved in a hard downward motion. He turned his back to them and trudged down the road with the barrow.

Will pushed the door shut and stepped back. He nearly tripped over his mother. He smiled. "I forgot you were there."

His mother laid an arm around his shoulders and laughed. "How could you forget me?"

Will sighed. She had a way of relieving tension when least expected.

"Momma, why is my father so mean? Even if he hasn't been drinking, I never know when he's going to . . ."

"Hit me?"

Will looked down and nodded his head. "Or even worse."

They drifted toward the wood stove.

His mother stared into a dark corner of the room, not seeing the darkness. "He wasn't always this way. He was actually kind, considerate, hardworking, but then, gradually, after the mine accident, he started drinking more and more, and sank into the boozer that he is." She looked back at Will. "Underneath, he's a good man. You don't know him like I do—or did."

"But he's so nasty and cruel all the time."

"Oh, Will."

"I want to like him, but I never have any reason to. I can remember some from when I was small—getting piggy back rides, and riding the horse."

"I think it was our mule."

"And the tractor when we got one. But now I . . . I hate him!"

"Will! He's your father."

"I try to like him, but I can't. The way he hurts you. And he's always drunk."

"I know he upsets you, Will. But you don't understand what he's been through."

"Tell me."

"Even before the mine. He's furious with how the government mistreated our nations, making treaties and always backing out on them. He hated it when Oklahoma became a state and took over the Indian Territory. There's so much to tell. He doesn't trust the white man. He got blamed for that tragedy at the mine and was fired. Then he couldn't get a decent job anywheres around. And Mr. North, he was a big part of that. Your father's smart—you take after him—and is more educated than any white man. Well, most.

"So he's angry, Will, angry. And the drinking doesn't help; it just brings it all out. When he's like he is, it's not you or me he's so mad about. He doesn't like being poor any more than you or me. I have to believe he still loves us in his own way. And, Will, I love you."

"I love you, too, Momma." He turned on his crutches to directly face his mother. "All you say may be true." A frown settled on his face. "But I still don't understand why he hates us. Or at least acts like it. Let him go pound on Mr. North."

* * *

Outside, the next morning, Will piled firewood into the carrier, stacked it into the wood box next to the stove, and then picked up the lantern from the kitchen table and went back outside. The lantern flame flickered in the wind. He lengthened the wick to make sure it stayed lit. The lamp made a wider circle of light. With a glance at the back door to see if anyone saw him, he made his way toward the barn.

Inside the barn, Will stopped. He peered into the shadows, squinting, his head jutted forward, to see past the ring of light. The odors of rotting hay and wood assaulted his nostrils.

He glanced behind him toward the barn's opening, fearing that his father's outline would appear. Raising the lantern high to cast light deeper into the shadows, he crept ahead, carefully planting his crutches amidst pieces of wood and unknown debris. He looked along the walls and poked a crutch into one dark corner after another and into old piles of hay.

About halfway through the barn, he came upon a suspiciously large hay pile. He poked it. The crutch hit an object near the pile's surface. He cleared away the hay and found three identical wooden boxes, one stacked upon the other. Were they not like the one he saw his father carting away? Will pulled open the first box. The lid lifted easily—it had already been opened. He sat the lantern aside.

A blast of wind struck the barn. It creaked and swayed. The lamp flickered. Shadows danced with the swaying of the barn, exaggerating the barn's movements. He had better hurry before the thing collapsed.

Will brought his attention back to the box. Inside it, he discovered ten bottles and space for two more. Trembling, he lifted a bottle and turned it toward the light. The label read, "Power's Gold Label Whiskey." His father's excursion to the railroad had been successful after all. So much for his father loving them. Will twisted his mouth in rage and cocked his arm back to heave the bottle, but then thought better of it. He replaced the bottle, closed the lid, and did his best to cover the boxes to make them appear as they had before.

Again, the barn creaked with a blast from the wind. Somewhere a board battered its neighbors. Will looked toward the open end of the barn. Its side now formed a more severe angle with the ground. He hurried outside. The wind blew out his lantern and tore through his clothes. Will shivered. He leaned against the wind and made his way back to the house. He would wear an extra shirt to school today.

* * *

That night, Will sat at the kitchen table, the lantern at its center casting a warm glow over the room. He was tired. And he had new pain, his neck was sore. He had managed to cut firewood himself. His stomach rumbled while he attempted to concentrate on schoolwork. He took a swig of hot tea sweetened with a bit of molasses his mother had begged from a neighbor. That was supper. He would be all right, but what of his mother? She sat across from him, staring into nothing. Her once lovely face sported hollowed cheeks under sharp cheekbones. Dark circles bled under her eyes. Although the woodstove had fared well against the Texana wind, the southerly wind off the Texas plain, she clutched her blue robe tightly around her and over her housedress. Tomorrow was Friday, and Mr. Whiz would pay him, and then he would go to Buttery's store. At least they would have food for a few days.

Valentine's Day. A pain jabbed Will's stomach and brought its rumblings to a halt. He wanted to buy Irene a valentine. He *had* to buy her one. He sighed and dropped his eyes, then put his forehead on his open book. And tomorrow was Dr. Grover's math exam. He wasn't worried about the exam, but what would Emery and Wade do after it was over?

The back door burst open and a swirl of wind tossed Will's papers from the table. The flame in the lantern flickered out. Except for the light which escaped from the woodstove, the room was black. His mother seemed to not notice.

Will heaved himself to his feet, intent on closing the door. The sparse light revealed a hand propping a piece of the barn's siding against the door. Cold air poured into the house, displacing its warmth. A gust ripped through the house. A glass tipped over, fell to the floor and shattered.

The old wheelbarrow rumbled into the kitchen, pushed by his father. In the sparse light Will could see that it was laden with bags and boxes. His father lifted the handles upright and gently twisted the barrow from side to side, causing its contents to slide and tumble to the floor. A few cans rolled across the linoleum. The odor of a grocery store wafted up to him.

Jumping to her feet, Will's mother crossed her hands beneath her throat. "Oh! Oh!" was all she managed. His father turned the wheelbarrow and pushed it outside. He reentered and closed the door against the cold wind. The darkness of the room prevented Will from reading his face, although he discerned that he was standing with hands on hips.

Will took a match from the matchbox on the table and struck it. It flared enough for Will to see that his father wore a half-smile. Will lit the lamp. The room brightened as the flame grew. He retrieved a can that had escaped from a bag, grabbed it and held its label up to the lamp— hominy grits. His face fell.

"How? What happened?" his mother asked. She rushed to the overturned bags and boxes and hefted them to the table, except one that she couldn't lift. A smile filled her hollow cheeks. "All this!" She looked at Will's father with an affection Will had not seen for months.

His father replaced his smile with a scowl. "It came at a high price. I sold some things for it."

Immediately, Will's mother's smile fled and her hands flew to her hair comb.

"You needn't have worried about that," his father said. "It's hardly worth anything. I had some things of my own."

Will looked into the box. He reached in and drew out a can. *A picture of hominy grits on the label—Forest City Brand.* He quickly picked up a few more. *Hominy.* His face fell. He peered into the box and recognized a sealed heavy paper bag. *I know these, too—too well. Corn Grits.* He pulled the bag from the box. The lamplight showed him to be right—*"Sunkissed Brand, Gurley Milling Company. 5 lbs."* The gnawing feeling in his stomach was replaced by a knot. *At least they weren't a fifty-pound bag of Jim Dandy's.* He felt around in the box again. There were more.

He looked up. His father was glaring at him. *I don't care. I don't even care if I cry.*

The large grocery bag on the floor! What was in the bag? Will pulled the side of the paper bag down enough to peer inside. Enclosed was a large cloth bag that filled the sack. He felt it. *Rice, he was sure. Ugh. Water-Maid.* A few moments ago, he was ready to giggle like a girl— and now . . . *The bag on the floor was fifty pounds of Water-Maid, no doubt. Nothing was cheaper.*

"That's it," his father said. "Grits and rice. Get the most food for my money. Oh, except for these." From a large paper sack his father pulled a smaller one and opened it. From it he lifted something wrapped in butcher paper. "For me," he said, grinning. He tore open the package and held up a sausage followed by four more, one linked to the next. "Polish sausages. Did you know Mr. Grabowski makes his own sausage?" He dropped them onto the paper and rubbed the palms of his hands together. "You can cook them for me now." The smile on his lips carried no joy.

Will stared at the cans of grits and at the bag of rice. *This, bought with stolen liquor. And I was an accomplice. Why didn't I go back home like I said? And sausage only for himself. He doesn't care about us. He should leave and never come back. I hate him.*

His mother stared blankly at nothing, unmoving, silent.

"Well, woman?" his father said.

She shuffled stiffly to the cabinet and pulled out the iron skillet.

Will picked up a can and let it slide back out of his hand. *Somehow, I'm going to get rid of him—before he gets rid of us.*

Chapter 14

The four boys squirmed on the office bench, Will and Sam next to each other, Emery and Wade together, waiting after school for Dr. Grover. Except for the occasional rattle of the mop bucket in the hall and the slam of a closing file drawer in the principal's office, the building was eerily quiet.

Dr. Grover's paddle loomed large in Will's mind. A lot of that had to do with the recent thrashing he received from his father. Over and over he told himself he had nothing to worry about; he was ready. Then there was Sam. He and Sam had studied hard. Never mind the licks for wrong answers; Sam could take that. He had to pass. The other two saps—well, they would get what they deserved.

Will felt Sam touch his arm. Sam pointed with his eyes at Emery and Wade, and then grimaced. "When you get done the test, wait for me by the office," he said in Will's ear. Will nodded.

Minutes dragged. Wade, antsy, whispered to Emery, but loud enough for Sam and Will to hear, "Grover probably doesn't even have a test made up yet, and he'll have to let us go."

"I'm not worried about it," Emery said. "He's not going to paddle me no matter how my test turns out, if he knows what's good for him. I'll give him a black eye."

"Me neither. I guess he'll have two black eyes." Wade gestured toward Grover's office door where a silhouette had appeared on its translucent glass. "There he is." The principal's office door opened.

A hush fell across the bench as Dr. Grover strode toward the boys with papers in hand. He loomed large over them. "This is a good sign—everyone is here. You must want to be in school."

Emery and Wade sniggered.

"Or at least your parents want you to be." Dr. Grover eyed the two, then continued, "Write out your answers on these blank sheets, in good form, showing all of your work. Do not write on the question sheets." Dr. Grover's beady eyes went from one boy to the next. "You do have sharpened pencils, right?"

Wade nudged Emery.

"You will work in separate rooms. Do not leave the room until you are done the test, and then bring it to me. Mr. Wyzowaty is buffing the hall outside and will let me know if you leave your room. Questions?"

"Ah, ah," Emery raised a hand to shoulder height, "Dr. Grover, I don't have a pencil." His face was bright red.

"Me neither," Wade said. His head dropped.

"You two aren't getting off to a good start. That will be your first lick."

Wade looked at Emery, but Emery was looking down at his feet with his lips pressed together.

"Come into my office and I will lend two pencils to each of you. Be careful that you do not break their points—you can't leave the room until you are done."

* * *

Will snatched up his completed test and swung toward the office. He hoped to get out of Grover's office and finish shoveling coal before Emery and Wade left for home. Mr. Whiz, who had finished mopping and was gliding a buffer back and forth over the floor, took one hand from the machine long enough to wave at Will scurrying down the hall.

Will knocked on the principal's door.

"Done so soon? I must not have made the test hard enough." Dr. Grover's eyes did not seem quite so pointy. His thin lips formed into a smile.

"I have to shovel coal for Mr. Whiz."

"Okay, we'll get this over with. Please get the Board of Education from off of the nail and I'll score your test. It won't take long with this answer key."

Will felt his heart thud. He watched as Dr. Grover ran his pencil over the work for each of Will's answers before granting it a mark. Will kept twisting to look at the wall clock behind him. Its hands raced along. Finally, Dr. Grover wrote "100" at the top of Will's paper. Will sighed.

"You can hang the paddle back on the nail," Grover said. "I won't need it, yet. Tomorrow, I'll send your test paper to Miss Whitaker. You will not be penalized for retaking the test. This is just between us—your parents will never be the wiser."

Will's jaw went slack. He couldn't move. What about the letter informing his father of the cheating? Did Sam or Emery or Wade get a letter? Who wrote . . .?

Miss Whitaker. He hated her.

"You may go." Dr. Grover moved his head closer and stared at Will's face. "Are you okay?"

Will wondered if Sam would receive any licks from Dr. Grover.

* * *

Although below ground level, Will felt the night closing in upon him. He jammed the shovel into the coal and lifted. Pain tore through his back. He was surprised; he thought his back was much better. He tried a small shovelful. It was tolerable. He picked up the pace, and then dropped the shovel as fire shot through his back. He missed Sam. He rested on hands and knees until the ache subsided.

Finally finished and washed, Will drug himself up the boiler room steps. At their top he slid aside the heavy metal door. He scanned the dim hallway, now lit only by the overhead globes. He could hear Mr. Wyzowaty's buffer around the corner. Will scooted in that direction, exchanged greetings with Mr. Whiz, and let him know that he had finished shoveling. Everybody else was probably gone, including Sam, who was not outside the office.

Will stood stock still, listening, but heard no sounds from inside, not even from Dr. Grover. Sam must have gone home. How would he handle Emery if Emery was waiting for him?

Will made his way down the front marble steps and onto the school grounds. Light still lingered in the western sky. He watched the last bit of red streak disappear, and then swung into the black shadow close to the corner of the building graced by a tall evergreen.

"Hey, Injun gimp. Stop right there. I want to talk to you."

Will's heart jumped into his throat. He knew the voice—Emery's. Emery and Wade ran to block his path. Will backed toward the brick wall.

"I told you I'd even things up," Emery growled. His breath reeked of tobacco.

"I offered to help you more than once," Will said. The handles of his crutches felt clammy.

"Yeah—but not the kind of help that does anybody any good. Where were the answers for this test?" Emery snarled. He gave Will a thrust with the heel of his hand. "We don't need dumb crippled Injuns in our school."

"And we can't help it if we're not good in math," Wade said. He mimicked Emery's hand thrust to Will's chest. "Lover boy! You should have failed Whitaker's test, too."

Lover boy! What is that about? Will caught himself by putting a hand on the wall behind him, and then stood as tall as he could. He mentally kicked himself for not going inside the office to look for Sam.

"If you would have come to the cafeteria on time, I could've helped you. How'd you expect to pass, if you don't do the work?"

"You should have helped us in Whitaker's class and kept your mouth shut. Then you wouldn't be about to have the pee-waddin' beat out of you," Emery said. "You're showing off for LeRoy's girl, Irene. Injuns and whites aren't supposed to mix."

Will's heart thumped at the mention of Irene. His blood boiled. There was no arguing with the likes of Emery and Wade. "Sorry you didn't do well on the test. Did Grover give a lick for every wrong answer?"

"What do you know about how we did on the test? It's none of your business. And Grover wouldn't dare touch me. My father said only he can paddle me," Emery said.

Will smiled. "So, your father is going to paddle you, too."

Emery screwed up his face and gave Will a hard shove. Will stumbled backwards. His backpack brushed the wall. "I'll help you anytime if you really want it," Will said, and reached for the wall behind him. He missed. Wade pushed Will hard while he floundered, making sure he fell. Will skinned his hand on the bricks as he went down.

Wade shook his fist. "Come on, Will. Get up, fight. Fight, you gimp. Fight like a man."

Will pulled on a crutch to right himself.

Too late. The two boys closed in. Emery cocked his leg and loosed a hard kick to Will's thigh. Will managed to brace the crutch with one hand to catch the next kick and sit up, his back against the wall. From Will's other side Wade aimed a kick at his head. Will rolled to one knee and attempted to rise. The movement caused Wade to miss and land a glancing blow to Will's head. To Will, everything looked like a blur.

Will saw that Emery's fist was drawn back, but the blow never came. Instead, Emery flew through the air toward the evergreen. Will got up and saw Big Sam with both hands grabbing fistfuls of Wade's coat lapels and heaving him backward onto Emery. He heard their grunts as Wade landed on Emery.

"Oww! Get off me, Wade."

Sam, fists clenched at his side, waited as the two hooligans untangled themselves and scrambled to their feet. "Get out of here while you still can," Sam said.

"Sam, you touch me again and I'll knock your teeth in," Emery said.

"Yeah!" Wade, his eyes wide with fright, stood behind Emery. "Emery, let's get him!"

Sam plowed toward the two. They threw themselves aside, then hightailed it toward the street, their shoes pounding the frozen lawn. Sam hustled after them, yelling and cursing.

Will heard a car's electric starter whine. The engine coughed and then started. His eyes found the car in the gloom as it started to roll. A passenger door swung open and Emery scrambled to get inside. He thumbed his nose at Sam before slamming the door shut. Wade sprinted alongside the rear wheel, falling further behind, yelling for them to wait. The car slowed and he hopped onto the running board. The engine strained as the car picked up speed.

The chugging sounds were those of a Studebaker. Will was sure of it.

Sam walked back toward him, panting, his face twisted in anger. "Those guys are nothing but trouble. I knew you should stay inside the school until I came out. Why didn't you stay?"

"Did you see who was in the car?" The idea that LeRoy instigated Emery's and Wade's hostilities pressed everything else from Will's mind. "Who was driving it?"

"What?" Sam said. "No. Emery. Wade was on the running board."

"No, not them. Who drove? It was a Studebaker, wasn't it?"

Sam shrugged. "I didn't notice. What you expect? I was busy."

"Shoot. If you ran into the car you would not have seen it. I bet it was LeRoy."

"You're right. Actually, he's the only one who would give them a ride."

"He even waited all this time after school." Will wrinkled his brow. "Why'd he do that? Not because he likes them so much. He and those two are nothing alike."

"Except they're mean," Sam said. "And he's always hung with Wade and Emery. He does things for them, gives them stuff—money, even. How do you think Emery gets all his tobacco? Of course, it's with a price, or vice-versa."

"Like what payment?"

"Like to get you to stay away from Irene."

"That's what they said. I don't have to be beat up to get the message. LeRoy already told me."

"I told you that, too. I tried to reason with you. But you don't listen," Sam said.

"Why doesn't he confront me himself? Not that it would make any difference. Irene is for me; that's all there is to it."

"Two reasons. One, he thinks fighting is beneath him, although he's done it. Fact is, I heard he trounced a big palooka at his old school—sent him to the hospital. Maybe the real reason LeRoy's at Enid instead of St. Worcester's. I think it cost him a promotion to the eleventh grade, too. Second, he wants to make the baseball team here. He said he was Worcester's ace pitcher last year. Coach doesn't let anybody on the team who gets into trouble. Actually, there's a third reason. Irene's the kind of girl that doesn't want boys fighting over her. It would make her look cheap. He knows that. And he wouldn't want to be seen beating up a crip . . ."

"Just go ahead and say it, 'a cripple.' Listen, Sam, I appreciate what you did this evening, but I can take care of myself." *If I have to.*

"Not from what I saw. Let me summarize this for you." Sam leaned toward Will, towering over him. "Irene is nothing but trouble for you. Keep pining over her, and you are going to get the snot beat out of you."

He poked Will's chest with his forefinger. "Look at you—look at her." He paused between couplets, like he was letting Will think about them. "Look at your clothes—look at hers. Look at where you live—look at where she lives. What does her father do for a living—What does your father do? Yeah, what *does* he do?

"You'll never have a chance with her. All it's going to do is get you hurt, one way or the other. Lots of boys like her. You think you are the first guy that's pined over her? It's a good thing you have me to set you straight. Forget her."

"All that lecture just because I got into a little trouble with a couple of dunderheads? They had their own reason for fighting with me. And I wasn't worried. I thought you were long gone. I can take care of myself." Will casually pressed his amulet against his chest. *The snake—defiant, persistent. Nothing will make me give up.* "And you won't change my mind about Irene." Sam was not going to tell him what to do. Will took a deep breath. He wanted to change the subject.

"How did you do on the *exam—Sam*?" Will emphasized "exam" and "Sam" and snickered at the little rhyme.

"I got one answer wrong—good for one lick from the Board of Education. Not very hard."

Will smiled and tapped Sam's shoulder with his fist. Sam got an "A" on an Algebra test!

"I don't think Dr. Grover wanted to do it," Sam said. "Actually, he congratulated me. And gave me a little pep talk."

"What did your folks say about the letter, before, about the cheating? They should be happy now." Will had been wondering if Sam had received a licking at home.

"What letter?"

"From Grover, about the math exam. Didn't you get one?"

"Nah. Nobody got a letter. You'll learn. Dr. Grover takes care of his own business. He doesn't need parents." Sam's eyes squinted. "You got a letter?"

Will couldn't move, not even blink. It felt like a cap, cold as ice, clamped itself onto his skull.

"You want proof that Grover takes care of his own business?" Sam continued, ignoring Will's silence. "Listen, I was late leaving because I took my time. I didn't want to get any wrong. I was sitting there, working the problems, when I heard lots of whomps from the Board of Education, all the way down the hall."

Sam's voice seemed to come from far away, from out of a fog.

Nobody got a letter, Sam had said.

"Dr. Grover talked between each whomp, but I couldn't' hear what he was saying. I waited until the whomping stopped before I finished my test." Sam gave a little nervous laugh.

"You can bet I rechecked all my answers."

There was silence. Will said, "Nobody's parents knew about the makeup exam with Dr. Grover?"

Sam regarded him strangely. "Not unless they told them. And who would do that, unless they enjoy getting a whomping at home."

Will curled his lips inward and pressed them together. *I was the only one that got a letter? And a 'whomping' at home—and I didn't cheat!*

Sam eyed Will. "You okay, Will?"

"Yeah, yeah." Will took a deep breath and forced his lips into a smile. "The way Emery tells it, he's got another paddling coming when he gets home."

And my letter was delivered personally, by LeRoy! Who has access to school stationery.

"You're funny," Sam said, and threw his heavy arm across Will's backpack. "Let's go home, Will."

Chapter 15

Window shopping around the town square excited Will. As he walked, he weighed the money he was earning, thirty cents per week, against the items he saw. But his mind was mostly on Irene; he had come to buy a box of valentine candy for her.

He carried a certain dread. There was risk in giving a Valentine's Day gift. Would she accept it—and him? His hands perspired at the thought. He pushed it aside and instead envisioned Irene, making the blood speed through his veins.

Stores announced, "Honest Abe Birthday Sale." This was February 12, President Abraham Lincoln's Birthday—and it was a school holiday. With his mind reeling with thoughts of Irene, he checked out Sanford Frazier's Drugstore's valentine window display. The day after tomorrow was Valentine's Day. He decided only a heart-shaped box would do.

Will crossed the square, looking for a store with a better price, and found himself staring at a pair of brown shoes in the small storefront window of *Tom and Tiddle Shoe Rebuilders*. Creases crossed the top of the shoes in the window; the shoes obviously had traveled hundreds of miles. But they shone like new and were tilted at an angle to show the handiwork of the shop—new soles and heels.

Will looked at his own shoes and his protruding toes. Cold from the pavement soaked through the worn soles. The February wind tore at his threadbare coat. He hunched his shoulders against the cold and shivered. The shoemaker looked back through the glare of the glass and smiled. Will shivered again. He decided he would step into the store and warm himself—for just a bit.

The bells hanging on the door tinkled as Will bumped his way through the doorway with his crutches. The aroma of worked leather and rubber and shoe polish filled his nostrils. The steady hum and click of the shoemaker's machines, the whack of his hammer and the warmth of the shop were comforting.

"May I help you?"

Will figured the cobbler was either Tom or Tiddle; he didn't know which. Will shook his head and, fascinated, looked at the shop.

"I don't think your shoes are worth repairing," Tiddle or Tom said. "You could buy a brand-new pair at Wards cheaper."

"I can't buy a pair." Will stared at the wall shelved with neat rows of worn but shiny shoes and boots, each pair tagged with its owner's name. He stood looking for a long minute, wishing one were his, then turned to leave.

"Some owners never return to pick up their shoes," Tom or Tiddle said.

Will glanced back. The repairman held a pair of shiny brown shoes in an outstretched palm. With his other hand he smoothed the long dark mustache that drooped around his mouth.

"I think these are about your size. You can have them for the cost of the repair."

Will decided the man was Tiddle. Tom was using the machinery at the back of the shop.

"Here, take them. Try them on." Tiddle thrust the shoes at Will and pointed to a rough wooden bench along the opposite wall for Will to sit on. Tiddle stood, smiling, between Will and the door.

Will shrugged and swung over to the bench and sat, his backpack pressed against the wall. He'd get warmed up good before going back outside. Tiddle placed the shoes on the bench next to him.

"Try them on," Tiddle said.

Will took off his shoes, wishing he could hide the holes in the heels and toes of his socks. Tiddle didn't seem to notice. Will felt the heft of the shoe—its sole, thick and sturdy. He pulled the shoes on. The warmth from the shoes bathed his feet. He looked down and smiled. The feet didn't belong to him. He couldn't stop smiling.

"Stand up and let me see if they fit. By the way, I'm Tom; that's my partner, Tiddle, back there."

Tom pressed down on the toes with his thumb. "A little too long. We can fix that, let me have 'em." Tom took them and Will's old shoes, too. "A little cotton in the front ought to do it. Growing room. Take the cotton out when your foot gets bigger."

Will sat opposite from the sign posted on the wall that read, "Springy Rubber Heels - 18¢; Genuine Leather Half Soles - 46¢; All Work

Guaranteed." His smile fell like a wounded squirrel from a tree. "How much for the repair?" To him, his voice sounded strange and far off.

"Eighty-six cents."

Will stared at the sign. Forty-six plus eighteen was sixty-four.

"That's because they have new full soles," Tom said, emphasizing the 'full.'

Will thought about Irene's valentine—the reason he had gone shopping—and felt relief. He couldn't afford the shoes. So, all the money he had for a valentine would still be intact. "I don't have that much money, Mr. Tom. May I have my old shoes back?"

"Take his old shoes for a trade-in." The voice was loud and coarse. It came from Tiddle yelling over the sound of the machinery at the back.

"I still won't have enough," Will said. "Could I have my shoes, please?"

"Maybe you don't like these?" Tom said. "Thirty-seven cents with the trade in." He looked at Tiddle. "A bargain."

With what I have left from last week, by Thursday, I'll have exactly that much money—I hope, Will thought. "No, I—I just started a job. I don't have the money, yet."

"He has a job, he says," Tom yelled.

"Let him have 'em on the layaway plan," Tiddle hollered.

"What payment pl—? Oh. Yeah. Ten cents down. Five cents a week, son. You got ten cents?"

What if I need all my money for the valentine? Will thought.

"Maybe he has something to trade in for a down payment," Tiddle hollered again.

"You got something, son?"

Will thought immediately of one of his most valuable possessions. He slowly put his hand into his pants pocket and felt the tobacco tin with the picture of Fay Wray inside. The image of Irene came before his eyes. And the amulet—he could never do that. He looked at the floor and slowly shook his head 'no.'

Tiddle hit a switch and the noise from the machinery stopped. He left his work and came over to Will, but stared at Tom. "We could use a little cash here of late. Sell them for about the cost of the materials. Make those shoes twenty-seven cents, five cents down now and three-cent-a-week payments, first one due Friday a week. Is that a deal, son?"

Will, his eyes big as saucers, looked up at Tom. Tom looked at Tiddle. Only five cents! He had five cents, but suppose he even ran short by a penny?

"Tiddle, it doesn't look like the young man is interested. I'd sure like to sell those shoes. I don't think the owner will ever come to claim them. How about seventeen cents, three-cents-a-week?"

Will stood speechless, trembling with temptation.

Tiddle went back to his machinery and turned it on. The humming started. He looked at Will, then Tom. Tiddle yelled, "He sure drives a hard bargain, Tom."

"Why won't you buy the shoes?" Tom asked.

Will dropped his head. Five cents down. That might be the difference between having enough for the valentine.

"It's not the price of the shoes is it, son?"

He shook his head. The shoes were a bargain. He'd love to have them. The words almost stuck in his throat and came out in a rough whisper. "No. I want to buy . . . a valentine, a heart." His face turned a deep red. He felt his ears burning.

"What he say?" Tiddle yelled over his machinery.

"He wants to buy a valentine."

"That's love, if I ever heard of it. Candy for a girl while you got holes in your shoes. Can we trump that, Tom?"

"Nope. He's got it ba-a-ad," Tom shouted back, grinning.

Tiddle rolled his eyes then closed them. "Mmmm, I'll bet she's a beauty."

Sweat broke out on Will's upper lip, trembling in his arms shook his crutches. He glanced around to see if anyone else was in the store to notice him. He'd have started for the door, but Tom had his shoes.

"Wish I could fix up those toe-holes a bit for you, son," Tiddle said. "But you'd never get them on. Your toes hang out too far."

"Tell you what we'll do, Tiddle. We'll—"

A loud screech came from the shoe Tiddle pressed onto the machine, drowning out Tom's words.

Tiddle made a face. "I can't hear you," he yelled.

"Then turn off that thundering thing a minute, will ya?" Tom yelled back.

In the sudden silence they stared at Will. He knew he looked like a glowing red beet. The store felt very hot.

"Now you've gone and embarrassed the boy," Tiddle said.

"Me?" Tom sighed. "I'm sorry, son. What I said was we'll hold the price on those shoes for when you get the money—if the owner doesn't claim them first. Or someone else doesn't buy them."

Will watched as Tom placed the shoes next to others on a shelf labeled, "For Sale—Unclaimed Shoes."

It wasn't the cold air that hit Will as he stepped out of the store that put him in shock. He'd left behind a great pair of shoes and just declared his love for Irene in front of two strangers. He wondered if somehow it would get back to her. At least, he hadn't given her name.

He looked down at his feet and imagined his new shoes. All he had to do was work another week and they would be his—if they weren't gone. And if he could face Tom and Tiddle again. His ears still burned.

He thought about yesterday. After shoveling coal, he had made his way down to Kress' Five-and-Dime on Main Street. Their window display included a red heart-shaped box edged with lace frill. It contained one pound of assorted chocolates, and it cost sixty-five cents.

That was the one.

Maybe the price would come down by Thursday, Valentine's Day. He hoped he could talk Mr. Whiz into paying him all he had earned thus far, even if payday was Friday.

But he couldn't bring himself to enter the store. What would Irene think? Anyway, he didn't have the money, yet.

* * *

The cold cutting through Will's jacket quickened his pace. Today was it, Saint Valentine's Day. He had summoned the courage to ask Mr. Whiz for his pay one day in advance, at least for the four days he had worked this week. He fingered the coins in his pocket—37 cents. With his first pay he had brought home some eggs, a few bananas, and a pound of sugar, proof that he had a job and saved the remainder, thirteen cents. So far, he had only worked nine days. Actually, five days, but Sam, thankfully, that first week had swapped the shoveling for the math tutoring.

The Kress store clerk had a round smiling face. "This is the third time you've been here, isn't it?" she said.

Will blushed and nodded. "How much is the valentine with the lace around it?"

"Sixty-five cents." She beamed at him.

Will looked down and grimaced. He had hoped, by some miracle, it had dropped to thirty-seven cents.

She picked up another box, a heart-shaped golden tin with the picture of a beautiful dark-haired woman holding a bouquet of red roses. Will's heart leapt; the woman on the box reminded him of Irene.

"This one has been selling like hotcakes," she said. "It's a better deal. I think it's a lot prettier and costs less. And look, the box is actually tin instead of cardboard. Your valentine will use it long after the candy is gone, and will think of you every time she opens it."

The lady had said, *"Your valentine."* Will's heart skipped a beat. His eyes danced. "How much is it?"

"Forty cents. But I must tell you, it has only half as many chocolates—eight ounces."

Will pulled the coins from his pocket and counted them. Not that he didn't already know the total was thirty-seven cents. His voice dropped to nearly a whisper. "How much is that one?" He pointed to a red cardboard heart.

"Twenty-five cents, but you don't want that one, Mister. This . . ." she held up the one with the beautiful dark-haired woman ". . . is the last one. But see, it has this little dent in the back. That's why it's still here. I can sell it to you for, ah, how much money did you say you had?"

"Thirty-seven cents."

"Five cents off. Thirty-five cents. Would you buy it, anyway, with the dent in it?"

* * *

Will tried to slip the valentine into his army surplus backpack, but there was not enough room. He gripped it in his hand along with his crutch.

If he could have, he would have skipped as he went out the door. *Good night, Irene, Good night, Irene, I'll see you in my dreams,* went around in his head until he was alone on the street. Then he sang aloud as he swung himself along. *Good night, Irene, Good night, Irene, I'll see—*

He heard a car slow beside him, then saw it was a clean, shiny Studebaker. It was LeRoy's father's; LeRoy had borrowed it again. LeRoy stopped, leaned over and rolled down the passenger side window. "Hey there, Will, what do you have there? Come on over, let me see it."

Will continued to swing along. "Valentine candy," he said.

The brown Studebaker rolled beside him. "Who's it for, your mother?"

Will felt his face growing warm. "No."

"Who then? A girl?" The Studebaker crept along next to him. "For Irene?"

Will swung along between his crutches.

The Studebaker stopped. Will felt relief. Then, suddenly, there were steps running up behind him. He turned. It was LeRoy. LeRoy grabbed the heart with two hands, tore it from Will's grip, then ran back to the car and started it rolling. When he drew abreast of Will, LeRoy slowed and held up the heart, sneered at Will through the window, then sped away.

Will swung furiously after the car, forgetting the patches of ice and sleet that still marked the walkway. He hated Studebakers. He couldn't stand their chugging. When it disappeared from sight he stopped and hung his head. Then, gritting his teeth, he pushed hard on his crutches to hurtle himself along.

Will drew near Irene's house. The Studebaker had pulled next to the curb. As he approached, he saw that Irene and LeRoy were inside the car, eating chocolates. Irene rolled down her window and called to Will, "Look what LeRoy gave me. Have one." She pushed the valentine box through the window toward Will. It was the heart with the beautiful girl and red roses. Irene glanced back at LeRoy and smiled.

Will's grip on his crutches turned his knuckles white. His lips curled back from his teeth. "LeRoy," he began, doing his best to speak pleasantly, "did you tell Irene where you got the valentine?"

"No, but that's not something one usually reveals," LeRoy said, simultaneously raising his nose and eyebrows.

"If you don't mind, as a gentleman, would you, in this case, tell Irene where you got it?"

"Yes, I would mind, since it's nothing to you."

"Surely you think this a joke. But to me, it is very serious, so I will tell." Will looked through the open car window at Irene. "Irene, I bought it. He parked his car, ran up behind me and snatched the heart from my hand as I walked along."

LeRoy jumped from the car and slammed the door. "That ragamuffin's lying. You know I wouldn't do that. He just wanted to take your candy."

LeRoy ran around the car and grabbed Will's arm. "Tell her the truth," he sneered. "Tell her how you don't have enough money to buy a valentine."

Irene frowned.

"I'd been saving up. I have a job," Will gritted his teeth and yanked his arm free.

"Oh, you do?" She stared at Will. "You do. Where?" Her lips curled into a smile.

Will didn't know if she was laughing at him or was pleased. "With Mister Whiz, at school."

"Okay. He does. But what would you do with a valentine, Will?" LeRoy's teeth gleamed as he poked his nose toward Will. "Give it to your mother?" he taunted. "You don't have a girlfriend."

"You're the liar, Le Roy. You think your fancy clothes and car let you do anything you want. You're nothing but a polecat."

"You thievin' hobo, trying to get the candy for yourself." He grabbed Will by the coat and pushed him against the tree. "You're the best liar I ever heard." Spittle sprayed Will's face. "Tell her the truth—you wish you were the one who gave her the valentine.

"See. He has nothing to say. He's lying," LeRoy said. "Beat it. Scram. And don't come near my girl."

Will pushed LeRoy away. He knew he should follow with a smash to LeRoy's nose, but he controlled himself. What would Irene think?

"Look at the back of the heart, Irene," Will said. "There's a dent in the bottom side of the tin.

It was the last valentine with the lady and roses. Turn it over. I'll show you."

Irene put the lid on the heart and turned it over.

"I'm sorry, Irene, about the dent. It was the best valentine. Even the clerk at the store said so, and I wanted it for you." He shrugged. "But the last one."

LeRoy's face twisted. "Wow! Can he ever make 'em up. I bought it just for you, Irene." LeRoy smiled at Irene, and then shook his fist at Will. "I'd beat you to a pulp if you weren't a cripple."

"Don't let that stop you. Just try it," Will said, thrusting his chin out. "Look at the heart, Irene."

Irene rubbed her finger over the back of the tin. She stared at the two boys, her mouth agape. Her eyes spat fire. "LeRoy Mattison, you're nothing but a liar. What's the matter with you?"

The boys' heads jerked back.

"I don't care whose old thing it is," she said. "Here, keep your disgusting old valentine." She threw the box at Will. He grabbed the valentine before it fell and clutched it to him.

"You're both . . . you're . . . animals, brutes."

Will stared at Irene. At her beautiful lips. Lips now turned down in disgust, then quivering. Tears rimmed her eyes.

Will's heart plummeted. Whatever little she cared for him had vanished. "I'm sor . . ."

While they looked on, she grabbed her school books from the car and stalked to her house. She glowered at the boys from the doorway, head erect, then slammed the door. Through the door's window Will saw her head drop.

LeRoy yelled to Irene, "It was just a joke. For fun." He glared at Will. "Tell her, Will."

LeRoy made his way around to the driver's side and got into the Studebaker. Before shutting the door, he called over the top, "You haven't seen the last of this, Cripple Boy." With that he shook his fist above his head, slammed his door shut and popped the car's clutch to spin the rear wheels.

Will, struggling, grabbed a hunk of ice from the side of the road and launched it into the air over the retreating vehicle. The ice smacked the roof and broke into smithereens. The brake light came on and LeRoy, now a silhouette, stepped out of the car and yelled something unintelligible. Then he sped the car away. Will watched until it was nearly out of sight.

He could still feel LeRoy's spit on his face. He rubbed it with his coat sleeve. He had shown himself to be a coward. And 'a disgusting valentine' she had called it. His head hung as he swung between his crutches to slog his way home.

* * *

Will slipped the valentine under his jacket before opening the door to his house. He went immediately to his bedroom. Scowling at the woman on the valentine tin, he shoved it under his bed. His chores and homework awaited. He sat on his bed with his elbows on his knees and his head in his hands. For all he cared, he wouldn't eat supper. Firewood? Let the house freeze solid tonight. At least his father would have a real reason to beat him. That would be all right, too.

"Will, what are you doing? We need some wood for the stove," called his mother.

Will didn't answer. His mother's voice was background noise for his thoughts.

His eyes fell on his backpack. *I have to write an essay for English class.* He sighed. *Let the teachers do their own homework.* For the essay he had decided on the adage, "Waste not, want not." He thought he knew something about that.

Irene was in his English class. *Irene.*

He started! He had something else to write. Will grabbed his crutches and slid from the bed to his feet. He rushed into the kitchen and grabbed his wood carrier.

"Will?" his mother said. "Your coat."

He gave a half wave, kept going, and was out the door.

He hustled back in, the carrier full.

"Will!" his mother said. He ignored her. Back and forth he went until the wood box next to the stove was full. He was perspiring. Next, the water. He worked the pump handle—hard. Water gushed into the bucket and splashed out the top. Inside, in his haste, he sloshed water onto the floor and had to mop it up. *Haste makes waste. I could write on that,* he thought.

When through with chores, Will flung his backpack onto the table and pulled out his books.

"I've never seen you in such a hurry to do your homework." His mother hitched up her apron. "You must have an awful lot."

Will shrugged, and began working. He wanted to get done before supper. He would need the rest of the evening to write to Irene.

Thankfully, his father hadn't come home—again—and it wasn't even Friday. His mother held supper for his father, giving Will more time to work. But when seven-thirty rolled around, he and his mother ate alone. They both knew it would be morning before his father arrived.

While they ate their grits and drank tea, his mother peppered Will with questions about his hurry to do his homework. Will was glad; it kept his mind off of the food. He told her about each subject's assignment, embellishing each a little, and about his English class essay.

His mother eyed him thoughtfully. "This big hurry you are in, it's not because you have so much homework, is it?" A smile crept over her face.

Will turned a deeper red. He started to shake his head "no," but stopped; she was watching him carefully. "Yes, ma'am." He looked down at his plate.

"Is it because of a girl?"

He didn't answer.

"Will, that's perfectly natural. It's what a mother expects—hopes for." She patted his arm. "Boys your age usually are interested in girls. "Is it okay if I take a stab at who it is?" She smiled warmly. "Don't worry, I won't tell anybody. And don't tell me if you don't want me to know."

Will barely nodded.

"I bet it's that girl that was here the other night—Irene. She's a pretty one. I thought you had looked at her special-like. She likes you, too—I could tell."

He worked at suppressing a grin.

"She must be really nice, or you wouldn't like her." His mother put her forearms on the table to turn and look into his face. "Why the hurry? You going out with her tonight?"

Will wagged his "no," even though he knew she knew the answer, but he liked the implication of the question. She had done that on purpose.

In spite of how worn-out his mother looked, he had begun to notice that she was more attractive than most women of her age. He wondered why she had married his father.

"Ma, how did you and my father meet?" He avoided referring to his father as "Dad," anymore. "Did he ask you out?"

"Hmmm, that's a little complicated." His mother's eyes rested on the wall where it met the ceiling. "I remember exactly when and where I first saw your father." A smile crossed her lips. "It was in Guthrie, on November 16, 1907 . . ."

". . . when Oklahoma became a state," Will said. "Every Oklahoman knows that."

Her eyes went back to Will. "Let me finish." Her eyes went back to the wall.

"Yes, and it needed a constitution. That day was the last meeting of our constitutional convention. That was really a big deal.

"A relative was a member of the convention. Another of his relatives was going to watch, and wanted company. He asked me, a distant cousin, to go. I jumped at the chance to travel. I was only eighteen. I was afraid my father wouldn't let me go. My heart was beating so hard.

"Of course, I wore my best dress. It had a high laced collar." She wore a wide grin and talked faster and faster. "I had a felt hat with little roses, and shoes . . ." Her eyes dropped to Will, again. "Oh, a boy doesn't want to hear about ladies' clothes.

"Well, when we got there, who was up on the platform but the most handsome man I had ever seen. I figured he must be important, even though he wasn't very old. You know, I never even heard a word that the speaker said. All I could think about was what a handsome man . . ." She giggled a little. "I couldn't take my eyes off him. He turned out to be your father."

"So, how did you meet him?"

"Afterwards, when it was over, I went right down to the platform steps and waited for him to come down."

"What happened?"

Will's mother shrugged. "Nothing much. I just kept staring at him, and when he came down the steps, he saw me staring. He was only this far away." His mother held her hands about two feet apart. "I was shaking so much, I couldn't say anything. He stared back, even turned around to look at me as he walked away."

His mother gazed glassy eyed at the lamp's flame. "Then the mine disaster and he . . ." She suddenly pulled her eyes away. "That was it."

"But how did . . .?"

"I already answered your question—Chapter Two can wait until tomorrow night." She laughed at her joke. "You better get busy; it'll soon be time for bed."

"One more question."

"Okay. One. But not Chapter Two. A little one."

"Is it okay to give a girl a valentine if she already has a boyfriend?" The words burst out of him. Too late, he knew it was obvious he had spoken of himself. The room no longer felt cold.

His mother grinned. "Of course." She rolled her eyes. "That ol' LeRoy, she likes you way better than him." She rose. "And looks—you have it all over him, even with his fancy clothes." She placed her arm across his shoulders and bent and kissed Will on the cheek. "Don't you worry none. You just keep on being Will and everything will turn out fine—as long as you remain a gentleman."

As soon as he finished helping clear the table, he sat back in front of the coal oil lamp and pulled out paper, pen and ink. Occasionally, the lamp's flame would prance, sending shadows dancing across his paper. The dinner dishes clinked as his mother washed and dried them. Tomorrow, it would be his turn.

The cold in the room sat with him at the table and contrasted with the warmth from the stove at his back, sending delicious chills through his body. As he thought of his conversation with his mother, a grin crossed his face. ". . .*she likes you way better than him.*" If it were only true. He brought the lamp close to glean whatever heat he could from its flame.

"Momma, what did you mean, 'as long as you remain a gentleman?' I'm not even a man yet, not until I'm twenty-one."

"A gentleman, Will, is a man, even a boy, who does what he *should*, not what he *wants*. It's that easy." She produced a deep sigh. "Your father used to be a gentleman—years ago."

"Suppose what you should do hurts somebody? Like you have to protect . . . a baby, or defend yourself."

"Your father means well. He has such high hopes for you. He's afraid your, ah—see, we can't even say it even when he's not here—condition will get you down, make you dependent." She placed the small stack of dishes on a shelf. "His drinking, that's what makes him so violent."

Beating us to make me independent? Will glowered. "It sure doesn't seem he's trying to help." *Do what you should, she said.*

Will stared into the flame. Through his mind's eye he saw his father backhand his mother across the face. He saw himself knock him to the floor and, straddling him on his knees, he clenched his father's throat and beat his head against the floor.

Will suddenly exhaled, aghast at his thoughts. *Is that what I* want, *or what I* should *do?* He stared blankly at his mother. The stare deepened into a frown.

"You all right?"

Will nodded.

"He wants the best for you." When Will made no response, she went on. "It's been dark a couple of hours, already. Better get busy."

Will's frown deepened.

"I know you're angry, but you can't go wrong if you act like a gentleman."

"I'll try, Momma." *I'll try. For Irene, I'll always be a gentleman.*

Will wiped the frown from his lips and let his mind settle on Irene. He sighed again, relaxing, letting his angry feelings go. He then picked up his pen, dipped it in the ink bottle, and began:

February 14, 1935
Dear Irene,

He thought about the *dear.* Could he really write that? The pang in his heart told him that he meant every bit of whatever *"dear"* meant. Would she accept it? Every letter starts with *Dear,* he reasoned. He dipped his pen into the ink and then wrote:

I am very sorry about what I said to LeRoy today.

No! That was a lie. Will smiled as he thought about calling him a 'polecat.' He wasn't really sorry. But it was not very gentlemanly. Maybe things would have turned out better if he had been less harsh.

He wanted to be honest about what he wrote. He crumpled the paper and threw it into the wood box. He couldn't afford to throw paper away. He had to think carefully. He smiled to himself. *"Haste makes waste." "Waste not, want not."* He had written his essay about that.

He started again:

February 14, 1935
Dear Irene,

Could he say, *I love you so much I never want to hurt you*? It was true, but he knew he couldn't say that, either. Instead he penned,

I am sorry that I hurt and disappointed you today. It was just the opposite of what I had intended. I wanted to make you smile, even laugh. Please forgive me and accept the valentine.

He held the pen over the paper for a long time. He wanted to sign the closure, *Love,* or at least *Fondly,* but he let wisdom prevail and wrote:

Sincerely yours,
Will Coleman

He let out a long sigh.

"You done with that . . . that . . . whatever it is, yet, Will Coleman?" his mother said.

She had been watching him while she worked. Somehow his feelings belonged to her, too.

"I was writing a letter to Irene."

"No wonder you were in such a hurry. You better be getting to bed."

"Just finished. And thanks, Ma." He carefully folded the paper into thirds with the note facing inside. He wished he had an envelope. Instead he wrote, *Miss Irene North*, on the backside of the paper and slipped it into his backpack on top of his books.

Chapter 16

In spite of having just gone through his morning ritual with Uba Pisku, Will felt uneasy. He touched his amulet and then pushed his hand into his pocket; the Prince Albert can was still there. He secured the valentine tin in his hand. The metal was ice cold. He left the house a little early so he could do what he had in mind, and get to his job on time. The sky had lightened, but a gloom prevailed at street level.

His father still hadn't arrived home, but he knew that was not what bothered him. It was LeRoy Mattison. He could hear LeRoy almost like he was in front of him waving his fist. "You haven't seen the last of me, Cripple Boy." It was an echo of his father's threat.

Would LeRoy really try to beat him up? More likely he would get Wade and Emery to jump him.

Will recalled Emery smashing his cookie and then crushing it underfoot, like a cigarette. "This is what is going to happen to you, if we fail the test." He envisioned Emery twisting his foot on the cookie. And they had carried out their threat—or tried to. If they got together with LeRoy, then they'd do most anything. Carrying the valentine made Will feel particularly vulnerable. He had to protect it.

Will still hadn't reached the end of his driveway when he saw the dark form of someone making his way slowly along Chestnut Street. Every couple of steps the figure lurched. It was his father.

"What you doing out at night, boy?" His father hiccupped. "S'cuse me."

The little niceties sometimes made their way back from his father's boyhood. Maybe his father had been a gentleman. He stopped walking to maintain his balance, then swayed. His shirt and coat hung open and loose from his shoulders.

Will kept moving. "It's morning. I'm on my way to school."

His father stepped toward him to block his path and stumbled. Will caught his father by the coat to keep him from falling. The stench of vomit and cheap liquor assaulted Will's nostrils.

"Get off me, before I knock you silly." His father made a roundhouse swing at Will and fell to the drive.

His father struggled to get up. Will moved closer and let his father pull himself up by grabbing Will's crutch. "Thanks," his father said. His head swung slowly from side to side. He continued to steady himself with the crutch.

He stared blearily at Will. "What you doing with that heart? Going to see that girl tonight, aren't you? I told you to stay away from her."

"It's morning, Dad."

"Let me have it." His father reached for the tin with both hands. Will gave a slight push with his crutch and his father tumbled to the ground. He cursed Will.

Will moved quickly away. "Leave me alone," Will said, and swung himself down the rest of the drive, without looking back, to Chestnut Avenue.

If his father had grabbed the valentine there might have been no end to the struggle and the heart could have been damaged. Upon reaching Chestnut, Will looked over his shoulder and saw his father staggering toward the house, none the worse for the fall.

Will worried about what his father might do to his mother, but in his father's current condition she would be able to defend herself. Anyway, Will bet his father would tumble into bed to sleep off his drunk and remain there for the day. And hopefully, his inebriated state would once more lend itself to forgetfulness. It had in the past. One more fall in a chain of falls. Hardly memorable. Otherwise, punishment for Will's defiance could be severe. Will shuddered.

Thankfully, he had left home extra early. He hurried by the lot at Grant and Randolph. Not a sign of anyone. He distracted himself by watching his shadow, cast by the corner street lamps, loom large in front of him and then disappear into the gloom.

Will thought about LeRoy, a real big cheese. One of the top students at Enid High. Trusted by the principal and office and coach. Thoughtful and helpful. Rich and an only child. Trusted by his father—even to drive his new car, a Studebaker, at that. LeRoy thought himself the cat's meow, a regular Joe Brooks, always dressed to the hilt. Wanted to be a man of the world and thought he was a gift to the girls. And some, like

Irene, bought it and fell in love. At the same time, LeRoy thought himself tough. Perceived of himself as a leader and popular. Adults thought he was wonderful.

Then there was the other side of LeRoy that Will learned about the hard way. He was sneaky, a bully and immature. Supposedly tough, with a reputation for fighting. That's what Sam said. Will relished the idea of LeRoy with a bloody nose.

Maybe LeRoy also got up extra early to waylay him. He wasn't afraid of LeRoy, anyway. It was less likely that Emery and Wade would get up early—unless LeRoy paid them to come with him.

Will heard a car approaching from behind him. LeRoy again? Will ducked into the shadow formed by the tree next to the walk. The car was a Model T and continued down the street.

He made out the gable of Irene's house. His heart quickened at the thought of placing the valentine on her porch. He imagined her opening the door and seeing it. She would see the note underneath and snatch it to her bosom so that her mother couldn't see it. Her mother would ask, "What's that?" and Irene would blush and say, "Just a paper," and keep on going.

Another car was coming. This time, toward him. He saw the lights looking like two dim lamps dancing among the shadows in the street. Then he heard the chugging of the motor. The lights grew larger and began lighting the street in front of it.

Will swung behind a tree trunk and turned sideways. He couldn't see the car with the tree in front of him, but the chugging grew louder as he waited. The motor sounded like LeRoy's Studebaker's. Its lights filled the street next to Will as the engine slowed to an idle, then stopped.

Will slowly moved his head from behind the tree, then jerked it back as he saw LeRoy emerge from his father's Studebaker. The car had parked in front of Irene's. Will barely heard the car door click shut.

He peeked around the tree and watched LeRoy, carrying what looked like a bunch of flowers, walk to Irene's house, up to her porch, then disappear from view.

Flowers! Flowers—he could never afford them.

Then, from behind the tree trunk, Will listened as footsteps grew closer. His heart pounded while he held his breath, hoping he would not be seen. The car started, its lights came on, then it pulled slowly away.

Will exhaled, then stared at the valentine in his hand. He made his way slowly down the pavement toward Irene's house and paused at her walkway. He thought of looking for a trash can; no, he would not give up. He turned up her walk and stepped onto the porch. A large bouquet of what looked like red roses wrapped in shiny white tissue paper, lay on the porch chair next to the door. A small card was attached. The only light came from a distant street lamp. "For Irene, With love—LeRoy," it said.

His mind raced through a number of scenarios, but he seriously considered only a few—removing LeRoy's card but leaving the flowers along with his box of chocolates and note to make it appear both were from him; taking the flowers and leaving his chocolates. Those two would make him no better than LeRoy. Or he could leave LeRoy's flowers and his own valentine to compete for Irene's favor.

The flowers would die. What had the lady at the store said? *After the candy is gone, your valentine*—Irene—*will use the beautiful heart and think of you every time.* Will chuckled and added, *And she'll throw LeRoy out along with the flowers. Besides, I left her a personal note with my valentine.*

Will could hardly wait for English class.

Chapter 17

Will thrust himself between his crutches, making long, fast strides. He must meet her in the hall before she entered their English classroom. He slowed as he neared the room and hugged the wall to hide behind students strolling to their classes. He looked behind him and then toward the room. There were many bodies moving in all directions, but he saw no sign of Irene. Why was she so late? He wiped perspiration from around his lips with the back of his hand, ran his fingers through his hair, and shifted on his crutches.

She would be alone this time. Not be with him. Will was certain. He would not even entertain the clod's name.

When Will saw her he would rush to her side. Her beautiful eyes would look deep into his and they would enter English class together.

Finally. There! Irene appeared from around the corner. Will swung out to intercept her. He stopped short, his breath knocked from him. Students trailing him stumbled against him, then glared over their shoulders as they passed by. Will didn't even notice.

The sap was there—LeRoy—effortlessly carrying their books under one arm. His eyes watched her every expression. The two chatted and drifted to the doorway. He, a head taller, looked down at her lovely smooth face. Her lips, above her upturned chin, invited. Invited a banned activity in the halls of Enid High School. He quickly handed her books to her. She spoke animatedly, still smiling. He turned and walked away, erect and confident.

She didn't even look for Will.

And now he would have to enter the classroom, lunge down the aisle while she watched him, thinking what a fool he had been for bringing her Valentine chocolates—in a heart, no less—even after she had thrust them back into his hands.

And his note to her. Had she shown it to LeRoy?

Will had written, *"I wanted to make you smile, even laugh."* He *bet* they had laughed. His crutches would not move, would not carry him out of the hallway. He could feel his face sagging.

Mrs. Johnson stepped into the hall and began to close her open door, but stopped. "Will, why are you standing in the hall?" Her voice came as from a distant cloud.

His mouth opened, but nothing came out.

She stood waiting, a smile pressed to her lips, her hand on the doorknob. "Come on, Will."

He made the first step, and then let his momentum carry him. He watched his shoes with their protruding toes swing forward between crutches and land on the floor. They landed again, and again. Down the aisle to his seat they carried him, down to where a desktop replaced the toes. The room was uncommonly quiet; not even Mrs. Johnson spoke. He did not look up.

There was no need. He felt their eyes. Why did they stare? He had only entered a little late.

Will Coleman stared down at his desktop. Mrs. Johnson spoke, students answered. Pens dipped into inkwells and scratched on paper. He stared at his desk. He would not think of her, even her name. He would not look up and see her beautiful hair, or wonder if she turned to look at him. Somehow, a rock had come to rest in his stomach. Mrs. Johnson walked across the room. A window opened. A desk seat squeaked. Chalk beat a tattoo on the blackboard. Pens scratched. Will Coleman looked at his desk top. The window closed. Papers passed to the front. Mrs. Johnson talked. A bell rang. Notebooks and books rustled around him. Feet scuffed their way to the door. Will's feet joined them.

Bells rang again and again. Sandwiched between the rings were Wood Shop, Study Hall, Latin. Shoes ran from the building. It was Friday, wasn't it?

Coal. Will shoveled it. He watched the black chunks fill the shovel blade. He tossed them. Chunks of coal lingered in the air before settling in the hopper. He filled the hoppers. Finally done.

Now home. Will slugged his way, watched his shoes with the protruding toes. Sam said, "Wait," then caught up to him. Sam talked, patted him on the shoulder.

"Goodbye," Sam said.

The image of his father grabbing for the valentine filled Will's mind. He wondered if his father had taken his anger out on his mother.

Will feared what would happen when he did get home. He forgot that he was walking, but now he was there, at her house. He did not look up. He just knew he was there.

Someone called to him. He kept going. It sounded like Irene, but he knew it was not her. Why did they torment him so? He heard feet scurrying down the front walk toward him. "Will, Will. Stop." Whoever it was ran right up to him and touched his arm.

It was her touch—he would always recognize it. It was she. Irene. This was the third time she had touched him. His heart pounded and pounded. The rock in his stomach grew. He stopped but did not smile. What did she want?

Will melted at the sight of her deep dark eyes with their thick lashes. He ached to touch her smooth, dark-honey skin. He hoped she would not see that his knees shook, or notice that his face had become a deeper rust color.

She smiled beautifully, with full, tender lips over even white teeth. Then her smile was gone and her eyes took on a glint he had never seen. It stirred a fear in him, accusing him. "Will Coleman, why did you hit LeRoy? He said you hit him. I didn't think you were the kind of person who picked fights." She turned her head just a bit so that she could look at him from the corner of her eyes to wait for his answer. Her smile was completely gone now. Red tinged her cheeks and neck.

Did she hate him? If she did, why would she even bother to confront him? She must have been watching for him. Would she believe his side of the story? She had already heard LeRoy's. Will's mind raced, but he did not answer immediately. He wondered if whatever he said now, she would think he was making it up.

He opened his mouth. Nothing came out.

Just tell the truth, he told himself. That was the best policy. Besides, how could he ever lie to her? He stared at her hair—black, thick, framing her beautiful face, now examining his. Deciding about him.

He licked his lips and gasped, "I admit, I was really angry when LeRoy snatched the valentine heart from me yesterday." The words tumbled out. "It was for you and I felt like—like killing him, but he ran to his car and drove away. And I never hit him, ever."

Irene's eyes softened a bit and she turned her head to look directly at him. She waited. "And there he was, acting like he had bought the candy for you. He probably hadn't even remembered it was Valentine's Day." Will's eyes turned away, out of focus. "When he grabbed me, and I had the chance . . ." Will's voice dropped, "I almost smashed his nose. I—I tried my best to be polite."

Irene said nothing, and when he looked back, her lips had turned up a bit. Her eyes searched his.

"And then, and then . . ." Did she believe him? Maybe he should turn away and go home where he could write her a note, explaining it all. He breathed deeply. She probably thought him pathetic. He couldn't even talk. She would pity him even more. Or find him disgusting. No, he was strong, a Choctaw. He stood straight, his head up.

She nodded for him to continue.

"I pushed him away. Called him a name. I never expected to hurt you."

She looked down. Will thought maybe he should have bought Tom and Tiddle's shoes. They would have been a better investment than a valentine. At least he had socks on today whose holes had been darned. When she looked back up there were tears rimming her eyes. Will wanted to crush her to him and smooth her hair.

"I'm sorry if I offended you."

"No, that's not it." She sniffed and wiped her eyes with the back of her hand.

Will wished he had a nice clean handkerchief to dab away her tears.

She smiled. "Thank you for the candy," she said, "and the beautiful heart." Her face became more solemn. "And the wonderful note."

She clutched her arms to her and shivered. "It's cold. Aren't you cold? Come on in and get warm."

Will felt the rock in his gut disappear. "No, I had better . . ."

"Just for a minute. Please. I want you to meet my mother." Her deep dark eyes sparkled. She hooked her arm about his and tried to drag him up the walk, crutch and all.

"I, I . . ." Suddenly his head was swimming. He could not resist. Invited into her house! Had LeRoy been dispensed with so easily? The blood pounded in his ears and he could tell that his face had taken on an even deeper rust color. He was glad for the twilight, but his face was exposed as he made his way up onto her porch and under its light. He hoped that his shaking was not apparent.

A frown crossed his brow. Suppose her father was home. Wasn't this about the time yesterday he got off the bus? Never get near his daughter? Why, she was hanging onto him. Will hesitated.

Irene's dark eyes sparkled. "Come on, Will." She clutched his arm and tugged until he stood on the threshold. The silver cross at her throat glimmered. "You'll like my mother," she said. "Mom," she called, "here's the boy I was telling you about."

Telling her mother about me? Will's heart pounded anew. Maybe Irene had talked her mother into joining her in making him a missionary project.

A delicious smell wafted from within the house.

A tall woman, almost stately, appeared at the entrance. She dried her hands on the folds of a kitchen apron that covered a flowered dress. "Please come in," she said.

Did he have a choice? How he hated to enter, but was never so happy to comply. Mrs. North held out her hand and introduced herself. Will knew she felt his hand trembling, but her smile was warm and accepting. She looked nothing like Irene, for she was fair and slim. The only similar features were her full generous lips.

She made him feel more at home, but the presence of Irene in this setting had the blood ringing in his ears.

"This is the boy who reads poetry so well?" she asked. Surely, this was not the reason Mrs. North wanted to meet him. She regarded him closely, and in spite of his ragged appearance, she looked pleased. Apparently, she was measuring his needs and what she could do to fulfill them. Was there a contest at their church? Maybe for attendance? "Maybe you could read some for us. The one you read aloud in class." Her eyes seemed never to leave him. "Irene, show Will to a seat."

Will felt sweat break out on his lip. If he were to read and had the same reaction in front of Irene's mother . . . could he control himself . . . what then? Irene led him to a davenport and, sitting, pulled him down next to her.

"Yes, let's do read. I have my English book," Irene said. Her eyes flashed, looking into his. She retrieved a book that was on a lamp table next to the sofa.

Already he felt overwhelmed with the same emotion he'd had in class, as if a string had pulled at his heart.

"Your mom doesn't want to listen to that." His voice sounded hoarse and weak.

"Of course I do. Oh, I almost forgot them," she said, finally taking her eyes from him. She hurried to the kitchen adjacent to the room in which they sat.

Irene turned the pages of the book in her lap. "We'll read it just like we did in class. You were wonderful, Will."

"You, too." The words came out almost in a squeak. "I mean it," he added to shore up his weak 'you, too.' She would never know how wonderful he thought she was.

Within minutes, Mrs. North was back, a plate of oatmeal hermits in one hand and napkins in the other. "Just a little overdone." With her eyes back on him, she held the plate out to him. The aroma of warm cookies filled his head, their taste already in his mouth. She handed him a cloth napkin. "Please, help yourself."

He gingerly took one and placed it on his napkin. Irene put her book back onto the table and grabbed a handful. "Here!" she said, and added three more to his napkin, keeping two for herself. Her mother smiled, nodding approvingly. Evidently, their intentions were to fatten him up. He would not break a cookie in half to save for later, as he had in the cafeteria. But maybe he could save a hermit for his mother.

"Will would like a glass of milk, too," Irene said.

Was it so easy to get a glass of milk? He hadn't thought of milk, but it sounded good with hermits.

"Of course, for both of you," Mrs. North said. "I wasn't thinking." She flashed an Irene smile, lips, teeth and all, and turned back to the kitchen.

Irene squirmed and pressed against Will, took a bite of cookie, and watched him intently as he bit into his own. The cookie—warm and soft, melting in his mouth—left delicate crumbs clinging to his lips. Irene half turned to look square into his face, putting her own close to his. With her finger, she gently brushed crumbs from his lips, and then smiled. Her eyes, shining, deep and liquid, and so close, searched his.

He sat, stunned. If his heart had pounded before, it was like nothing compared to now. His half-eaten cookie was still in his hand, resting in his lap. She took it from him and brought it to his lips. He opened his mouth and she gently placed it on his tongue. He heard the clink of a glass. Irene straightened up and, imperceptibly, edged away. Her mother appeared with two glasses of milk.

Mrs. North sat across from them, nibbling on a cookie of her own, while they ate and sipped the milk. Never had anything tasted so good.

When they had finished, Mrs. North smoothed her apron and said, "Now, how about that poem? I think all those hermits should have bought a poem."

It seemed reasonable, but Will again felt edgy. He had forgotten about Mr. North. And, surely, by now, it was time, as much as he hated to go, for Will to leave.

But Irene picked up her English book from the table and, while opening the book and placing it on their laps in front of them, squirmed close to Will, all while her mother watched.

It made perfectly good sense that you would have to sit close in order to share the book. His mind raced back to when he was four. His mother had wrapped an arm around him, snuggled him up close, and read to him from his storybook.

Thoughts of Mr. North fled. Irene turned the pages, her arm brushing Will's, until she found the place, and seemed to have taken a long time doing it, although, as chills went up and down him, he cared not if it took her an hour to find the page. Upon locating it, she glanced at Will, took a breath, and began.

Will fixed his own eyes on the page. He could not look at Mrs. North or else his throat would surely close up altogether from embarrassment. He did not need to look at Irene. Feeling her warmth along his side was enough, although alone with her would improve the situation even more. Everything else had fled his mind. He did not want the present to ever end.

"'*Duet,' by Alfred, Lord Tennyson*," began Irene. "'*Is it the wind of the dawn that I hear in the pine overhead?*'"

She nudged him, just barely, to signal his turn, but the movement left her nestled that much closer, pressing against his side. Before he spoke, Will's eyes flicked involuntarily but Mrs. North, sat calmly with her hands in her lap, a smile upon her lips, unaware of the nudge.

Will read even as Irene's foot pressed against his own. "'*No; but the voice of the deep as it . . .*'"

The front door knob rattled and the door swung open. Looking against the light from the open door, all Will could see was the silhouette of a man, turning to close the door and shedding his coat.

Chapter 18

"Oh, Daddy!" Irene sprang to her feet and ran to her father in the entrance way. She threw her arms around him and hugged him tightly.

Mr. North! Will's body went from warm to ice. If he had his coat on and knew for certain where the back door was located, Will would have fled for his life. Instead, he froze and let jealousy barge in. Would she ever throw her arms around him?

"Wait, wait, hold this, and let me get out of my coat." Mr. North handed Irene a package wrapped in brown paper and tied with twine, and then shook himself free of his heavy garment.

Irene smiled broadly. "We have a guest. Somebody special."

"It must be LeRoy." Mr. North, only a few inches taller than his daughter, craned his neck to the side, attempting to peer past her. He revealed a face resembling hers, including the bright smile.

The smile collapsed. "That's not LeRoy."

Will sunk back into the davenport and froze.

"Come and see." Mrs. North slipped from behind her daughter, exchanged pecks on the cheek with her husband, took his coat, and lifted the hat from his head.

"But first, my present?" Mrs. North said. She took the package from Irene, lowered her chin, and smiled coyly up at her husband.

Mr. North laughed and turned toward her. "No, I'm sorry dear. I stopped for my shoes. The package is from Tom and Tittle's. They told the dangedest story."

Mrs. North discarded her burdens and held both of her husband's hands to look intently into his face. Irene, too, turned in her father's direction, blocking Will's view of Mr. North so that he could only see Mr. North's forehead.

Mr. North chuckled again. "Some fool boy, his frostbitten toes sticking right through the ends of his shoes, refused a practically free pair of shoes. Guess why? He had his heart set on buying a valentine for his sweetheart—with his last cent!"

"Would you spend your last cent on me, dear?" Mrs. North asked. She squeezed his hand and brought it to her lips.

"Why—why I would certainly hope so. I mean, I certainly would."

She giggled and this time kissed him on the cheek.

"I smell cake," Mr. North said. "No? Ahh! Oatmeal hermits. Let me see who this guest is that gets cookies."

Will, his crutches now under him, stuck out his hand as Mr. North stepped toward him.

"Daddy, this is Will Cole . . ."

"I know who he is." His voice turned low, guttural. "And I want him out of here—now!"

Will's hand remained empty. He withdrew it. He felt anger rising through his body and into his temples. He was a Choctaw. He stared hard into Mr. North's eyes.

"I've known about him long before he even came to Enid. More than a week ago we met outside on our walkway." His voice became louder. "I had told him then to stay away from my family, and now he's dared set foot in my house. Get him ou—"

"Ira! He's our guest," Mrs. North said.

"How dare you say that? He's no guest of mine. Stay away from him. His father is nothing but a sopping, drunken Indian." Mr. North stared at Will and pointed. "There's the door!"

Will's grip on his crutches turned his knuckles white. What did Irene think? Will glowered at Mr. North. Through clenched teeth he said, "Not true," and tried to pick his way to the door past the two women barring his way.

Mrs. North frowned at her husband. "Will's done nothing to deserve yelling at. Why are you so angry?"

Mr. North's jaw jutted out. "Charlie Coleman was responsible for the '23 mine explosion that killed seventy-two men. Practically murder and he got away with it. Can't ever trust a redskin."

Will glared. Now he understood why his father didn't want him to find out about the mine disaster, especially from Mr. North. Well, now he knew, and when his father discovered he had heard North's side, how could his father still object to Irene. But what did Irene think of him, now? He could not read the frown on her face.

Will leaned onto his crutches to head toward the door.

"Daddy, that's his father, not him." Irene moved toward Will's side, but her father stepped into her way and, inadvertently, into Will's. "And he's one of my friends," she said.

He stared at his daughter. "You listen to me, young lady! The apple doesn't fall far from the tree."

"Ira," Mrs. North said, "he was going to go to church with us Sunday, weren't you Will? And we're having donuts and hot chocolate before the service."

"Beth, you of all people," Mr. North said. "You lost husbands of church friends. How could you let that Indian in here? Let alone take him to church. Look at him!"

Will stood dumbfounded by the argument. But Will figured he had been right about his being a church project, although this was the first he had heard of an invitation.

"We don't need members like that. And stay away from him," Mr. North said. "Evil's in his stinking Indian blood." His brows knitted together. He stared at Will's neck. "Here, I'll prove what a heathen he is, before I toss him out." He pointed at Will. "What's that string around your neck? Let us see it."

Will hesitated, knowing no good would come of it, but slowly pulled the amulet from inside of his shirt by its leather thong. "My father gave it to me. I am not to take it off."

"What is that? What's that on there?"

"My amulet." Will began tucking it back inside his shirt.

"I knew it." Mr. North's tone was smug. "Leave it out." He nodded to Irene and her mother. "I want you to take a good look at it."

As Will held the amulet away from his chest for them to see, Irene, her father and mother bent closer to the gem. A tapered baguette of polished emerald stone, two inches long, lay in Will's hand.

Mr. North straightened up and sucked in his breath. "That's the exact same amulet his father showed me." The blood drained from his face and he sank to the chair behind him. "That thing is evil."

"Why, Ira, I didn't realize you were superstitious," Mrs. North said.

"I'm not."

"Is that a snake on it?" Irene asked, referring to the silver carving wrapping the stone.

"A diamondback rattler."

Mr. North leaned forward in his chair. "Get that Indian and his rock out of here," he said in a hoarse whisper.

Will's eyes darted toward him. Why is he so upset over it?

"It'll kill us all. Only an evil person would carry it," Mr. North said.

Irene grimaced and bent closer, her face near Will's. "I can see the diamond shapes in its back, and the rattle."

Will inhaled the fragrance of her hair and caught himself leaning toward her, forgetting Mr. North. "And the snake imparts my character—persistence." *And I'll never give up on Irene.*

"And wisdom," Will added.

Mr. North cleared his throat. "Wisdom! If you were wise, you wouldn't have come in here." He waved a forefinger in the direction of the talisman, "After Coleman showed off that thing, people died." He examined his wife's and daughter's faces. "You understand? Listen, at the mine, he came to my office. He insisted on showing me that inane object—waving it around. That Indian was on the warpath—still is. He knew what he was doing." He was loud now. "Then the mine blew. He should have been in the mine with his men. He caused that explosion."

"Why, Ira, how could you say such a thing? You know that couldn't be true," Mrs. North said.

"I know. It was his fault, one way or the other." He raised his eyes to glare at Will. "Just get him out." Mr. North wiped a handkerchief across his brow and upper lip. "Young lady, you stay away from him." Color came back to Mr. North's face and he rose from the chair. His chin jutted in Will's direction. "I want you and that thing and all it represents out of my house!"

"Oh, Daddy, stop it. I want to find out more about it."

"Yeah, find out what that rock really is," Mr. North said, throwing up his hands. "You'll be sorry. And stop your impertinence.

"An amulet, you say, eh? Why do you wear it?" Mr. North's face wrinkled into a snarl.

"The sun god, Abu Pisku—as long as I wear this, keeps evil spirits away."

"Like the one that saved those men," Mr. North growled. "I suppose you've seen this before, Irene?"

"I knew he had it, but it was always under his shirt. Finally, I get to see it."

"Irene wears an amulet, too," Will said. "A cross, that means two paths crossing—hers and mine." There—he had added the last part.

Mr. North's face turned blood red. His body appeared to swell until it would burst. His cheeks, which looked like red balloons, only allowed him to sputter. Finally, he got himself under enough control to speak. "That's sacrilege. I told you, he's nothing but an ignorant savage!" He looked at Will and spoke through gritted teeth. "If you're not out of here in seconds, I'll . . . I'll . . . throw you out by the seat of your pants. Now git!"

"Ira, don't be so . . . so . . . crude. He doesn't believe that stuff anymore than you do."

"Give me my coat and backpack." Will slipped the amulet inside his shirt and attempted to move toward the door, but the three boxed him in. Mr. North glared, seeming not to realize he blocked the way.

Irene slid next to Will and gripped his forearm. "Oh, don't go, Will. Daddy will get over it." As angry as Will was, her touch went to his heart. How could Mr. North possibly oppose her?

She looked at her father. "You don't know him. Wait. Talk with him. You'll feel better about him."

"Huh! And you better have no feelings for that Injun!"

"My feelings come unbidden, Daddy. Just like . . . I love you."

Will and Mr. North stood facing each other, her father expecting, no, demanding, Will to go around him. The two women frowned, not wanting him to leave. No one spoke. Finally, Mr. North spied his package lying on a chair and deliberately picked it up, opening the way. Will swung between his crutches to the doorway.

Mr. North thrust his finger at Will. "Now you beat it, and never come back!"

"Honestly, Will, you don't have to go," Irene said, steering her eyes from her father to Will.

"Don't you be so impudent, young lady!" Mr. North said.

Irene, her brow furrowed, snatched her own coat from the coat tree as Will headed for the door. "Wait for me," she said.

Mr. North shook his finger. "Miss Irene North. You're staying right here!"

"Wait, I'll be back," she said to Will at the doorway, brushed past her father, and then disappeared into the kitchen.

Will swung out onto the porch, down the front walk, and up the main walk toward home. Even though the air was crisp, he still felt warm from the struggle he had been in. Yet, his heart felt as if it were gripped in ice. He tried to fathom its ache. Irene. Abu Pisku. His father. The amulet. Her mother was right. Will knew what the sun really was. So did Mr. North.

From behind him, he heard Irene's father's voice, "Stay in—" and then heard the front door slam shut. Feet clattered across the wooden porch and then scurried toward him. Irene arrived slightly out of breath.

Coming to reclaim her missionary project, he supposed. He turned and faced her in front of the neighbor's house.

His heart skipped a beat, then thudded. The ice encasing his heart melted. Maybe he wasn't a pawn for her contest, after all. But, he said, "Irene, you better go back. I don't want you to get into trouble."

Will heard her front door reopen. Her father yelled again.

Irene paused to take a few breaths. "He's just wrong, Will. I'm ignoring him. He can threaten all he wants." She shrugged. "If he punishes me, I'll accept it.

"Here, I went back for these. Put them in your pocket." She didn't wait for Will to take them, but thrust them into his coat pocket. Automatically, he put his own hand into the pocket and felt a wax paper package.

She smiled. "Cookies, what did you expect?"

"You shouldn't—your family, your father might . . ." He thought of his own beating. Surely, Mr. North would do nothing like that, not to her. Will would not stand for it.

She waved at him. "He doesn't care about cookies. We've plenty, and can make more."

"You better go back."

"No, I'm going with you. I wore my coat."

Will's jaw fell slack. "To my house? You can't."

"Part way. Up to Grant Street." She rolled her lips together.

"Girls don't walk boys."

"This one does, sometimes." She smiled; her white teeth were even more striking in the gathering twilight. "You can pay me back. Stop by my house tomorrow morning and walk me to school. You can carry my books."

They were walking now, and Will, his heart pounding in his chest, struggled to think. He finally said, "What if your father finds out about tomorrow?" *And what of LeRoy?* he didn't say. Surely, she has decided to end her relationship with LeRoy.

"You don't want to stop by?" She turned her head away with chin uplifted, pretending to be miffed.

"I don't want you to get into more trouble." *Besides, if my father finds out . . . So what, he can't stop me from walking with her.*

She shrugged. "There is only so much punishment he can mete out." She laughed. "I suppose I'll be punished until I'm married."

Will felt the red warm his cheeks. It was probably too dark for her to see the color. Did she mean marriage to refer to him? Nah, just a way of speaking, he decided.

She hooked her arm around both his arm and his crutch, reminiscent of her mother and father at the door. Irene pulled Will's arm close to her, causing him to plant his crutch behind his center of gravity. He stumbled and fell headlong, twisting just enough to land atop his backpack, striking the hard, cold walk, and pulling her on top of him.

He lay there, stunned. Her soft hair and cheek rested against his face. Her body, even through their coats, felt warm and soft. He basked in sensation so pleasant that it overwhelmed the pain from his back and legs.

But why was he unsettled? Was it the fall, or her nearness?

She didn't move!

Will was aghast. Had he hurt her? He was so clumsy. She would never talk to him again. "Irene!" he shouted. "Irene!"

She stirred, then pushed herself to an arm's length away and looked into his face. She began to laugh and snort and laughed. Will recoiled with turned-down lips, his feelings hurt. She tried to speak, but laughed all the harder. She managed to place her hand on his forearm, signaling that she was not laughing at him. Puzzled, he smiled, but soon could not help but join her. They sat convulsing in laughter, making it impossible for them to arise. He could not recall ever laughing so hard. It felt wonderful. Finally, Will pulled himself up with a crutch and, with one hand, fairly lifted her to her feet.

"You're so strong!" she said. Embarrassment reddened his cheeks once more, yet he felt proud.

She brushed herself off, still giggling. She looked into his eyes.

In that moment, his understanding of what had just happened went deep, deeper than he could put into words.

"Are you okay? Is that dirt or is your hand bleeding?" Will asked. "I'm sorry." He brushed at his own clothes. He wanted to tell her what he felt inside, but no words came.

"Just a scratch, I should have worn my gloves." She rooted in her coat pocket, found a tissue, and wiped it clean.

Will sidled up to her, again said, 'I'm sorry,' and, leading with his lips, his emotions welling up in him, bent to kiss her cheek.

She waited while he drew close, then jumped aside, laughing. "Oh, no you're not, Will Coleman. Let's go. Here." And with that, she wrapped her hand around his hand holding the crutch. They walked along silently, and awkwardly, for a bit.

He was amazed. His having crutches didn't bother her at all. But right then he decided he would start the exercises and whatever else Coach told him to do. He would soon walk holding hands as any boy could.

"Irene?" he said.

"Yes."

"I'm sorry, I didn't mean to get you into trouble with your father."

"You didn't. I did that. Just look for me in the second story window, staring forlornly from my room." She giggled. "What more can he do? Besides, it won't last long. My mom will talk him out of it, and eventually, he'll like you."

They walked a little further, with Will doubting if her father would ever accept him.

"Irene?" This time he stopped. They faced each other.

"Yes."

Although her eyes were beautiful and her gorgeous hair framed a lovely face, and undoubtedly, she was fun, kind and intelligent, it had come to matter to him, so he had to ask, "Irene, are you being nice to me just so . . ." He took a breath. "so that I'll go to church with you?"

The faintest smile alighted upon her face. She regarded him carefully. "No, silly, I'm not being *nice* to you. I'm just being *me* with you. Okay? I don't feel sorry for you, either, if that's what you're going to ask me."

He continued to watch her face. "That apple you gave me—why?"

"You looked hungry. Maybe back then I felt a teeny bit sorry for you."

"But your mother . . ."

"Okay, she really wants to get you to church, but she likes you, too. I can tell."

Will waited, expecting more.

"I admit, I was a little like my mother at first. But not now, not a bit."

They resumed walking.

"Irene, I would go to church with you, if you want. Even if they don't serve donuts."

"Could you face my father?" She half-smiled.

"I'm not afraid of him. I can't imagine he would act that way in church. Would he?"

Irene's hand went to the cross at her neck. "No, but when you said my cross meant our paths crossed, I thought he would explode. Why did you say that?"

"A cross, drawn with the arms the same length—that's the Choctaw symbol for 'paths crossing.'"

Irene looked at him intently. "And, you said, *our* paths?"

They stopped.

Will focused upon her black tresses caressing the side of her face and resting on her shoulders. His looked to where the cross lay under her coat. He breathed deeply. His eyes found hers searching his face. "When I see your cross, that's what I think."

"Think what?" She smiled—the smile meant only for him.

Will stopped. "Our paths crossed for a reason." His heart really pounded now. He didn't know if he could say more, but down inside he wanted her to know. His voice dropped to a near whisper. "I think about you all the time."

She continued to smile, but was more serious than Will had ever seen her. She then turned and led the way. He had said too much.

Finally, she spoke. "The shoe story my father told—was that you?"

Will's eyes dropped and inadvertently pointed to the toes sticking out of his shoes. He quickly looked back up.

Irene followed his glance. "Oh, Will." Her hand found his arm. She smiled as a tear rimmed her eye. "I loved the Valentine heart. I'll keep it forever. And Will, about the apple, I think what I really wanted was just to share with you."

Will gazed into her eyes, not knowing what to say, wanting to pull her to him.

"May I see your amulet, again?"

Will pulled the gem out and, bending close to her, took her hand and laid the amulet in it. With that act, a tingling surged through him.

She stepped toward him. Their heads nearly touched.

"It's beautiful. That silver, it looks like real diamonds."

Irene tilted her head up to look into his eyes. Her lips were so close.

"Did your father make it?" she asked.

"No, he got it from his father, and he got it from his father, going back generations."

"Why did he give it to you?" The water vapor from their breaths mingled.

"The first son receives it when he becomes worthy, a brave." Will remembered the time his father placed it around his neck. Those were better days.

They turned and continued their stroll, not speaking. She placed her hand on his, on his crutch, as before. Will really wanted to speak of his feelings—dared he even think it, lest they come aloud—that he loved her? Instead, he settled for, "Here's Grant Street. I'm glad you walked with me."

They stopped and turned to each other again.

"And we didn't even talk about your father or mother. 'Bye, Will." She looked long and seriously into his face, and then started to back away, but he grabbed her arm and pulled her to him. Second chances, and even first chances, didn't come every day.

"Unh-unh," she said, shaking her head and wagging her finger "no." "I'll see you tomorrow in front of my house." Her lips gathered and her eyes danced, teasing, as she pulled away. Reluctantly, he let her go.

He watched as she hurried down the walk. She turned once to wave and then quickly grew smaller and fainter in the near dark. He watched until he could see her no more. His fingers closed around the cookies in his pocket while his mind filled with images of their walk, and the fall, and her face and body pressing against his. Absently, he shoved a cookie into his mouth. His heart pounded. The cookie crumbled and melted in his mouth; its moist taste lingered on his lips—her kiss.

Will sighed and forced himself to start north on Grant. The lot at the corner barely stirred his memory of the snowball fight. However, fear again gripped him as the image of his own father berating his mother entered his mind. If that was all, it would be okay, he told himself.

But, try as he might, he could not squelch his doubts. He should not have stayed at Irene's house. Now he was late, giving his father reason to beat his mother. Will kept hoping his father had stumbled away early to a saloon. Yet, that was unlikely, considering his father hadn't returned home until this morning, and probably only recently awoke. Then he'd yell at his mother and blame her for his headache and nausea. When he discovered Will was not home, he'd hit her.

Will tried to hurry, but his feet felt like logs. He wiped a cold wet spot from his cheek, then felt one on his hand. He looked closely at his coat sleeve. Flakes of snow rested briefly, and then disappeared as they melted into the fabric. They provided some impetus, a distraction, and he picked up his pace. He turned and looked at the street lamp on the corner of Grant and Rudolph to see if snow swirled beneath the lamp. It was too far away to tell.

Will paused at the foot of the long drive to his house. The flakes were coming faster now. The house looked very dark. Usually, he saw some hint of light from the window. He dragged his legs between his crutches.

As he closed the distance to his house, its darkness loomed greater. It struck him that the doorway itself was black, a blacker rectangle within a black house, a house that emanated gloom rather than light. A tremor went down his spine.

The wind picked up speed and flung snowflakes into his face. Snow coated the front of his jacket.

He was nearly home. His breaths came hard and fast, but it was as if he could draw no air. Flakes obscured his vision, but through them, he saw why the black rectangle had replaced his door. The doorway framed the dark gloom from within the house, for the door sat wide open. Not a hint of a light came from inside, not even an ember was visible in the woodstove. He faced a wider blackness. Will trembled.

The wind buffeted him and the door. The open door swung back a foot and hit the wall with a bang, ricocheted forward, but stopped and remained wide open.

The building briefly blocked the wind and the snow, allowing Will to see more clearly. The door was being held open by something lying across the threshold.

Chapter 19

Fear stabbed Will's gut. As he drew closer, he hoped against hope that the something was not his mother lying at the entrance to his house. Two quick strides on his crutches and he was there.

Will lowered himself to his knees. He ignored the snow swirling around him and it's growing depth. The darkness and falling snow obscured his vision. He bent close. He brushed snow from the face, pleading within himself that it was not whom he thought it was.

"Momma!" Will screamed. He gently shook her by the shoulders. "Momma, wake up! Please! Momma." He grabbed her wrist and felt for a pulse. There was no pulse. He probed along her wrist—nothing. Was she even alive? He put his ear to her chest to listen for a heartbeat. Her chest rose slightly. Certainly, there was a beat. Encouraged, he patted her face, rubbed her arms, and yelled for her to wake up, but to no avail. Against the cold, snow, and blackness of the night, it seemed hopeless.

Only her lower legs were inside the house, over the threshold, but her upper body lay exposed to the storm. He needed to turn her around and, to keep from hurting her, pull her inside headfirst.

From a kneeling position, he grabbed her under her arms and pulled. Instead of her moving, he slid on the snow. He could not budge her. At best, he only lifted her upper body and head. Carrying her would be impossible for him.

All the boards he had drug to the sawhorse—surely, he was strong enough to drag her. She was thin, light. The sill wouldn't hurt her that much if she went feet first. He went to her feet, positioned himself in a sitting position inside the doorway, dug in his heels, and tugged again. Pain shot through his back, but he didn't care. She slid! He backed up a little and pulled again. He managed to get the entire length of her legs inside, but could move her no further.

Her clothing must have caught on something. He ran his hand under her body. Her dress was free. Maybe the sill, against the curve of her body, impeded him. He knelt there, and now encumbered by the doorframe, worked his arms under her. He lifted. Pain seared his back. He gritted his teeth, twisted, trying to get her over the sill and inside. Sweating with pain, he let her down. He had not moved her one inch further.

"Dad! Dad!" he yelled into the black void of the house. He wanted to curse him. "Come help! Help me!"

In frustration, he turned to face the wide space behind him, hoping someone would hear. "Somebody, help! Help!" A blast of wind knocked his call down. Will shivered. The temperature was dropping. He yelled again. His voice went nowhere against the heavy snowfall.

Even to his cold hands, her face felt ice cold. He slid his fingers up into her hair. It was wet with crystals of ice. And the side of her head, above and behind her ear, felt swollen, misshapen even. It was sticky, with blood probably. In the darkness, it was all black and white. Had she fallen and banged her head—or was she struck? The top of her dress and apron were icy and sopping wet, too wet to have been solely from the snowfall. He recalled his father pouring water on her when she lay in the kitchen.

"Da-a-ad!" This time his yell was angry, vitriolic. "Da-a-ad!" He yelled with such force, it hurt his throat. "Dad, what is the matter with you? Help!" The air, heavy with moisture, soaked up his words. He hated his father.

He brushed the snow and ice off her with his hands, then covered her with his coat. Even though he shivered, he was now barely aware of the cold. He again yelled for help. The wind whistled along corners of the house and battered the door against the wall in reply, then kicked the door against his mother. Will worked his way to her other side to put himself between her and the slamming door. "Somebody, help," he pleaded, and held his amulet. In anger, he banged his fist against the door behind him.

Looking toward the inside of the house, Will saw only a void. He jammed one crutch beneath the door so it would not strike his mother and hobbled inside on the other crutch. Inside and out of the wind, it was notably warmer. He wished he could bring his mother inside. The darkness was overwhelming. He banged his thigh into the corner of the cold cookstove. It hurt, but helped orient him so that he could find the kitchen table and the coal lamp that sat perpetually at its center. With a lamp he could find what he needed and then place it near his mother to warm her.

Will patted around the center of the table, but did not find the lamp, only the box of wooden matches. He struck a match on the side of the box, and, once the flame caught, held it high. What he saw in its dim, flickering light made him suck in his breath. He marveled that he had not tripped on something when he had entered the lightless room. Chairs were scattered and broken. Pieces of china and glass littered the floor. The curtain dividing his parents' bedroom from the kitchen lay in a heap at the base of their bedroom doorway. Anger with—no, a hatred for—his father welled up inside of him. His heart beat hard and his breath came in short gasps.

The match's flame burned Will's fingers and, having wandered a bit, he quickly noted what lay between him and the box of matches on the table before he shook the light out. He berated himself for not bringing the box with him and wished he had looked to see if their old beat-up lamp sat in its usual place by the rear door. He again retrieved the matches, felt inside the box—only four matches. Never had matches been so precious.

He knew his mother was getting colder by the minute, so risked another match in order to find his way to his bedroom as quickly as possible.

First, he looked toward the rear door. The heap strewn on the floor blocked his view of the place where the old lamp usually sat. Pushing his door curtains aside, he saw that his room had not been subject to the chaos he had found in the kitchen. He located the nub of a candle he had in his room, lit it, and breathed a sigh of relief. Not everything was against him. Even from below the rim of the earth and through the snow, Abu Pisku smiled upon him—if indeed there was an Abu Pisku.

Taking the candle into the kitchen would take time and, more importantly, subject it to the wind coming through the open door, so he allowed it to remain on his table. He stripped the blankets from his bed and pulled his curtains down. Enough light emanated from his bedroom candle for him to see in the kitchen. With one crutch, Will dragged his load of curtain and blankets, dodged the rubble scattered on the floor, and finally reached the front doorway. At his mother's feet, he dropped his burden and once more, without pausing to check for a heartbeat, cleared his mother of snow and ice, and then briefly rubbed her arms. Having done that, he pulled the blankets over her, then his curtains, all the while shouting into the night for help, hoping someone would hear. Not even a dog barked. Immediately, he went back into the kitchen, feeling somewhat more relieved, but knew that he was far from finished helping his mother.

Will thought he would try to rebuild a fire in the stove, even though it would be some time before it produced any heat. At that moment, the candle in his bedroom went out. Within a few steps, he tripped over an object and fell forward onto his hands and knees. "Ow!" he cried. It felt like jagged glass had cut a palm and the fingers of one hand. He carefully pulled himself upright with his crutch and gingerly felt his palm and fingers. He winced as he touched shards imbedded in his skin. In the dark, he picked glass from his hand as best as he could, but grimaced as pieces continued to stab with each slight movement. He would be able to do very little until he cleaned out the glass, but to do the job needed to see.

Could he hold a match to see well enough and have time to remove the glass splinters to make it worth burning another match? He would be left with only two matches.

Tongues like fire stabbed his palm and fingers as his hand made its way into his pocket and grasped the box. He gritted his teeth, pulled out the matchbox, and lit the match. He held the lighted match in his injured hand to work on it with his free hand. The blood made his hand sticky. One wound was deep, but it seemed to have no glass in it. Working quickly, Will pulled and brushed a number of shards from his wounds. He cringed as he worked, but forced himself to race the match's flame.

It reached his fingers and he involuntarily shook the flame out. He flexed his injured hand slowly. It was better, if not pain free. Two matches remained. He had spent too much time on himself, but reasoned that he had to be able to function or else he would be of no help at all.

Using his crutch to clear the way, Will inched his way forward until he again bumped into the table. He yanked the oilcloth from it. A utensil clattered to the floor. Turning toward the brighter opening of the doorway, he made his way to his mother. In the relative light of the storm outside, he shook the snow from the outermost layers covering her, then re-covered her, adding the oilcloth. With the latter, he was quite pleased. It provided a waterproof covering and a good break from the wind. He only hoped he was not too late.

Of course, his mother needed medical attention. Without telephone or car, he would have to walk to the hospital. As slow as he was, he did not think his mother could survive that long. Perhaps his father was with his whiskey in the barn. Together, he and his father could carry her into the house. Together they would get the fire going. Together, they would take care of his mother.

Leaving his mother at the front doorway, Will rounded the corner of his house and headed in the direction of the old barn. Immediately, a white sheet of windblown flakes hit him in the face and overwhelmed his vision. He could not even see the barn. He pushed forward, but soon was not sure if he were headed in the right direction.

Although his work inside the house had warmed him, in the storm, without a coat, the cold cut to his core. He shook violently. With but one crutch, the snow underfoot, and the battering wind, Will struggled to keep upright. He moved slowly. It seemed that he was never going to get there. He despaired that he had veered from the path and had passed the barn.

A blast struck his back and rocked him forward. He made a lightning move with his crutch to keep himself upright. Then, the wind and snow, as if repentant, fled. Having overcompensated, Will pitched to the snow-covered ground. In the wind's lull, he struggled to his feet, and for a moment caught a glimpse of the barn before the snow resumed its furious assault. He had indeed wandered off course, his heading that to the rear of the barn, leading him beyond it.

He altered his course and struggled toward the opening, now wide from his family's cannibalism of its wood for their stove. He realized he was inside the barn because of the sudden calm and the lack of cold snow wetting his face. Moving carefully so as not to fall in the dark, he set his direction for what he thought were the cases of whiskey. The relative warmth of the barn made him aware that his feet were like blocks of ice. His mind wandered momentarily to Mr. Wyzowaty's foot baths that had thawed his feet not many days ago.

The familiar but repugnant odors of whiskey, vomit and urine signaled that either his father had recently visited the barn or was still there.

In the eerie still blackness of the barn, Will felt watched. His head swiveled from side to side as he peered into the darkness. He saw nothing.

"Dad, you in here? Where are you?"

Silence.

Will yelled again, but louder, then held still, listening. A snort and some grunts came from not many feet away. "Dad, help! Mom is freezing to death!" Again, noises—he was sure they were human. Will moved in that direction. Someone or something stirred. Will stopped. Someone breathed deeply.

"Dad!"

Two matches remained. Will slipped his hand into his pocket. His fingers closed around the matchbox. He paused, and then withdrew the box.

The flame danced and he immediately shielded it with his hand. Will quickly looked around him.

His father, his coat on but unbuttoned, lay curled on his side on the earthen floor in scattered bits of rotting hay. An empty and a half-filled whiskey bottle were within his reach, the boxes of stolen whiskey two yards further away, the lid of one missing.

Will's heart leaped. The kitchen lantern sat on one box, unlit. Will, careful to keep the match lit, hurried to the lamp, raised the chimney and put the match to the wick. The flame died before the wick caught fire.

One match. Will sighed. What else was it good for? he reasoned. Making sure his back was to the barn's opening to shield the match from any wind current, Will lit the match and put it to the wick. He held it there, turned the wick up, but it did not light. The match went out.

He shook the lamp in frustration. There was no sloshing of oil. The lantern was empty.

Empty. His stupidity may have cost his mother her life. He stood there in the darkness, his head hanging.

"Dad, get up!" Will fumbled for the lamp and hurled it in the direction where his father lay. The only response was the crash of the lamp and the tinkle of broken glass. His father was useless, broken, an empty shell. He couldn't fix him.

"Get up!" he screamed. He waited a few seconds, searched for the lesser darkness that pointed to the barn's opening, and hobbled to it. Outside, the snow fell heavily. In places, it already stood in drifts.

He shuddered. He had never been so cold. He hoped that his mother was warmer than he was. He thought of pulling his coat out from under the wraps he had piled upon her, but that would take more time—and maybe cause her to lose heat, heat that might make all the difference.

It seemed impossible to him to become any colder, but standing there increased the cold's bitterness. He had to do something. Looking about, he saw a dim light. It lay in the direction, Will was sure, of Mr. Sutter's house, the farmer who owned the property and old house Will's family lived in. It wasn't but several hundreds of yards away.

Will struck out for the light. He wished he had his other crutch, and he wished he had his coat. But he felt much encouraged. And though he hobbled rather than swung along smoothly, he thought he was making good time, but the light seemed to not get any closer and to even move away. At times, it flickered or disappeared altogether, but it always came back. He realized that this variation was in response to the intensity of the snowfall. Finally, he saw the side of the house, very much coated with snow, and the window that had been casting the light. In his excitement, he stumbled, fell and lost his grip on his crutch. It buried itself in the snow. Pain shot up his legs and back.

Will crawled and felt beneath the snow for his crutch. His hands were so numb he could barely determine what he was touching. He had to have his crutch! There, that was it. It had traveled several feet under the snow in front of where he had fallen.

Caked snow covered his clothes and his hat. His hands and feet ached terribly. His teeth chattered and he shook uncontrollably. Mr. Sutter's house no longer seemed close. Stiff with cold, Will edged himself along.

At last, he stepped onto the house's porch. Light from the window next to the porch illuminated the maelstrom of flakes and cast light in front of him. Never had a light been so welcome.

Will pounded on the door and waited. When it seemed that no one heard, he used his crutch. He struck so ferociously that the racket hurt his ears.

Maybe he should have spent the time bumbling about, making a fire in their stove. But was there any firewood cut? And how much heat would have reached his mother?

Please answer the door. He struck the door again.

"What's the matter with you, pounding on my door that way? Go away!" It was Mr. Sutter from behind the door—finally.

"Pleashh, it's m-m-m-" Will chattered through stiff cheeks and lips. "Hep! Sh-sh-she's freee—"

The door cracked open a few inches. What Will could see of a bony face, topped with thin gray hair, appeared.

"Who is it?"

"Me, W-Will C-Coleman. Li-Li-in y-house."

"Oh, you Colemans. Why should you be cold? You been burning up my old barn. It's late; go home and get warm. I can't let the heat outta' my house. I don't have no barn to burn up."

"For land's sake, John, let him in," a woman's voice said. "We got plenty of coal. Give him some if he needs it."

The door swung open. The snow, itself cold, gladly leaped ahead of Will through the door. The warmth inside, hospitably, came outside to beckon Will into the house.

Mr. Sutter, a tall man with sunken eyes and pronounced cheekbones, stood to the side of the doorway to allow Will to enter.

Will shook his head. "N-No. H-H- My, my-C-Come with . . ." He gestured stiffly for Mr. Sutter to come out.

"Bring him in here, John, so we can understand him."

"I'm holding the door open for him. He won't come in." Mr. Sutter motioned with his head. "Come in here, son. We're old—having a hard time hearing you." He reached out and gently grasped Will by the arm. Will allowed Mr. Sutter to guide him into the house.

"Look at that boy, covered with snow. You must be cold," the woman, evidently Mrs. Sutter, said. Will nodded his head, but it was masked by his shaking. He followed them through a short hall into a brightly lit kitchen.

The contrast between the warmth of the house and the bone cold of his body set Will into spasms. His teeth chattered. "My m-m-other . . ." was all that he could get out. Will squinted to shield his eyes from the globe light in the ceiling.

"Goodness, boy, where's your coat? Don't you have a coat?" Mrs. Sutter said.

"Them Indians don't mind the cold. Isn't that so?" Mr. Sutter said.

"Choctaw," Will managed. He wondered why he responded with that answer. "Please, help m-m-m-my mother." He felt embarrassed at his difficulty in forming words.

"Don't you worry none, we'll help, won't we Henry?" She wiped at the snow clinging to his shirt then wiped her hand on her apron. "Let me have your shirt before the snow melts and has you all wet."

"N-No. No t-time."

"Then stand here by the furnace and get thawed out a bit, so you can talk and tell us what you need." Mrs. Sutter gripped his arm without the crutch and led him to a hole in the floor with a large grate over it. Will was too cold and stiff to resist. She brushed snow from his shirt. The snow made little sizzling and popping noises as it hit the grate.

The circulation was gradually returning to his face. "I-I have to go." He turned toward the door although the heat was wonderful.

"Son, you're not ready to go out there yet. You'll freeze to death and won't help nobody," Mr. Sutter said. You have to explain what the problem is so we can help. You thaw out while you tell us. Now where's your mother?"

"Lying in the s-s-s-snow." Will's teeth still chattered when he spoke.

"Oh!" Mrs. Sutter said

"And where?" Mr. Sutter said.

"F-Front . . . the house," Will said. "I-I. . . c . . . She wouldn't wake. S-Snow piling on her."

The heat from the furnace was considerable and Will's shivering, except for an occasional shudder, ceased. The numbness in his fingers and toes was replaced by severe pain as they warmed and the blood waged war with his capillaries. The cuts from the broken glass made their presence known again.

"There's not much time," Will said slowly. His cheeks were still stiff. He spied the phone on the wall. "My mom's freezing. Please, call a doctor or hos—"

"We can't call nobody 'cause the phone company's already closed—six o'clock. They're hurting like everybody else. It opens in the morning, though," Mr. Sutter said.

"We can't wait that long, she'll f-freeze."

"What about your father?"

Will grimaced at the mention of his father. "He—He couldn't help."

Mr. Sutter lowered his head and grimaced with disgust.

"I—I can't stay. Got to go help her. Get her in your car, Mr. Sutter. Right now. Help me get her to the hospital."

Mr. Sutter looked at him for a bit, measuring what Will had said. "I think I best be getting the Model T started. It's contrary in this cold." He headed for the coats on pegs along the wall. "'Time I get it snorting and bucking, and the chains on, you ought to be thawed out some." He reached for a coat.

Will leaned on his crutch to make his way to the door, even though he hated to move away from the grate. "Please, hurry, Mr. Sutter."

Mr. Sutter stuck an arm in a coat sleeve. "I'm doing my best."

"John Sutter, you just leave that tan coat for Will." Mrs. Sutter said.

Mr. Sutter's jaw dropped, but he allowed his wife to help him slip his arm from the coat. He retrieved another coat that showed considerable wear.

Mrs. Sutter handed the tan coat to Will. "Here, put this on." She had Will's arm in a sleeve almost before he knew what was happening. The coat reached below his knees.

"Land's sake, Will, that coat fits you perfectly, she said." She stared at her husband. "It's his now."

"What!" Mr. Sutter said. "That's my new coat." He shook his head as he buttoned his old coat around his neck.

Will thought the coat was the warmest and softest he had ever put on. "I can't keep it," he said, but wished with all his might that it was his. With fingers still aching, he fumbled with the buttons.

"Sure you can. Here, let me help," she said, and took over the buttoning. She glanced over her shoulder at Mr. Sutter wrapping a scarf around his neck. "Henry, you better hurry."

She swiped a pair of galoshes with rows of buckles from beneath the coat hooks. "Now, Will, sit on that chair and put these on."

"I'll help put the chains on, Mr. Sutter," Will called.

The door slammed behind Mr. Sutter, leaving a blast of cold air and swirling snow. Mrs. Sutter sat the galoshes next to Will. "You pull those shoes and socks off real quick while I get you a pair of dry socks before you put these boots on. You got time—it'll take Henry a bit to get his auto going. It cranks hard in the cold."

The door swung open, bitter air forced its way in, followed by Mr. Sutter. "Forgot my flashlight," he said, and tracked snow across the linoleum. He banged open a kitchen cabinet drawer, rooted around until he found the flashlight, tested it, then left, sending another blast of cold inside. Will shuddered.

Mrs. Sutter was back half a minute later, a folded quilt under one arm and waving a pair of socks with the other hand. "For your mother," she said, referring to the quilt.

Will's fingers and toes still ached terribly, but his shaking hands managed to exchange the holey wet socks for the thick ones she handed him. Their warmth crept up his legs, soothing him. The socks seemed strange without toes sticking out. While Mrs. Sutter, holding the blanket, waited, he slipped his shoes back on, wishing all the more that they did not have holes in them.

"No," he said, indicating the galoshes she held out to him, and leaned forward to reach for his crutch. "I've got to help Mr. Sutter put on the chains."

Mrs. Sutter pushed him back into the chair before he got his feet under him and stood in his way so he couldn't stand. "We'll hurry." Together they tugged and pushed the boots over his shoes. Will heard the clatter and chugging of the Model T. He closed the top buckles and reached for his crutch, leaving Mrs. Sutter stooped, attempting to close the lower buckles.

"Thanks, Mrs. Sutter," Will said, and scurried to the door. Mrs. Sutter helped him stuff the quilt under his arm and placed his cap on his head. He hobbled into the cold.

Chapter 20

Although he was inside Mr. Sutter's Model T, and even though he was wrapped in Mr. Sutter's new wool coat, Will shivered as the vehicle bounced and slid over the frozen field. "No use going long way around by the road; field's just as clear," Mr. Sutter said, and they cut across the field. Will stared hard past the headlamps, past the swirling snow, wanting to see his mother and imagining she was cold blue ice. How did Mr. Sutter see where he was going? It was like being blind.

The rear end of the car slid to the side, threatening to pass the front end and turn them around. "Got to keep giving her the gas or we'll get stuck," Mr. Sutter said, and turned the steering wheel against the slide. They sashayed back the other way and bounced and slid through the ruts. Will gripped the door handle with one hand, the other arm braced against the dash.

Suddenly the old barn and Will's house loomed close in the headlamps. His heart pounded against his ribs. Was his mother alive?

Mr. Sutter managed to skate the Model T to the front of the house. He gassed the engine and wrestled the steering wheel until the headlights illuminated the doorway. Will opened the car door and swung his legs out as the car slid slowly to a stop. His feet and crutches skimmed the snow, then caught a snowdrift and yanked him out. He hit the snow face first but he bounded up on his crutches.

Nothing looked like his mother, like a person. He plowed his way through the drifts toward a mound of snow lying in front of the door and dropped to his knees next to the mound. "Momma, Momma," he gasped.

Madly he swiped snow away with his arms and hands, then yanked the tablecloth aside to reveal dry covers. He felt underneath them for her arm. It was cold. He saw no water vapor rising from her nostrils. "Momma!" he shouted. He patted her face, but got no response.

"Will, let's get her into the back seat and out of this storm as quickly as we can," Mr. Sutter said. "We can't help her lying out here. You hold the car door open, and I'll carry her over." Mr. Sutter bent and slid his arms under his mother and lifted, but within a few inches he was jerked back down. "She's caught on something." He ran a hand beneath her, lifted again, but could not raise her.

"Will, I'll raise her much as I can, and you look with the flashlight. See what you find."

Will turned on the light and swept it back and forth beneath his mother. The earth beneath her looked dark and somber amidst the sea of white. "The tie for her apron is caught between some boards." Will grabbed the tie and pulled, gritted his teeth and yanked one way and then the other. "I can't budge it. I can't tear it."

"Let me try." Mr. Sutter felt for Will's hands, took the tie from him and yanked until he was winded. "Oh, my, what are we going to do?"

"Just a minute." Will hurried to his feet and made his way into the house with Mr. Sutter's flashlight. He returned with a butcher knife. "Hold her up, Mr. Sutter, and I'll cut her free."

"Careful, Will."

Once his mother was loose, Mr. Sutter, from behind her, wrapped his arms around her midsection and backed into the car's rear seat. Will helped by lifting her legs up over the running board and sill. They covered her with Mrs. Sutter's quilt, added Will's blankets and curtains, and tucked them around her.

"You'll have to sit back there. Make sure she doesn't fall over," Mr. Sutter said.

Will's driveway leading to the street was not visible, but Mr. Sutter aimed the Model T for the street light at Randolph. Will wrapped an arm around his mother and braced himself with his other arm.

The Model T bucked through a drift and bounced into a rut, snapping Will's teeth together. The car hit an uneven patch and slid. If they cut across anyone's lawn no one would know—they certainly didn't. Will repositioned himself and his hold on his mother.

The Enid General Hospital was only two blocks from the high school, ordinarily a ten-minute ride from his house, but it was taking forever.

Suddenly, across the windshield, an image of his father's big fist punching his mother's head appeared. Will's breath came fast and shallow. He clenched his hands. He shook his head and stared at the windshield. He must have fallen asleep. Blowing snow reflected light back onto the windshield from the headlamps.

His father's cruelty enraged Will. He felt as if he would burst, but he pushed it down, down, the pressure built like steam in a boiler with the valve closed. That his father would hurt his mother and then let her lay there, perhaps even die, he could not understand. Who could understand? No one could do anything about it—except for him. It was up to him.

And Mr. North said that his dad was responsible for the deaths of all those miners.

Who next? Please, not his mother. He grasped his amulet. *Dad, you are going to pay, I'll see to that. Momma, he'll never hurt you again, or me, or anybody else.*

* * *

Two strong-looking orderlies hurried out into the snow and placed Will's mother on a gurney along with the blankets. With the snow swirling at their backs, they disappeared into the hospital.

Except for the yellow pine floor, everything inside was bright white—the walls, the ceiling, the window frames, the furniture—white as the snow outside. An antiseptic scent pricked Will's nostrils. Standing in front of the desk that faced the entrance, he stared at the young nurse behind it asking him questions. Not so much did he stare at her, but at her starched white uniform and hat; this was the first time he had been inside a hospital. The girls taking nursing classes after school at Enid High wore ordinary clothes.

Will told the nurse everything he knew about the circumstances in which he found his mother, but was careful not to reveal anything that would implicate his father. Some things were family matters, things that he would take care of when the opportunity presented itself.

"Is my mother going to be okay?"

"Your mother is in one of the finest hospitals in Oklahoma," the nurse said.

A blast of wind buffeted the doors and drew Will's eyes. The window curtains flickered. The nurse pulled the blue cape she wore around her shoulders a little closer about her neck. Will actually began to feel hot in Mr. Sutter's coat. "But is she going to . . . to . . .?"

"She'll be fine. We'll let you know as soon as you can see her." The nurse's name tag read, "Jo Anne Steele, R.N."

Will took a seat next to Mr. Sutter on a cushioned bench with a spindled back. He propped his elbows on his knees and put his head in his hands, holding it up, thinking, wondering what else he should have done for his mother. If only he had looked harder and found the apron tie. He could have cut it and dragged his mother into the house. And this morning—he should not have left her alone with his father. He should have wrapped the valentine so that his father didn't see it. That morning in the kitchen, he should have . . . He couldn't bear to finish that thought. But now he was going to do that which he dared not think.

The bench cut into his legs. He repositioned himself.

Sooner or later everybody would find out how his mother got hurt. But they couldn't, really. Nobody saw what happened. *I know what happened, and my father knows, I'm sure of it. He did it.*

But nobody else has to know. If Mr. North finds out, he'll say, "See, what did I tell you?" then add, "The apple never falls far from the tree," and "you'll never see Irene again." She gave me an apple—so she could share with me. Mother, you have to get well or there'll be no more apples.

Will looked for a clock. The cushion on the bench was terribly thin. He pulled himself up with his crutches and went over to the desk. "How is my mother doing?"

The young nurse gave Will a wooden smile. "Don't you worry none. She'll be all right." She bent to her task of writing, leaving Will to lean on his crutches in front of her. Then, again noticing his presence, she asked, "Is there something else?"

Will shook his head and returned to the bench. As he sat, the nurse rose and disappeared down the hall.

Mr. Sutter had fallen asleep, or looked like it. His chin rested on his chest and he had those slow heavy breaths of the sleeping. Will wished he could sleep, too. When Will sat back down, Mr. Sutter stirred, and then spoke, leaving his head in place. "I expect I better be getting home while I still can. You want a ride home?"

"I have to stay with my mother." He hated to think of home. Home meant a drunken father and a cold, smashed up house. Besides, he was hungry. What could he cook on a cold stove? Even if a warm bed and a meal awaited him, he wouldn't leave the hospital.

Hungry! The cookies! Irene had thrust them into his coat pocket. He reached inside his coat pocket. Oh, no, it was Mr. Sutter's. Will had not eaten since Mrs. North had served him hermits. It wouldn't be the first time he had missed a meal. His mind turned to Irene and the cookies and her gentle touch on his lips, wiping the crumbs.

Mr. Sutter lifted his head and pushed himself up from his seat. "Suit yourself. I'll be back to get you in the morning, if I ain't snowed in." He buttoned his coat to the last button at his neck and pulled his wool cap with its earflaps onto his head.

Will, as a courtesy, followed him to the main entrance's double doors. Snow and ice clung to the doors' windows through which a few swirling flakes were visible. When Mr. Sutter pushed the doors open, he paused instinctively. A blast of snow buffeted him and swept into the entrance way. The light above the stoop revealed snow blowing horizontally. Will had never seen so much snow.

"Thanks, Mr. Sutter," Will said, forcing his words against the blast.

Mr. Sutter nodded and waved as he trudged beyond the ring of light at the entranceway.

Will waited at the door, listening, and finally heard Mr. Sutter's car sputter as he cranked it. At last the car's chugs, muffled by the snow, kept a steady beat, and then faded away. Will, confident in Mr. Sutter's ability to reach home, returned to his seat.

Miss Steele was at her desk and had placed his blankets, neatly folded, on the bench. She called to him, "Doctor Fisher said your mother is still asleep. He'll let you know when she wakes up. By the way, he said she was not injured by the cold at all. You did a good job of protecting her." The nurse's smile seemed genuine. "You can spread your blankets on the bench and take a nap, if you'd like. Nobody'll be bothering us tonight."

The blankets tempted him to lie down, but Will wanted to be awake when his mother awoke. He pulled a blanket about him and put his head in his hand. He wondered if he would have school tomorrow. He hoped so because he wanted to see Irene. Enid's schools hadn't closed for the previous snow, but it wasn't nearly this heavy. He figured it would be easy to find out if school was open, since it was only two blocks away. He could fuel the furnaces and continue to earn money. He thought about how dirty he would be and the impression he wanted to make on Irene. After working, he would clean himself up really well in the furnace room. Nobody would have to know that he had not slept at home. He could walk back to Irene's house so that he could carry her books to school.

Will leaned his head on the blankets piled next to him. His eyes closed.

* * *

A sharp, burning pain jerked Will awake. The pain wracked his joints, muscles and bones. He had a headache. Where was he?

His mind raced in jagged spurts. Light—he had overslept. It was always dark when he awoke. Everything was white, a white ceiling— clean. He examined the covers under him. They were his, and they cushioned a bench. This was not his room. There was a lady with white hair with a white cap in a nurse's uniform at a desk. Now he remembered. He was in Enid General Hospital because his mother was unconscious.

He grabbed his crutches and pulled himself to his feet. The pain shot down his back and legs, nearly knocking him to the floor. He leaned on his crutches for several seconds, and then forced his body to respond. He made his way toward the desk.

"Mr. Coleman," the nurse began. He was only halfway to the desk. "Dr. Flanagan said that you can see your mother now." The nurse was much older than Miss Steele, the one from the previous night, and heavyset.

"Is she okay?"

The nurse arose from the desk, looking tired and slightly disheveled. Her badge said, "Mrs. Lucille Sears, LPN."

"Come with me," was all she said, but she forced a smile. She led him past a hallway of doors with little windows in each one. She paused to turn toward him and put her forefinger to her lips, which again formed a stiff smile. Her back was broad and she waddled along. Will easily kept up with her.

They made a right turn and met a set of double doors through which they passed into a wide room, a dormitory, with a row of fifteen beds on both sides, the foot of each bed toward the passageway between which Mrs. Sears led him. Two weary looking nurses tended patients in the beds. In spite of the large number of patients, the only words spoken were those of necessity. Body odors spoiled the antiseptic atmosphere he had come to expect. Against the quiet, water poured from a pitcher into a glass at the far end of the dormitory resonated in his ears.

Mrs. Sears and Will made a right turn and went through another set of double doors that opened upon another hallway of doors.

"Wait here," Mrs. Sears whispered, indicating the second door on the right with a black "4" stenciled on it. She walked on, passing another nurse who exited one room and then entered another.

Will peered through the small glass pane and saw the bottom half of a bed with sheets gathered over someone's legs. He looked back down the hall. Mrs. Sears had disappeared, but soon reappeared with another nurse,

"This is Miss Collins. She cares for the critically ill. She's in charge of your mother."

Miss Collins, tall, ramrod straight and angular, had a no-nonsense look about her. She reminded Will of his math teacher, Miss Whitaker. She had his attention.

Critically ill? Will's heart thumped in his chest. "What's wrong?" he choked on the words. He hardly noticed as Mrs. Sears sighed and trudged away.

"Your mother suffered a severe blow to her head." Miss Collins looked Will directly in the eyes. Her voice was low, but strong. "Dr. Fisher is certain it will be a long time before she wakes up."

"Oh, no!"

"Please keep your voice down. You may visit with her for five minutes. But you must be quiet. She must get rest for her brain to recover."

"Her brain?"

"Please, Mr. Coleman, if you wish to visit her, you must restrain yourself." She stood staring at Will. She made no move to open the door until Will stood straight and calmed himself.

"Quietly, Mr. Coleman. You may hold her hand." She looked at her large wristwatch.

They entered the room. Although it was white like the remainder of the hospital, its window was shuttered, giving the room a gloomy gray cast. Hung from a pole near the head of the bed was a bottle of liquid with a tube running from it that was stuck into his mother's arm by means of a needle. The back and one side of her head were wrapped in white bandage. What he could see of her head and face appeared swollen and ghostly white, but she lay peacefully and took regular breaths. He gently picked up her hand and slowly bent to kiss it. *Oh, Mother,* he wished to cry out. What was he going to do? He straightened up to help control the tears that threatened to spill down onto his cheeks.

Choctaw braves don't cry.

Miss Collins finished writing on a chart and hung it at the foot of the bed. She looked at her watch. Will bent to bring his mother's hand to his cheek. His breath came in silent choking sobs.

Miss Collins walked next to him and whispered, "Five minutes are up, Mr. Coleman."

He straightened. She pointed to the door and stepped to open it, then nodded for him to go through the doorway. Once in the hall, she closed the door carefully behind them. "If she is to recover, she needs all of the quiet and rest we can give her. It's a race against time. Your mother was already very thin. She can't eat. The only food she is getting is through that tube."

If she is to recover! If? She must.

Miss Collins placed her hand on Will's shoulder. Will thought that touching someone was probably difficult for her to do. "There is very little you can do for her here. Go home and get some rest," she said, and looked straight ahead past Will at nothing. "I wish—" She straightened herself even more and seemed to talk to no one. "With this storm we have had very few nurses come in to give our girls relief." She turned and entered the room marked "6."

Will stood staring after her.

Wind howled against the eaves and buffeted the side of the building. Cold crept through Mr. Sutter's jacket. Will fastened its buttons while standing in the empty hall, staring at room 4.

If she is to recover . . .

Chapter 21

"Mr. Coleman, Mr. Sutter called for you," said Mrs. Sears, the desk nurse. "He apologized and said he wouldn't be able to come pick you up. He's froze in.

"You can stay here at the hospital if you want. You must be hungry this morning."

Will's worry about his mother had wiped out thoughts of food. The mention of it sent his stomach into spasms, bringing him an awful ache. He nodded, fearful that a definite acknowledgement would bring disappointment and sharpen his hunger pangs. It was better to ignore some things.

"I stopped by the cafeteria on my way back," Mrs. Sears said. "With us all snowed in, they're running out of things." She held a brown lunch bag out to him. "A drumstick—that was the last of the chicken—and a peanut butter and jelly sandwich."

His hand trembled as he reached for the bag. "Thanks."

"Pull up a chair next to my desk so you have a place to eat." She cleared a spot from the edge of her desk.

"Thanks, Miss Sears. Thanks a lot."

"Miss Collins said you can visit your mother at 4:55, sharp."

Will dragged the chair to the desk, removed Mr. Sutter's coat and tore into the bag. Food never tasted so good. He tried to allow the howling of the wind and the snow outside to distract him, but he bolted the food down, anyway.

Was his father eating? More likely, he was huddled in the barn, drinking his whiskey to keep warm. He should be here, caring for his mother. Actually, if he really cared about her, she would not be here.

Will watched Mrs. Sears complete a form. It seemed to Will that she was old enough to be his grandmother. When she put the paper in her "OUT" box, Will spoke. "Do people, like my mother, sometimes never wake up?" His grip on the paper bag showed the tendons on the back of his hand. "She's in a coma, isn't she?"

Mrs. Sears laid down her pen to look into Will's face. She pursed her lips and frowned. Almost imperceptibly, she rocked to and fro, nodding. "Let's see. Mrs. Coleman was just admitted last night. Let's give her a chance." Mrs. Sears' lips and cheeks formed a smile, but her eyes were dead serious.

Will sat still and continued to look at the nurse. To him, the food inside the bottle above his mother's head had looked almost like water. She must be starving. "Miss Sears, can my mother get enough food through that tube?" He held the last of the sandwich in his hand, refusing to eat it, feeling that somehow, it would be taking food from his mother.

"You really are worried about your mother, aren't you? Feeding her through a tube can take care of her for quite a while."

"But what if she doesn't wa—?"

"Mr. Coleman, there is no use worrying about the 'what if's.'"

"But maybe she is awake and they are feeding her right now—chicken broth, that's what she always gave me when I was sick, if we had any chicken."

The nurse made no response and reached for her pen.

"Miss Sears, they would come and tell me if she was better, wouldn't they? If she is awake now, I could go see her again." Will looked hopeful.

Mrs. Sears put her pen down again and regarded Will with soft eyes. "Please understand, Mr. Coleman, even if your mother awoke, she still needs her rest. You can visit her this evening at 4:55, like Miss Collins said." Mrs. Sears dipped her pen's point in the inkwell for a long moment before she resumed writing.

Will unmindfully minced at what was left of his sandwich. "If she's asleep, what difference does it make if I visit, even make noise? Maybe she'd wake up."

Mrs. Sears did not even look up; she shook her head and kept working.

And his father? He didn't care if his father froze to death—it served him right. At the notion, Will shivered in the chill of the room. He chased the thought of his strong hands about his father's throat from his mind—for his mother's sake. She said there was always a better way than violence. Will wasn't so sure anymore. Sometimes it seemed to be the only thing left. He reached for Mr. Sutter's coat, but stopped. He would need to feel that warmth when he went outside—if he went to school.

A blast of wind rattled the door. Cold air swept through the room like a ghost. Mrs. Sears quivered and frowned at the radiator, its steam keeping clear a spot on the window. Ice formed around that spot and on the window frame beneath it.

Will dreaded going out in this storm. Maybe it was so bad, even Mr. Wyzowaty was not at the school. Will would trudge through the storm for nothing. He would earn no money, plus he could get sick and die—maybe freeze to death. His mother would have no one, not a person to comfort her. He took a half-hearted bite of his sandwich.

On the other hand, he could stay in the warm hospital, probably get fed, not have to work, could even sleep. Who could blame him? Not even Mr. Whiz.

Maybe he could sell something instead of working, but he could not think of a thing he owned anybody would want. He laughed at the thought of selling his father's stolen whiskey.

No one expected him to, but he had to go to work. When his mother came home from the hospital, there would be medicine to buy and huge hospital and doctor bills. He would need money worse than ever. He sat the sandwich aside and began pulling and tugging to get Mr. Sutter's boots started on his feet.

He recalled the previous snow; it was nothing compared to this storm. The image of Irene running to him through that snow came to mind, making his heart beat hard, but he pushed the thought aside.

His mother needed him worse. She had no one else. She might become bedfast and would need him to cook and scrub and wash clothes and do the dishes—no more sharing of that chore—it would be all his. She might need special food—like chicken broth. He saw himself spooning rich broth into his mother's mouth. In time, he would get her well.

He stood with his crutches and worked the boots on with his weight, then sat to buckle them.

No, he would not even get a pair of shoes from Tom and Tittle.

Hurt and ache stabbed his chest and then lingered. He gulped down the rest of his sandwich, hoping to chase the pain away.

The radiator's valve blasted steam into the room. Maybe they needed someone at the hospital to help shovel coal. He could work both jobs. He would ask when he came back.

Will stood, slipped on Mr. Sutter's coat and buttoned it.

His mother needed him, loved him. He loved his mother. She had taken care of him and stood up to his father to protect him—and gotten hurt for her troubles. And now, she was terribly hurt. He would do anything to help her.

The wind whistled and battered the doors, threatening to bust them open. Snow blew by the windows in sheets. Mrs. Sears drew her coat up about her neck with one hand and wrote with the other.

"Thanks, Miss Sears. If you would set my blankets aside, I'll pick them up later. I have to get to work." He liked how that last sentence sounded. He buttoned the last coat button at his throat.

"You can't go out there, you're a crip—." She clasped her hand over her mouth. "Normal people shouldn't—." She threw her hand over her mouth again. "Oh, my!" She blushed. "Be very careful."

Will put on his hat and swung on his crutches to the doorway. With the image of his mother in the hospital bed in his mind, he leaned hard against the door. The door cracked open a few inches, letting in a shower of snow and a blast that stirred the papers on Mrs. Sears' desk, then the wind slammed it shut against him.

"See, I told you," Mrs. Sears said.

He heaved against it again. Pain shot down his back and legs. His arms were powerful enough, but he didn't have the strength in his back and legs from which to push.

"Wait. Let me weigh my papers down, then I'll help," Mrs. Sears said.

* * *

Outside, Will pulled his hat tightly onto his head, faced the direction of the school and leaned against the wind. Sky and earth looked all the same—grey-white. A fierce wind rocked him and tried to fling him aside. He sighed. He had to do this.

To move, he swung forward on his crutches and dragged his boots through the snow, leaving a furrow. He managed but a foot. Again and again, he set his crutches in front of him. He paused in front of a waist-high drift, set his crutches, and swung his legs to plow through the snow. The drift almost stopped him cold. He replanted his crutches and pushed again. He could almost hear Mrs. Sears starting to say, "You can't—"

Maybe she was right. He should go back.

No one would blame him; walking with crutches through a blizzard was impossible, foolhardy. He could barely see where he was going. Already he felt tired. He turned and looked behind him.

After all that effort, he was still on hospital property.

A cold blast hit him, reminding him that he could not stand there. He had to decide.

A large sign, torn loose from its post and carried by the wind, twirled end over end to plant itself in his drift. He thought himself no better off than the sign, planted in the same drift.

If he went back, he would be useless, a nobody, unable to help his mother. He would hate himself. He must get to work. Through the coat he pressed the amulet with its snake against his chest. Persistent. Stubborn, some would say about him.

From now on, he knew, his life, even his family's existence, depended on him.

He looked ahead. Sidewalk, curb and street blended into one. He barely recognized his surroundings. The waist-high snowdrift stretched across his path in either direction as far as he could see. There was one way—through it. Again, he pushed against the snow. Again, it pushed back. Will stopped and sighed, staring at the sign gathering snow, wedged in the bank. Was he not stuck as surely as that plank?

The plank reminded him of the barn. It was so cold, Will wondered if his father had frozen to death out there. Will's stomach turned sick. After all, Charlie Coleman was his father. However, if he were gone, what a relief—except Will would have to saw wood alone. He smiled at his inane, cruel thought. But it was true. He'd probably have a lot of other things to do, too.   Even if his father was not dead, Will might have to do everything. His father's drunken orgies were lasting longer. And when he was sober, he still wasn't reliable. Will might have to feed him, but he surely wasn't going to get his whiskey for him. Nor was his father going to hurt either of them anymore.

Will stared at the sign. He struggled his way over to it, inching his way, puffing like a steam engine. He stretched to reach the sign, worked it out of the snow, and turned it over. "Emergency Entrance," it said. It was much smaller than the barn's boards, but wide enough, and it was not going to do the hospital any good.

Will turned back toward the street and laid the plank flat on the drift in front of him so that the end nearest him sank in the snow. He straddled the board with his crutches and pulled his feet onto the board. It sank some more, but supported him. He leaned forward on his crutches and swung his feet along the board to stand farther along it. When he got to the end of the board, he swung down into the snow, removed the board from behind him, put it in front of him and started the process again. Finally, through the drift, he stopped to catch his breath. He slipped the board under his arm for use when the snow was again too high.

Snow fought with the wind to cover every surface. Trees bent and waved, their bare branches stripped of any snow except in their crooks and deeper clefts. Evergreens shook themselves free of most of their white blankets, letting the snow crash to the ground. Drifts built up against buildings and crept up first floor windows. The wind howled so loud it muffled Will's movements, even the crunch of his boots on the snow, and surrounded him with a deafening silence. He caught whiffs of smoke blown down from chimneys, reminding him of the coal furnaces awaiting him.

He squinted and lowered his head to screen the flakes and glare from his eyes. He peeked up. A half-visible building, suspended in clouds of blowing snow, floated directly in front of him. He readjusted his direction to center his path between the buildings lining the street.

Silently, he thanked Mr. Sutter for lending him the coat and boots.

He didn't see a soul. They could be ahead of him, or behind him, or walk toward him and pass him by, and he would not see them. Except for the wind's roar in the treetops and its battering against buildings, he heard nothing. The world had become a vast, all-but-invisible, grey-white.

A great loneliness welled up inside of him. How he longed for his mother, and for the man his father had once been many years ago. Will recalled the times, as a young boy in Haskell County, when he begged his father to let him ride on the backs of the farm mules while his father plowed the fields. With a smile, his father lifted him high and settled him on Hank's bare back. His father bragged to his mother about how the mules obeyed Will's commands, how fast Will had learned to milk their cow, and what strong but gentle hands he had. But that was before he fell from a mule. He was sure of that. His mother always feared Will would get hurt, especially after the fall, but his father treated him like a normal boy. For that, he loved his father. Will hated, more than anything else, to be treated differently because of his legs. If only he could bring those days back. One good thing, the doctor explained that it is usually worse in those who are born that way.

A silent calm hit. Will pitched forward and flailed to keep his balance. He stuck out a crutch that kept him from landing face first, but then a blast buffeted him and put him on his back.

Snow cushioned his fall. He scrambled to his feet and bent into the wind again. It caught hold of the board and threatened to tear it from his grip.

Glancing up, he saw a wide, flat expanse, almost black, like a pit, looming below. No buildings or trees about, not even any snow to be seen, as if the depths had swallowed them up. He stopped short lest he meet the same fate, his heart pounding, and then laughed at himself as he realized that the wind, unimpeded by any structures, had scrubbed the road bare and whipped the snow to farther reaches.

He had never worked so hard to travel such a short distance. He paused to undo the top coat button to release the heat building inside. By now, he should have arrived at the school. He would earn at least twelve cents today. He grimaced as he thought about how he would probably have to spend it at the Randolph Street Market for food. He would never make it all the way home to fix some grits. He pushed aside the thought of the mess in their house.

He began to worry that Miss Collins would say, *Sorry, Mr. Coleman, but the doctor does not think your mother will ever wake from this coma. You may take her home.* At the thought, the blood pounded in Will's ears and he trembled. How would he, only sixteen years old, take care of his mother, a grown woman? He clenched his teeth. He would do whatever he had to do.

His surroundings seemed brighter, and he looked up. In the distance, patches of blue revealed scudding clouds alternating with gray blankets through which shafts of light hurtled earthward like arrows. It appeared the storm was over, but the wind buffeted him and snow stung his face. The clouds reunited. All was a low grey ceiling once again. He buttoned the collar button. He could barely make out buildings that sat back from the street.

Nobody was at school—that was certain. Except Mr. Wyzowaty. As custodian he had to take care of the school; it was his baby. He said it had to have heat all the time so the pipes wouldn't freeze and burst. The coal in the hoppers was eaten up every night and had to be refilled in the mornings.

With all of the snow piled around, it hardly looked like Enid High School. No interior lights showed in the windows, no sign of footprints led into the building. Of course, footprints would have been obliterated in minutes.

The sky opened once again—this time, directly overhead. The clear sky was punctuated by a blast that rocked Will and pelted him with snow. He squinted against the glare. Great sheets of snow, blown from the roof, fell upon him.

He made his way to the back outer stairwell that led down to the boiler room. He shoved an end of his board down into the snow; he might need it later. The stair's steps, obscured by snow, looked like a giant sliding board. Will hesitated. The wind hit him on the back, rocking him forward, and nearly pitched him headfirst down the steps. He stepped back from the edge. Climbing out looked impossible. Once at the bottom, he had to get inside the building, or he would be trapped.

The sides of the stairwell shaded the door's darkened window. He could see a glimmer of light. It might mean someone was there, or perhaps it had been left on.

He hadn't fought through this storm for nothing. He'd figure a way to get back out—or inside. If he had to, he would break the window with a crutch, but that would be difficult with the wire mesh sandwiched inside the glass.

Will sat at the top of the steps, scooted to the edge and gave himself a push. Down he went in a swift slide, the edges of the steps giving a slight ripple to his ride. The brief thrill of the slide over, he pulled himself to his feet on the snow piled at the landing in front of the door. Evidently, a great deal of snow had fallen from the roof into the stairwell. Snowfall remained heavy, but swirled down around him in relative calm. After the buffeting he had endured, the stillness stifled him.

He knocked on the door and shaded the window with his hand so that he could peer inside. A light was very definitely on, but it did little to dispel the gloom inside. He saw no one. He banged harder and waited. When no one came, he rapped hard with his crutch, producing a sharp hard knock. Putting his hand up to his brow and the window again, he saw Mr. Whiz, shoulders slumped, moving slowly toward the door.

Mr. Whiz unlocked the door and pushed hard. The snow, piled against the door, fought back. He pushed again and again, gaining an inch. "Ah, Will, it's you. I don't know how you made it," he shouted through the crack. "I'm trapped. I can't get out."

"Wait until I clear the snow from behind the door," Will called back. He dropped to his knees and dug with his hands. When he paused, Mr. Whiz gave the door a shove, opening it a half-foot. He stuck a shovel through the opening. "Here, use this."

Once inside the basement boiler room, the storm seemed nonexistent. Its noise was replaced by the familiar roar of the furnaces. However, leaving the brightness of the snow made the furnace room a dungeon and before him, a shadowy, menacing figure. His father! No, it had to be Mr. Whiz.

Inexplicably, Will's hands clenched his crutches and he trembled with effort to stifle a curse for his father rising at the back of his throat. How could he be angry with Mr. Whiz? Will clamped his teeth together, even as his lips curled. Finally, he slumped on his crutches, allowing the air to fall from his lungs. He relaxed, letting go of the image of his father as his eyes adjusted to the artificial light.

Mr. Whiz gently shook Will by the shoulder as they exchanged greetings. Without explanation, Mr. Whiz hurried to his office and brought out a chair while Will shucked his coat and hat. Heat from the furnaces struck him. This must what equatorial Africa is like. Not needing to take another step, he sighed as he settled on the seat.

Looking up, he noticed dark circles beneath Mr. Whiz's eyes.

Will started to push himself up from the chair. "Here, Mr. Whiz, you sit."

Mr. Whiz put his hand on Will's shoulder. "No, no, you rest. But I did get tired and had to take a nap." Mr. Whiz shook his head as if regretting his nap. "I got a cot from the nurse's office. I'm feeling better now."

Mr. Whiz answered Will's questioning look. "As soon as I realized we were having a blizzard, I came over before it got too deep. The wind and the cold have been stripping the heat right out of the rooms and the furnaces had to go full blast. I hardly got a break from shoveling since eight last night. Good thing you came along, though. I overslept. Look, the coal hoppers are about empty."

Will's glance told him the furnaces were dangerously near starving.

"How'd you make it in this blizzard?" Mr. Whiz bent to throw shovels full of coal in a hopper.

Will reached to unbuckle his boots. "I only walked from the hospital." The heat, thawing his ears, made them ache.

Mr. Wyzowaty stopped shoveling. "The hospital?" Mr. Whiz turned and looked at Will with genuine concern. "You all right?"

"I'm fine. It was my mother."

"What's wrong?"

Mr. Whiz waited, looking at Will expectantly, his brow furrowed.

Will's cheeks darkened to an even deeper red as he thought about what his father had done to her. Hatred for his father welled up inside him. *If he were here, I'd kill him right now.* "What do you care?" Will shouted. Immediately, he saw hurt in Mr. Whiz's eyes.

"I had a mother once, too, Will. I'm really sorry."

"I'm sorry I yelled, Mr. Whiz. My mother might be dying . . . and . . . I think it was. . ." *I can't, shouldn't tell about my father.*

"Was what?"

"Was . . . was an accident. A bad one." Will tried to slow his breathing, talk naturally, gloomily, about his mother, how he had found her lying unconscious in the front doorway and then had taken her, with Mr. Sutter's help, to the hospital. Will pushed the anger down. There could be no talk about his father. White men would blame him and arrest him.

Mr. Wyzowaty looked at the floor for a bit with his lips rolled under, shaking his head. "I'm sorry," he said. "And it's okay to be angry, too."

Will thought back. Had he let something slip about his father? Angry because your mother is dying? No. Sad and hurt—yes.

Wyzowaty took Will's coat and hat from the back of the chair. "Sometimes life is unfair." He shook the snow and wet off, and hung them near a furnace to dry. "New coat and boots?"

Will sensed Mr. Whiz had deeper questions; the ones Will didn't want to answer. "Mr. Sutter lent them to me." Mr. Whiz kept his puzzled look.

"He saw me out in the storm when I was trying to help my mother."

Mr. Whiz stared into Will's eyes. Will felt the heat creep up his neck and burn his cheeks.

"How did your mother end up unconscious in the doorway?"

Will's mouth went dry. He swallowed and wet his lips. The question hung over Will like a black cloud. The cloud emptied itself upon him. Will shrugged. The furnaces roared in his ears.

Mr. Whiz stared at a furnace, threw a shovelful of coal, and then looked back at Will. "We can't let them freeze up and burst the pipes. And it looks like its clearing up out there. It's going to turn real cold tonight."

Will turned his head to look through the door window. Bright sunlight filled the stairway.

"What about your father?"

The question hit Will like a hammer hitting his chest.

Will swallowed. He couldn't answer. It was his turn to stare at a furnace. "That's why I came over, to help shovel coal."

"Wasn't your father at home?" Mr. Whiz was a bulldog.

Will tried to hide his shaking. "No," he lied. Technically, that was true—his father had been in the barn. Will rose from the chair and headed for the shovels. "I'll start shoveling coal into the cart," he said. He felt weak and shaky.

"And we got to get the school ready to open Monday—only two days, counting today," Mr. Whiz said.

"Today is Saturday, not Friday?" Will's heart thumped. He didn't work on Saturday. Would Mr. Whiz pay him?

Mr. Whiz laughed. "You thought today was Friday?"

Will nodded.

"Does your father know what happened? Didn't he go to the hospital?"

Will grumbled to himself. Mr. Whiz would not give up; he had a snake for an amulet, too. Will thrust a shovel into the coal pile and threw the coal at a coal cart. The cart rocked.

Mr. Whiz joined him by tossing a shovelful. "Your father?"

Will threw another shovelful. The coal nearly went out the other side of the cart. "I don't know," he rasped. The weakness of his voice shocked him. He cleared his throat and repeated, "I don't know." He let the blade of the shovel clang hard on the concrete floor.

Mr. Whiz acted as if he didn't notice. "Even as cold as it is, the sun'll melt it a bit. We got to clear as much of the walk and the steps as we can before it freezes into ice—or it's going to be a real job on Sunday. The ash we saved up we'll spread on the steps and walks."

Will thought about his father going to the hospital. Not likely he even got up. He'd awaken with a terrible headache and open another bottle of whiskey to kill the pain. One look at the snow and he'd crawl back under some hay in the barn. He wouldn't care, let alone know, what happened to his mother.

"Will, while you finish filling those hoppers, I'll start on the walks. God knows I'm getting too old to do all this myself. He must have sent you over." Mr. Whiz stomped into his boots. "No, wait. Slip your gear back on. I'll never get that door open wide enough for me until a little more of the snow is shoveled aside."

Will swung over to get his boots and coat; rather, to get Mr. Sutter's boots and coat. It was Saturday. Again, he wondered—was he going to get paid? Will berated himself—thinking of money at a time like this. He needed to visit his mother; he needed to get done.

"Take your time shoveling that coal. Pace yourself," Mr. Whiz said. "You're going to be at it a long time, not like your one-hour stints on weekdays."

"Do you get paid more for all this extra work, Mr. Whiz?" He looked at the custodian from the corners of his eyes.

Mr. Whiz smiled. "I get a salary, on contract. It doesn't matter how little or how much work I have to do. I'm the custodian. My job is to take care of this building, no matter what it needs. Remember, I told you and Sam about the budget and all the things I had to do and buy for this building? Anyway, it will probably never snow like this again in my lifetime—maybe yours."

The corners of Will's lips turned down. He risked his life to get here, had to leave his mother, must work until exhausted, and get paid nothing. And his own house—how would he ever get it all cleaned? He banged the door hard against the snow—again and again—twisting the door.

"Hey, don't break my door!" Mr. Whiz said.

Right then, Will didn't care if it did break, and shoved it extra hard one more time. He then squeezed through the small opening. With his shovel, he dug out more snow from behind the door. After Mr. Whiz got out, he had a good mind to keep on going. Maybe the hospital would allow him to visit his mother now.

* * *

After Will filled the hoppers and Mr. Whiz checked all the gauges, he had Will fill a bucket with ash and tie a rope to the handle. Mr. Whiz, from the top of the outside stairwell, pulled the bucket up and began spreading the ashes on steps and sidewalks while Will filled another bucket to be pulled up. Besides keeping the ash buckets filled for Mr. Whiz, Will also kept an eye on the coal hoppers and made sure they did not run out of coal.

But Mr. Whiz seemed to come back for ashes faster and faster. Bucket after bucket after bucket. Will wondered if he would ever get to see his mother.

He struggled to keep up. Of necessity, he rested for several seconds between shovelfuls. He stopped for a drink of water. He pulled off his shirt. Using a sleeve, he wiped the sweat from his eyes.

Will's rests between shovelfuls lasted longer and longer, and the coal in the hoppers got lower and lower. He had to work more quickly or the furnaces would go out. And Mr. Whiz would have to run up and down the steps to fill the buckets himself. Mr. Whiz would think him a slacker and fire him. Or was he working for nothing, anyway?

Suddenly the door opened and Mr. Whiz stuck in his head. Will stood upright in front of the hopper, hoping that Mr. Whiz would not be able to see into it. Will pretended he hadn't seen Mr. Whiz and shoveled more coal into the hopper.

"Will, you have to see this," Mr. Whiz said. "Grab your shirt and coat, and come on out."

Will felt his ears and neck burning. What could he say? He'd have to admit it. "I can't. The hoppers are low."

"Never mind them. We'll get them later."

Will donned his coat and began buttoning it.

"Hurry. Forget the buttons and the boots. I don't know how long this will last," Mr. Whiz said.

Will shuffled toward the door.

"Hurry!"

With his crutches, Will pulled himself up the cleared stairway as quickly as possible while Mr. Whiz waited at the top. The sun gave some warmth, but mostly had turned the world into a world of blinding light. After the dark boiler room, Will had to squint his eyes almost shut in order to be able to see at all. A bitter wind continued to rage, sending sheets of snow into the air. His body, having built up so much heat, was refreshed by the cold.

Mr. Whiz led Will along a cleared pathway toward the corner of the building.

Once past the corner, he pointed and laughed. "Will, will you look at that?"

"The farm tractor?" Will asked. "Whose is that?"

"No, not on the street, the walk."

At first, all Will saw was a dark object inside a low cloud of flying snow. It moved slowly down the sidewalk next to Wabash Avenue. He heard yelling, but did not see where it came from. Gradually, Will could see inside the heavy cloud the forms of two men heaving shovelfuls of snow as fast as they could. *I don't have time for this, I should be at the hospital with my mother! Don't you understand, Mr. Whiz?*

"It's Dr. Grover and Sam, in a shoveling race. It seems as if one can't get ahead of the other." Mr. Whiz laughed. "But I'm betting Grover poops out pretty soon. Besides, Dr. Grover offered Sam a dollar if he won."

A number of men at the other end of the walk leaned on shovels, watching and yelling, "Come on Sam, don't let that old man beat you."

Will frowned. The cloud turned the corner and started down the Washington Street walk. The cloud slowed perceptibly. Will wished he could walk without crutches. He'd be out there and beat them both and collect a dollar in just a few minutes. He could sure use a dollar, a lot more than Sam could.

Soon there was just one person shoveling; the other leaned on his shovel, watching, his breath rising like smoke from a chimney. The onlookers clapped and shouted. Lots of snow got shoveled in a short time, and Dr. Grover owed Sam a dollar. Will thought if he had won the dollar, he'd buy flowers for his mother.

"In a storm like this, a lot of the farmers, if they have a blade for their tractors, scoop out their own places, then come on into Enid to help push snow out of the streets," Mr. Whiz said. "It gets the city up and going again real quick. Teachers volunteer, too. You can bet school will be open Monday—unless it snows again."

Will picked out the men with the shovels. All of Will's male teachers were there—Mr. Bender, Mr. Goldstein, Mr. Bitterroot, and Coach Mattingly. No wonder Will couldn't keep up with the ashes and the coal with so many outside shoveling.

Sam had fun and would get a dollar. Will didn't know if he would get paid at all. He suddenly felt cold and turned to Mr. Whiz. "I need to see how my mother is doing."

Chapter 22

When Will had started the short trek to the Enid General Hospital from the school, he had hoped that he would find his mother sitting up and able to talk with him. With each swing through his crutches, his fear mounted until he had convinced himself that he would find her pale and stiff. He ignored the cleared but slippery surface and planted his crutches in front of him at ever-increasing speeds.

His father's fist pounding his mother's temple, the same phantasm he had seen on Mr. Sutter's Model T's windshield when they brought his mother to the hospital, tormented him. A fiery wrath sprang up in Will's throat. He clenched his teeth. Somehow, he would settle the score with his father.

Will looked up, amazed that he stood at the hospital entrance. He paused to gather himself. He had left school only a few minutes ago. What a difference the farmers had made with their tractors and snowplows.

He struggled against the wind to open the hospital door a crack, then levered it open with a crutch. He stepped inside. Wind whipped papers about the room. The nurse at the reception desk lunged for the papers still lifting from her desk.

"Shut that door before you turn this place inside out," the nurse said. It was Miss Steele, the young nurse who had manned the reception desk the night they had brought his mother in.

He stomped the snow from Mr. Sutter's boots and yanked his own hat from his head. He cupped his hand over his cold nose to warm it and ward off the hospital smell.

He again hoped for the best, but shook with dread. A rage smoldered in his breast, fueled by hatred for his father and fear for his mother. How anger and fear and love and hate could be so intertwined, he did not know. He was sixteen years old.

The welcome heat had not yet made it through his coat, and he shivered from the contrast between the cold under the coat and the warmth caressing his head. The late sunlight had burned the windows clear of frost and cast the room in long shadows.

Dark circles about the nurse's eyes spoke of a restless night at the hospital and long hours in service. She clutched her blue cape at her throat with one hand as she picked up papers with the other. Even though it was just yesterday, it seemed long ago since he had first seen her doing just that. She had been kind, though impassive.

He walked to the desk as she sat back down. His jaws, stiff with cold, were slow to work.

She spoke first. "I'm so glad you came, Mr. Coleman. I have a message from the doctor. All the phone lines seem to be down."

Will's temples throbbed. "I don't have a phone."

"Pardon me." She looked down. "I see that, now. And we couldn't send someone out. With this weather we have been so short-staffed. I'm sorry, I'm rambling on."

Will's ears buzzed . . . *glad you came* . . . s*end someone out* . . .sounded terribly serious—fatal. It didn't matter what else she said; he had barely heard. The room blurred. His mother must be worse.

No, coming in from the cold made him dizzy. He reset his crutches and focused on the nurse's desk name plate, *Miss Jo Anne Steele, R.N.,* and managed to stay upright. "What's the reason you're glad I came?" he mumbled.

"Please excuse me. I'm tired. Dr. Fisher . . . Let me see the exact message." Miss Steele bent and ran her finger across a line in the chart in front of her. "Dr. Fisher thought you would want to see your mother now."

Will's heart was pounding. He wondered what else it said. "*Wants* me to—*now*? She's worse, isn't she?" he managed.

"Sorry, it's the only message I have for you." The chair scraped as she stood and then walked across the room toward the hallway entrance. "Wait here a minute." He watched as her back, then her white stocking, and then her white low-heeled shoe disappeared through the doorway. The door closed.

It seemed she would never come back. Finally, the door opened. He heard whispering, followed by Miss Steele's appearance with Miss Collins, the registered nurse in charge of the critically ill. Although Miss Collins's face was gray with fatigue, she continued to hold herself stiff and erect. "Come," she said with a slight motion of her head. Will followed as she walked slowly down the hall. Will wondered if her shoulders would slump after he was out of sight.

The cold, drafty hallway clawed at Will, but he shivered from fear for his mother. He took rapid, shallow breaths.

Miss Collins stopped at room 4, placed her hand on the doorknob, and, with a keen eye, looked back at Will. She stood unmoving. "Are you okay?" she said. Only after Will nodded his head did she open the door. Inside the room, curtains darkened the windows, allowing but a dim light.

Will went immediately to his mother's side. Her head remained bound in white bandages. Her face was pale and puffy. The usual black circles beneath her eyes were blacker still. Several blankets covered her to the chin, giving her the appearance of having no body. Will, his arms wide, cried, "Momma," and then threw his body across the side of the bed and buried his face in the covers. His crutches clattered to the floor. His mother made no response.

Miss Collins moved to the other side of the bed, felt his mother's wrist with practiced fingers, and watched the second hand of her watch. "Forty-six," she said. "Forty-six beats per minute." Considering, she hesitated, then added, "That's dangerously slow."

Will nodded his understanding without lifting his head. He held back tears.

She held a glass of water with a straw to his mother's lips. His mother did not respond. She then swabbed his mother's lips with a moistened cloth. From the foot of the bed she took a small cane chair and placed it so that Will could sit near his mother's head.

"Your mother spoke your name this morning. I think she wanted you. Doctor Fisher gave his okay." Miss Collins helped Will rise. "You may talk softly to her and hold her hand." Miss Collins went to the door and backed out, carefully closing it behind her.

"Momma, it's me, Will." He lifted the cover from her side and found her hand. It was cold. He leaned toward her ear and spoke a little louder, "It's me, Momma. Will, your son." His lip quivered as he hesitated. "Momma, I love you. Wake up."

He waited, watched her breathe, and then held his own, waiting, hoping for her next breath.

"Will."

Momentarily startled, he looked into her face and tenderly drew his hand across her cheek. Her eyes remained closed. "Momma, I want you to come home."

She breathed slowly. "Where . . ." She took another breath. ". . . am I?" Her eyes fluttered beneath her lids.

"The hospital."

Her hand weakly squeezed his.

"Yes." She breathed. Her hand went limp.

"You've been sleeping almost three days."

"Will?" His mother's eyes flew open. She looked at him, but seemed not to see.

"Yes, Momma, I'm right here."

She gripped his hand with surprising strength and turned herself slightly toward him.

""I love you!" Her eyes shut, but a frown crossed her brow. "But . . . " She took several shallow breaths. ". . . your father, he can't help it—the mine." Her voice was a hollow whisper. Again, her head lay more heavily in the pillows; her grip relaxed. Her chest rose and fell slowly. Suddenly, she thrust her head forward, "Lee's dead!" And then it dropped back to her pillow.

Yes, I never had a chance to know my Uncle Lee.

Will's mother lay still for a long time, each shallow breath separated by long intervals. Will watched, and then spoke. "Dad escaped."

She seemed not to hear. And then, after long moments, she unexpectedly said, "Your father . . . loves you."

Will shook with shock. "What?"

Except for her breaths, his mother remained still. Then she stirred, seemed to gather her strength. Her lips and jaw moved. He couldn't hear her. He pushed himself up from his chair and leaned across to put his ear to her lips.

With a breath she formed a word, barely audible, hardly more than the sound of air escaping. "I . . ."

He caressed her hand. "What, Mom? 'I' what?"

"Did . . ." she breathed.

"Did what?" He spoke into her ear.

"It."

Her breaths came faster, as if she had just run.

"It?"

She breathed. "Threw . . ." She took a breath, then another. Then. ". . . dishes." Breath. A smile, one so faint only her son could read it, rested on her lips.

"You threw dishes at Dad?" His mind's eye saw his mother heave a plate at his father, striking him in the head. Will, pleased with the impossible, remembered the chaos of the kitchen and the likely furor that had put her in the hospital. But his mother had defended herself.

She made no response. Her breaths slowed once more. Her smile lingered.

Will again leaned to her ear. "Momma, I'll get him," he said, in a whisper, but with such ferocity it would have stopped the heart of a madman. "He'll never hurt you again, I promise." He felt the blood rising, pressure building in his head. He ground his teeth.

He sat there, waiting, hoping. "Never again," he heard. Had he whispered it aloud, or to himself?

The light outside the window had become gray. Will sat, hands folded, staring into the deepening shadows, allowing the pressure in his head to die down. He exhaled.

"Will," she sighed. Her eyes remained closed.

He quickly put his ear to her lips. "What is it, Momma?"

"For . . . give. . ." Again, shallow breaths came between nearly soundless words. "him."

Will, stunned, fell back into his chair. *Forgive—him?* But she, *she* threw a plate at him. How could he promise he would forgive his father? The anger rose again.

"Look how he has hurt you . . . and me. And spent all our money on whiskey. And we didn't even have enough to eat. I'm sorry, Momma, so sorry."

I'll get him!

Will watched her face—nothing. Her mouth hung open; her breaths, at irregular intervals, passed through her mouth. The sound she made was like snoring. Had she heard him?

"Momma, are you thirsty?" He got up from his chair and held on to the bed as he made his way around it. Then he took the moistened cloth and swabbed her lips as he had seen Miss Collins do it.

"When you are well, we'll go someplace far away," Will said, desperate for an encouraging word. He returned to the chair and reached for her hand.

Her chest rose. Her lips moved. She coughed once, and then her chest rose and fell rapidly, trying to get air into her lungs. She stopped as if worn out, not having the energy for another breath. A coarse gurgle rose from the depths of her throat. Will waited for her chest to rise again.

She didn't breathe. Then a gurgle, a rattling in her throat, her chest barely falling, and then no more.

Will's eyes opened wide with fear. He involuntarily squeezed her hand. "Momma, Momma, wake up!" He shook her gently. "Nurse! Miss Collins!"

Grabbing his crutches, Will raced to the door and swung it open. Light from the hall swept into the room, hurting his eyes. "Miss Collins! Help! She stopped breathing."

Remaining in the doorway, he turned toward his mother. He heard another gurgle. His own breathing was rapid and shallow. "Help!" He hurried toward the bed.

A shadow from the hall fell across the room. The light from the hallway framed the silhouette of a nurse rushing into the room. The silhouette became Miss Collins. "Get out, Mr. Coleman, please," she said.

Will, immobile, mouth agape, stared at the nurse.

Miss Collins held the door for him, hesitated, and then pushed the door shut, leaving him inside. She hurried to the far side of the room, clicked on the lamp, casting the room in a soft yellow light that lifted the shadow from her face. She hurried to the bed. "I must care for your mother now." Will moved away from the bed. She turned his mother on her side, taking care not to pull on the drip line.

Light from the hallway once more flooded the room. A large man in a white lab coat entered, reclosed the door, and brushed past him.

Miss Collins addressed the man. "Dr. Fisher, Mrs. Coleman has not been doing well. I was about to—" She glanced at Will. "And now it appears . . ."

Will shook his head, "no." Blood drained from his face. *No, his mother could not die!* He felt weak. He sagged on his crutches. Hearing it said heightened his dread.

Dr. Fisher put his stethoscope's ear tips to his ears and with its chest piece probed Will's mother's neck, chest, and abdomen, and then lifted the blanket and felt her feet.

He moved swiftly, continuing his examination, and then looked into the nurse's face, nodding his head almost imperceptibly. "But it's worth a try," he said.

The doctor turned toward Will. "You may want to leave, son." Pale blue eyes found and held Will's. "It would be best."

Trembling, Will managed to retrieve his crutches and slip into the hall. Before the door closed, he heard Dr. Fisher say, "Let's get started." Then the door closed behind him. Will strained to hear what they were saying, and then he heard hollow thumps, like someone being pounded on their back. Again, he heard talking, then pounding. After a long pause, the pounding resumed once more. Then there was silence.

Will stood in the hall, slumped on his crutches, his breathing ragged.

Finally, the door opened and the doctor stepped out. Upon seeing Will, he placed his hand on his shoulder. "I'm Doctor Fisher. I'm very sorry. This was not the first time your mother had stopped breathing. We did everything we could. You are a brave young man, Mr. Coleman. Your mother died peacefully and without pain. I'm sure she left happy because of your visit."

Will's chest expanded and rose uncontrollably, bringing in a great gulp of air.

His breath released in spasms. He would not cry, not in front of anyone.

Dr. Fisher waited several moments. "If there is any way we can be of further help, let us know. We'll leave you alone with her for a few minutes."

The doctor held out his arm to usher Miss Coleman into the hall. The black around her eyes was darker than ever. She laid her hand on Will's arm as he swung into the room. "I'm sorry, Will."

The door closed, leaving Will alone in the lamp lit room with his dead mother. He slumped in the chair and stared at the form in front of him. He felt drained and could barely think. Only minutes ago, it seemed, he had left for school, bid his mother goodbye and left her looking down the drive after him.

How could he live without her?

No one disturbed him. He sat for a long time.

Finally, he pulled himself up from the chair.

Will swung himself through the door and out into the hallway. Light glared off pure white walls into his eyes. He expected no one, but Miss Collins waited there to escort him to the vestibule. Pure willpower held him upright. Neither she nor Will spoke. The only sound heard in the hallways was the shuffling of their feet, the creak of Will's crutches, and the wind moaning at the eaves and cracks of the building. They entered the waiting area. Although almost dark outside, the evening was still early.

Miss Steele, the nurse on reception desk duty, sat with her face nearly to the top of the desk. Her hand, unmoving, gripped a pen. The inkwell was open. The staff had been on duty for brutally long hours.

Miss Collins cleared her throat. Miss Steele stirred, then jerked upright.

"Miss Steele, Mr. Coleman's mother has just passed," Miss Collins said. "Perhaps Mr. Coleman could remain here until he is ready to leave."

After a pause to get her bearings, Miss Steele looked steadily at Will. Her face was drawn and troubled. "I'm very sorry about your mother's passing, Mr. Coleman. I had been fearful of that. Won't you have a seat?"

Will nodded. He wanted to cry, but again could not. He sat stone still, gripping his gut to keep it from convulsing, and stared at the floor.

Miss Steele said, "Stay as long as you like. We could possibly get you a bed."

Stay here? No, he had a sudden urge to get away. "No, thank you. I want to go home. I have to go home." Will pulled himself up. He pulled on Mr. Sutter's coat and grabbed his hat. "Thanks for everything." He felt weak, unsteady, but waited a few moments until he took his first stride. The unsteadiness dissipated. He pulled his hat onto his head and went to the door.

"Wait, I'll help you with the door," Miss Steele said.

Chapter 23

For a long moment, Will grimaced against the glare and the wind and the heat and the chaff and the dust. One hand held his hat in place; his other arm fiercely encircled his father's waist for fear that the rhythmic bouncing would dislodge him from the tractor seat he shared with his father. His father drove with one hand; his other arm gripped Will about the shoulders.

The image of that long-ago event fled Will's reverie and was replaced by the harsh wind-driven snow that stung Will's cheeks and eyes and even bit his skin beneath his winter garb. Now Will rode with the farmer who had noticed his struggle against the bitter wind. He glanced at the man's bronzed face and tightened his grip on the seat to keep from falling beneath the tractor's huge wheel.

Mr. Whiz's prediction of a plunging thermometer was certainly true, and was backed up by the unbridled wind howling down Randolph Avenue. Will hardly cared; the sting on his cheeks could not compare to the pain which tore his heart. That the kindly farmer had picked him up after he left the hospital meant that he would be home sooner to confront his father.

With emotions roiling inside, Will grew oblivious to the cold and the occasional waves of warmth coming off the tractor's engine. The trauma of losing his mother buried itself; fear for what lay ahead replaced it. Images of the cold, dark, shattered kitchen and his father lying in the barn hugging a bottle of whiskey flared through his mind. There was no chance that his father had cleaned up the mess he had created, nor started a fire in the stove, let alone prepared something to eat.

Seemingly shortened by the snow surrounding them and bent beneath their white burden, the evergreens at the corner lot looked strange. "This is my road," Will shouted above the roar of the wind and the engine, barely in time to keep from passing it.

The farmer turned onto Grant, stopped, and geared the tractor down so it could push through the unplowed road. "You'd never make it up there on foot," he shouted above the noise. "I'll take you right to your door."

Sharing the hard, bouncing seat had been uncomfortable, but as they approached Will's house, Will lamented the end of the ride.

"You sure someone is home, son?" the farmer yelled. He cut off the engine. "It looks mighty dark."

"Yes, sir, my father's home." In the barn, anyway. Maybe frozen.

"I'd be glad to come in with you, make sure everything's okay. Don't see no light in the window or nothing. It's getting mighty late. Seems it's turned dark here in the last thirty seconds. Kinda spooky."

Will started. He had almost forgotten. "Shoot, I could use some matches for my lantern."

Without them, he would be in a pickle. He held his breath and watched the farmer's hand as it unbuttoned the top two buttons of his coat, then fished around inside it. His hand extracted a small box of wooden matches. "You can have these. I've plenty more at my place."

Weak with relief, Will said, "Thanks. You sure?"

"Glad I could help. It's getting so dark and cold, think I'll go back to town and give Hotel Youngblood a whirl."

Will hadn't thought about the farmer getting home. He probably lived far from Enid. The drifting snow and the night would make it difficult to see the roads in open country. Will wanted to invite him to stay the night, but considering the condition of his house, he couldn't.

The farmer helped Will to the ground. Will struggled through the snow bank that guarded his door. As he reached the threshold where he had found his mother lying, and standing on that very spot, he suddenly wanted to kill his father, so much so that his hands shook. He turned and waved to the farmer. He tried to make it look natural. His voice trembled as he called out, "Good-bye."

Angry tears came into his eyes. Feeling weak, he stood a few moments longer to regain his strength.

The house was darker than Will expected, and colder, too. Leaving the door open to glean as much illumination as possible from the fading light, he dodged around the chaos in the kitchen to the opposite side of the room. There, near the back door, he found their old spare lantern under an upended chair and a kitchen towel.

He lit the lantern and sighed, and then closed the door. He was tired, cold, thirsty, and hungry, and the house was hours from being put into a hospitable condition. Remarkably, the tea kettle still sat on the stove. He picked it up. Its weight suggested it contained water, but it would not slosh around—its water had frozen. Suddenly, his body felt leaden, his breaths deep and slow. Even though standing, he fought to keep his eyes open. His exhaustion precluded any expression of anger, not even about his father.

He would have to work to solve the last three of his four problems, but his fatigue bid him take care of it first. Perhaps his blankets would provide enough warmth for sleep. He made his way to his bedroom, pulled the door curtain aside and raised his lamp. His countenance fell. His blankets were still at the hospital. If he were to bed down immediately, he would have to use his father's, still filthy with vomit and urine, and strewn on the floor.

He opened the kitchen cabinet and found exactly the food he expected. Grits—and more grits—and they would have to be prepared, which meant cooking.

Fortunately, the wood box contained a quantity of firewood. With all the strength he could muster, he cleaned the ashes out of the stove's firebox, retrieved the hatchet and set about shaving the lumber to create some tinder. He then split the wood to produce some kindling.

The tasks warmed his body and drove away the sensation of fatigue. He hung Mr. Sutter's coat on the back of a chair.

He thought back to when he was nine years old and his family had lived on their Haskell County farm. Will, supposedly chopping kindling, had instead imagined himself a great warrior and threw the hatchet at the rough outline of a man formed by the wood grain of the outhouse siding. Again and again his tomahawk bounced harmlessly off the wood. His father stepped out from behind the side of the outhouse, caught the hatchet in midair and hurled it into a wooden post twenty feet behind Will. He then taught Will how to throw a tomahawk. It was one of Will's best memories.

But now . . . his father had beaten his mother and killed her. He stared at the hatchet and imagined his father lying in the barn. He raised the hatchet over the wood, and with lips pulled back over gritted teeth, brought the blade down. He saw it cleave his father's skull into two.

No! Will tossed the hatchet into the box with the firewood and looked at his hand with repulsion. His father deserved to die, but not with a split skull. Or, maybe he did. He would be asleep; it would be quick. He wouldn't even know that he had died.

But the police would know who did it. That would mean running and hiding forever, or the electric chair.

And what of Irene? He would never see her again. A longing and sadness welled up within him. No, that would not work. He wanted her to be in his life forever.

She would hate him now if she knew what he was contemplating. He would never let her know about this, not these thoughts.

He picked up the hatchet and brought the blade down hard on a length of wood. It split with a crack. He chopped again. There—the piece that split off—that was his answer. It went to a point with a long sharp blade, shaped like a dagger. After he used it on his father, he would burn it in the stove. There would be no incriminating murder weapon for the police to find.

Will's heart beat hard. Could he really do that? Even if not suspected, he would have to hold this terrible act inside for his entire life. For his mother, it would be worth it. He must do it.

Will chopped. Better daggers split off. He stopped and clutched the amulet at his breast. Were the daggers a sign from Uba Pisku?

After setting aside three of his best daggers, Will opened the stove's damper, placed his tinder in the stove firebox, lit it, and then fed the growing fire increasingly larger pieces of kindling. Finally, he filled the firebox with firewood and readjusted the damper. He cleared the kitchen table and pulled it and a chair closer to the stove. The coal lamp and matches he placed in the middle of the table. He sat in the chair, turned off the lamp, and with the warmth from the stove behind him, laid his head on the table and promptly went to sleep.

Will shivered awake. Something had awakened him. He looked around stiffly. There—

the silhouette of a man appeared in the rear doorway, backlit by the approaching dawn. Then the door slammed shut. A cold blast swept the room. Coals in the stove flared. Dim light danced across a shadowy figure, then was lost to the darkened stove. A chill coursed across Will's scalp, down his spine, and froze him to the spot. Surely, the figure was his father.

Unsure of whether he had been seen, and not wanting his presence to be known, Will remained silent in the nearly black kitchen. He carefully reached for a crutch leaning against the table and with it lowered himself to the floor, then pulled himself silently to the nearby firewood box. He felt for a dagger, but in doing so, rattled the wood inside the box.

The figure standing motionless in front of the door spoke with thick tongue. "It's me, Charlie. Who's there?"

Hearing his father's voice brought back Will's emotions of hate and anger and confusion. He crouched lower and felt in the box for a dagger, but his hand found the hatchet.

"I know you're there; you're by the stove. Why you hiding? Answer me!"

"I'm not. I'm getting some wood." Will slipped the hatchet into the box to free his hands and swung the fire door open. He threw in a stick of wood. "The fire's getting low. I'll put in another piece." He fumbled for the hatchet again but his fingers finally found a dagger. Good; he had no desire to go to prison. He shoved another stick of firewood into the stove and slammed the door shut. Slipping the dagger into a belt loop, he pulled himself up. Old pains shot through his body. He made his way back to the table.

The fresh wood in the stove caught, popped. Light flickered from stove joints and vents, seeming to cast shadows rather than light.

His father moved toward him.

"Wait. I'll light the lamp." Will struck a match. It flamed.

His father spoke before the lamp light spread through the room. "You can't be up to go to school with weather like today's."

"It's Sat—no, Sunday. School's tomorrow. I'll go unless it snows again."

His father's eyes swept the room. "Why is this stuff all over the place? What you been up to, boy?"

Will kept at a distance while his eyes followed his father shuffling stiffly toward his parents' bedroom, knocking items aside with his legs. His father's wrinkled clothes hung on him, and his coat sagged open. Straw stuck out randomly from his hair and clothes. Although his father hated any semblance of having a white man's facial features, he had not plucked his few facial hairs, as had been his custom.

He stumbled on the door curtains lying at the foot of his bedroom doorway. He stuck his head around the doorjamb. "Vera, where are you? Woman, why aren't you cooking breakfast?"

The stove clanged as it picked up heat.

"I'll beat you to a pulp." He almost seemed to have forgotten Will until he awkwardly turned back to the kitchen. Lamp light caught the front of his clothes. He raised his voice. "Where's your mother?"

Will gasped. Dark burgundy blotches had splattered the front of his father's coat. And his knuckles were black. Will's mother's blood! His own blood went cold.

"'Where is she? I said.'" Light from the lantern cast long shadows across his father's sunken cheeks. He seemed darker than ever.

"She's dead." Will said. Suddenly he wanted to hurt him as much as he could.

"What do you mean, 'dead'?"

"Dead! Dead! You killed her. Look, on the front of you—her blood!"

"What you talking about? I haven't even seen her." His father squeezed the back of his neck—another one of his headaches.

"You clubbed her unconscious, and then left her out in the blizzard to freeze to death. Me and Mr. Sutter took her to the hospital in the blizzard. She's there now."

"I'll knock *you* unconscious." He moved stiffly toward Will, stumbled, but regained his footing. "Where is she?" Will swung carefully out of his way, remaining on the other side of the table. His father was strong, even when drunk. Will pulled his dagger from the belt loop and held the weapon low, behind his thigh, just in case. He'd never let his father beat him again.

"I told you, at the hospital. Enid General Hospital. They probably want to know what you want done with her body."

"Watch your mouth. Show respect for your mother. I'm not fooling with you. She probably got caught at the neighbor's in this storm. And get this place cleaned up, boy. I don't know what's got into you. Leave you alone and you tear the place apart. You haven't learned your lesson yet." His mouth twisted cruelly. "Come here, so I can give you one." He staggered around the table toward Will.

Will brought his wooden knife from behind his leg and pointed it at his father's stomach. "You'll never hurt me again. Stay away—or I'll kill you!"

His father brought back his ham of a fist and aimed it at Will's head. Will pushed himself inside the blow and his father's jab glanced harmlessly off Will's shoulder. With all his might, Will thrust his wooden blade at his father's belly. The dagger hit the whiskey bottle his father had shoved inside his pants waist. Will heard the blade crack as his fist holding the handle sank into his father's gut. His father doubled over. Taking advantage of his momentum, Will jabbed his blunted weapon into his father's neck. His father gagged, and already off balance, fell sideways onto the litter-strewn floor. With his crutches, Will propelled himself at his father until he was standing over him. Taking one crutch, he pile-drove the crutch down into his father, again and again, until the man seized Will's crutch and pushed Will back. Will stumbled backwards and landed on the floor. Using his other crutch, he fought to rise before his father could get up.

His father, clutching his stomach with one arm, pulled himself up using an overturned chair. He put his fingers to his neck and then stared at them, but in the dim lantern light saw little. "Sticky—my blood," he panted, still holding his stomach. His eyes gleamed with surprise and hatred. Hauling the bottle from his beltline by its neck, he smashed it against the iron stove. Shattered glass clinked on the stove and the floor. Liquor from the broken bottle sizzled on the stove top, sending the odor of Power's Gold Label through the room. His father brandished his newly formed weapon high, its jagged edges finding whatever light they could.

Will backed away from his father and circled around the stove, seeking to get to the wood box and his hatchet. Backing more, he ducked under the hot stove pipe, and waited at a crutch's length as his father marched toward him. Seeing the pipe, his father lowered his head. At that moment Will struck the pipe with his crutch. Hot grey dust and smoke spewed from joints onto his father and into his eyes.

"Ow! The mine blew! North! You snake!" his father shouted and covered his eyes with his hands. "You let this happen. Seventy-two men. You buried them alive, North. Seventy-two. Fred, Orrie, Ted, Ronnie, Jimmy—you killed 'em, you killed them all, you long-eared jackass." He shook the jagged bottle in front of him.

"Dad, Dad! It's me, Will." Had the situation not been so serious, Will would have laughed. Circling the hot stove, he reached across it with his crutch and jabbed his father. "It's me, Will."

His father, unseeing, swatted at the crutch. "Lee! Lee! Are you down there?" Tears streamed down his face. "I'll get you, North. I'll make you pay." Not realizing he faced the back of the blistering stove, his father blindly thrust the shattered bottle at Will and fell across the stove. His hands met the scorching top. He screamed. The bottle clattered to the floor. Wiping at his eyes with his sleeve, he lurched for the back door and fumbled it open. Once outside, he plunged his hands into a snowdrift near the house.

Will hurriedly retrieved the hatchet from the wood box and raced to the door. Behind Mr. Sutter's house rested a long band of burnt orange sky, split in half by the old barn. High overhead a gray dome slowly assumed a blue tint. Against this backdrop was centered his father's shadowed outline—a bullseye. He looked on as his father knelt in the snow, soothing his burnt hands. To kill his father now would certainly send Will to prison. There had to be a better, safer, way.

Finally, his father rose, wiped at his eyes with his sleeve, and, leaning against the icy blast, staggered across the wind-scrubbed ground toward the barn and his whiskey. His drunken state twice brought him to the ground.

"Forgive him," Will's mother had said with her dying breath.

Just words. She had not understood. She died because of *him*. Will saw nothing but a repulsive, hateful, pathetic man—a monster.

Will's world turned red. Blood thundered in his ears. *Life imprisonment, even execution*—so what?

His face twisted in rage; he hefted the hatchet a few times. He cocked his arm back and hurled his tomahawk at his father. It spun perfectly to bury its sharp blade deep into his father's back. But his father stumbled again and the handle struck first. The weapon fell, ringing on the frozen earth.

Will sucked in his breath and then stood transfixed while his father turned to face him. His father's eyes searched the ground until they found the hatchet. Gone were the unsteady legs. He crouched and grasped the hatchet with a burned hand, rose, drew back his arm, the other arm forward in balance, and yelled, "This is how—" The wind flung the words away. His arm shot forward. The rotating hatchet grew larger, whirled toward Will's head, only to whistle by his ear and bury its blade with a thunk into the porch post next to him.

Will's heart froze. He leaned on his crutch and fought to remain upright.

His father shook a fist. "Next time, I won't miss." He turned and continued toward the barn. Meeting a snowdrift near the barn, he again dipped his hands in the cold snow, and then slogged toward the opening.

The wind rose, buffeted them, and prodded the barn until it leaned further still. A few more inches of snow, and it would fall down. Will looked hopefully at the clear blue sky. A few white clouds scudded before the wind; no hope for snow soon.

He watched his father plant himself to keep from falling. Then the wind abated, and his father disappeared into the barn.

Will went back through the open door through which much of the house's heat had been stripped. With the whirling blade large in his mind's eye, he slammed the door against the wind. He threw himself into the chair at the table, put his brow upon the tabletop, and listened as his heart sped to recover its lost beats.

Anger and hatred had raged through him, but upon flinging the axe, had his heart, at the last instant, kept him from killing his father? Or was it his father's slight stumble? Had his father, by the same love, returned the favor? Or had he drunkenly missed his target? *"Next time, I won't miss,"* his father had said.

Will pushed himself to his feet, put on Mr. Sutter's coat and retrieved the broom. *There won't be a next time.* He swung himself out the back door. Outside, he shut the door behind him. He surveyed the snow piled against the back of the house. Somewhere near the door was what he wanted. He swept the snow aside until a long-handled tool presented itself. Lifting it and holding it with two hands, he examined the head of his father's maul like it was a gift. "12 lbs" had been stamped in its side. A smile crossed his face with thoughts of his plan. *"Third time's the charm,"* so the saying goes. But his stomach turned sour as he contemplated its conclusion. But it had to be done. *Momma, it's really for you.*

In one hand Will gripped a crutch and the hammer handle near the maul head. He swung through the opening into the barn. Its low overhead added to the gloom. His father's deep snoring guided him through the dark as he moved slowly into the barn's depth.

When his eyes adjusted, Will discerned his father's prone form and, as expected, the stacked boxes of liquor. Will ducked his head below the leaning side so that he could move to a position where he could examine his father more closely.

His father lay on his back, his arms wide. A hand gripped a whiskey bottle. His coat remained unfastened and open. The whiskey in his veins undoubtedly numbed the cold, also lessened by the insulating snow piled on the side of the barn. The wound in his neck had stopped bleeding.

This man was the exact opposite of the one who had cared for him when he was a boy. Lying here was the man who beat his mother and him unreasonably, even to the point of death. This man, his father, Charlie Coleman, had killed his wife, Will's mother, the one person who had been willing to sacrifice everything for them. His father's only promise had been to continue to hurt them.

No one but Will himself recognized that Charlie Coleman was a killer who deserved to die. Only he, Will Coleman, would carry out that sentence. Now was the time of execution. And it would look like an accident, as if fate had decided it.

Will's eyes found the two posts that ran from the floor to the roof's beam. Because of the barn's imminent collapse, they leaned at an extreme angle along with the barn's sides and roof. They no longer bore the core weight of the roof. Knocking these timbers out from under the collapsing barn appeared an easy task. Getting out safely would be the trick. In the stillness he heard the blood pounding in his ears. He'd worry about escape when the time came.

He went to the post furthest from the entrance, set his crutches beneath him in order to swing the maul, screwed his face into a snarl, brought it back behind him. *Momma, this is for you!*

He struck the base of the post hard. And again. *Take that you dirty killer!* The handle stung his hands and his momentum pitched him to the side, but he hardly noticed. He lifted the sledgehammer once more, but stopped suddenly. The post bore indentations and chips from the maul's head.

Will retrieved an empty whiskey box and carried it outside, knocked it apart with his sledge hammer, and then returned to the same post with one of the box's sides. Leaning the side against the post to shield it from his blows' marks, he planted himself with crutches spread, lifted the maul high over his shoulder and brought it down. There was a dull thud. He examined the post. Only his shield bore the scar from the blow.

He replanted his crutches to keep from falling and swung again. After the fifth swing, Will feared he would not be successful at all. He paused a few moments to catch his breath, and then put all his might into the stroke. His blow knocked him completely from his feet, but the post had skidded a quarter of an inch.

He'd make it slide until it came down.

With several more thunderous blows, the post gave a loud "crack." Large, jagged splinters opened near where he had struck the beam. The old post creaked and groaned as it splintered apart. The barn shifted. Cracking and screeching sounded from the whole barn. Overhead, openings between boards spewed snow and dust and bits of wood. The rear of the barn picked up speed in its descent and landed with a "whomp!" Dust, straw and snow exploded into the air. Will held a crutch upright and went to his knees. He held his breath and froze as the section near the opening creaked and settled lower. When the movement and noises stopped, he exhaled. Debris settled to the floor. The whole barn, in a mighty twist, sloped away from the last post at a severe angle. In the direction where his father lay, the building sagged nearly to the ground. No one would be able to even kneel there, let alone stand.

Will watched and listened—nothing from where his father lay.

Gathering his gear, he crawled his way beneath the toppled roof toward the second post. From where he stood there was good passage to the barn's opening. When he brought the second post down, that opening would disappear. At the first sign the barn was in total collapse, he would flee.

He leaned the shield, the whiskey box's side, against the post. He didn't want to take any chance that an investigator would detect that either post had been pounded.

He squared himself up with the post, readied his maul, looked briefly over his shoulder at his exit, and slammed the hammer into the shield. As Will prepared for the next blow he heard a screech overhead. He looked up. The top of the barn, where post met ridge, was shifting. It picked up speed and dove downward. Pieces collided with each other. The barn groaned.

With crutches and sledgehammer in hand, Will pressed for the exit. He jerked to a stop and reached back for the shield. A piece of overhead lumber swung loose and broke free. Its end crashed into the bottom of his crutch, his probable location had he not stopped. He threw the shield and the maul as far as he could toward the opening and thrust himself after them. Then, as everything above him caved in, he launched himself at the floor. He tried to keep a crutch upright while putting his other arm over his head. He squeezed his eyes shut. The rending of lumber and the screech of nails pulled from their resting places assaulted his ears. Another section of roof tore loose and sailed down. Its corner thudded into the floor.

Then all was quiet except for the rush of wind. Will felt the crush of lumber. He opened his eyes. Where the roof had been torn apart, light made a rough circle on the floor just feet from his head.

Will snorted and blew dust from his nose. With his back he pushed against the piece of siding that pinned him down. He could not lift it. He squirmed and rotated his body enough to shove the board aside and crawl from the rubble. The sun, directly overhead, blinded him. Cold wind penetrated his coat to reach his body, damp from his efforts. Squinting, and from his knees, he pushed boards aside to find his crutches.

A large section of roofing leaned on something. Will shoved the section hard, again, and then again. Finally, it slipped to the side and crashed to the ground, revealing his crutch. Will sighed. His oak crutch had saved him. He examined it—not even a crack. His other crutch lay nearby.

Will became aware of a searing pain in his cheek. He gingerly touched it with his fingertips. They came away bloody. Otherwise, surprisingly, he felt very little pain, not even in his back. Also, he had nearly made it out of the barn before it trapped him. Assuredly, Uba Pisku had protected him.

He picked his way to the edge of the rubble and there gathered the maul and a little farther, the well-pounded Power's Gold Label box side— the shield. He leaned the maul back against the house and worked the hatchet from the door jamb.

Will paused at the doorway to scan his suddenly strange surroundings. The barn, flattened, seemed to have disappeared. Distant trees and the horizon soared in its place. Nearby, boards lay loose and splintered. Collecting them to cut firewood would certainly be easier.

Snow, blown from the roof, came down; its icy particles stung Will's skin. An icicle, dislodged by the wind and sun, plunged from an eave and disappeared into a mound of snow.

Chapter 24

Will stared at the collapsed barn. His heart pounded. He had really done it. Fear and self-loathing enveloped him.

He'd killed his own father.

He was a murderer.

He would get the electric chair.

Irene would hate him.

And his mother! Gone! Forever! His chest rose and fell rapidly. Tears rimmed his eyes. He shuddered as he fought for control.

What was he to do? Slow down. Take one step at a time. Blot everything else from consciousness.

First, burn the battered whiskey box.

He carried the box inside, split it with the hatchet, and added the pieces to the stove's glowing coals. The dry wood quickly flared. If he was going to keep warm, he would need considerably more fuel.

But there was no point building the fire. He must get away—his father's body was lying out there. Hopefully, the weather would be cold for a long, long time. More snow would be good. Right away they would see that the barn had collapsed; they wouldn't be surprised. But it would be long before anyone cleared away the wreckage. By the time anyone discovered his father's body, he would be far away.

Even if they found the body right away, "What a shame," they'd say. "A terrible accident."

His father had told him many boys younger than him were hobos. He would hop a train and start a new life somewhere else. He had no reason to stay here—except Irene. He wasn't worthy of her, especially now. He would never forget her. His heart already ached for her. She would probably forget him and would marry LeRoy. She deserved better than LeRoy. The thought of LeRoy with Irene set his teeth on edge—so much for blotting out his thoughts and taking one step at a time.

But if he ran away, it would show his guilt. He had to do the opposite. That was why he went to all the trouble of making the barn fall—to make his father's death seem like an accident. To prove his innocence, he had to find his body. Or try to. Get him out from under the barn. And maybe get someone to help.

Mr. Sutter again? "What a pity," Mrs. Sutter would say. "That poor boy lost his mother and now his father—so tragic."

No! He did not want people to feel sorry for him. He must take care of things himself. But to find anyone under that wreckage, no one would expect him—a cripple . . .

"Never use that word again!" Will's head jerked around. He half expected to see his father standing over him.

* * *

Will hustled from the house, found a shovel to use as a pry, and swung to the collapsed barn.

There, where the siding was raised a little, that was probably the rubble under which his father was buried. Will jammed the shovel between boards and pried. He worked at several points before the board gave way enough for him to lift. He bent to peer inside. Surprisingly, warm air from the opening caressed his face. He figured the sun's rays had pierced the siding. At the same time, the blanket of snow kept in the generated heat, like the greenhouse effect he had learned about in biology class. He pried another plank loose and threw it aside.

The siding was higher off the ground than a person's body would hold it. The reason became apparent. Two whiskey boxes, one stacked upon the other, supported the fallen side of the barn. Maybe they had saved his father. Will shuddered. He stooped to look beneath the shored-up lumber. He allowed his eyes to adjust to the darkness, but saw no body. Strangely, he felt relief. But surely his father was dead, somewhere near this spot, near his beloved whiskey—Power's Gold Label.

Will tore at the boards adjacent to the hole he had made. Perspiration dampened his shirt. He removed his coat. Cold air, finding his moist skin, set him shivering, but he kept working. He freed a board, set it on end, and then pushed it out of the way. He struggled to lift a large section, but gave up and returned to loosening each piece separately. More and more of the dirt floor showed itself. No father. Inexplicably, a cold fear gripped Will's heart. He looked around, half expecting to see his father.

To make sure his father had not slipped away, Will hurried to the immediate perimeter of the house to examine the snow. No footprints led from the barn or the house in any direction. And his father would have had to pass him to enter the house.

Will moved to the other side of the opening he had made. He attacked a piece of siding. Pain wracked his back and seared his legs. He must block the pain and the fear. He thought about Irene, how beautiful she was. Her eyes had lingered on his as they read "Duet" to each other in English class.

The wind swept the sky of clouds and his skin of perspiration. The sun, from directly overhead, warmed his body.

Unexpectedly, cold air won his attention. He looked for the sun. It had slid behind him, already resting on the roof of his house. He pulled on his coat and then stood there, leaning on his crutches, aware that he had become terribly hungry and thirsty. He needed to find his father soon or he would be too weak to continue. But he couldn't stop, or he'd lose the last of the day's light.

He tested the water pump. The sun had freed it from the storm's icy paralysis. He drank deeply.

Would the pump freeze up tonight? He retrieved the kettle and a pot, filled them both and returned them to the stove inside the house. Outside, he cast about for pieces of wood which had splintered from the fallen boards, then filled the wood box by the stove to overflowing. He threw a few chunks into the firebox to keep the fire from the Power's Gold Label box from going out. Soon, he would need hot water.

He resumed his search. By dusk he would not be able to see his father lying among the fallen planks. He paused to rest and then freed a board to peer below it. The dirt was strangely dark. Blood soaked—he was sure. A lump rose in his throat. Gritting his teeth, he thrust the shovel between the next two boards and put all his weight on the handle. Nails squealed and the board popped up. There lay his father, face down, the earthen floor dark around his head and next to his side. So still, like his mother had been barely days ago. Shocked, Will straightened.

Very little blood stained his father's back.

"Dad! Dad!"

Will let himself down onto his knees and pulled on his father's shoulder with all his might, slowly turning him over. Blood ran from his father's head and side. That meant he must be alive. He could not let him bleed to death.

Will pulled himself up with his crutches and sped to the house where he searched for clean cloth to use as bandages. The shelf beneath the sink produced dish towels. From his room he retrieved a pair of clean underwear. With these, he hustled back outside. He tightly bandaged his father's head and pressed a wad of cloth on the wound in his father's side. Something needed to hold the cloth in place. His eyes rested upon his father's suspenders. Will slipped them off and tied them around him and the dressing. His father moaned.

"Dad, I'm here. I'll help you."

His father's lips moved.

Will lowered his ear to his father's lips. "What, Dad?"

"D . . . drink."

Will hustled to the house and returned with a curtain he had yanked from his bedroom doorway and his father's old tin cup, which he filled at the pump. He set the cup on a board, rolled the curtain into a pillow, and placed it beneath his father's head. Will fed him sips of the water. His father coughed and stared up into Will's eyes.

"My arm . . ." His father moaned again. "I think . . ." Blood had soaked through the coat sleeve and darkened the front of the coat.

Will tugged at the coat sleeve. "Let me loo—"

"Oww! Let it be. Ahh."

"I've got to get someone to take you to the hospital."

His father's chest rose and fell rapidly. "No . . . a drink . . ."

Will brought more water to his father's lips. He sipped a little but then pressed his lips shut. His face twisted in pain.

"I'll get you a doctor."

His father slowly wagged his head from side to side. "No. Dammit! A drink. Whiskey. Power's . . . Gold," he said in a hoarse whisper. "The barn."

"You've already been drinking day and night. Maybe the barn smashed the bottles."

His father's eyes pleaded.

Will frowned, but made his way to where the boxes of Gold Label stood. He cleared debris from the top of an opened box and pulled out a bottle. Will stood looking at the label. Maybe this would put his father out of his misery for good. It would be his own doing. And a lot easier for Will.

Will returned with the bottle.

"Open it," his father whispered.

Will removed the cap. The odor of whiskey brought a frown to Will's face. He handed the bottle to his father who swilled the golden liquid until one-fourth of the bottle had been drunk. His head fell back onto the rolled curtain.

"I'll be all right now," his father said. "Help me up." His head fell back. "No, wait while I get my breath."

Will, leaning on his crutches, pulled his father up while he got his legs under him. Then, clinging to Will, and thus seeming to share a crutch between them, they made their way slowly through the downtrodden snow and into the house. Will settled his father onto a chair and tossed some wood into the stove. The water had not yet boiled.

Will leaned on his crutches. Exhausted, they looked at each other, waiting. His father's arm lay limp in his lap.

His father spoke first. "I heard that racket you were making. Then I saw you strike the post. I tried to get out, but I was too late." His eyes narrowed. "You knew I was there. You try to kill me, Will?"

Will wondered why his father asked. He knew Will had thrown the hatchet at him.

"Mom's dead. You killed her." Will spoke evenly, keeping his emotions in check.

"You egg. I know. Leave me be; stop telling me about it. She's in the hospital. We had a fight, a bad one." He swallowed and slumped lower on the chair. "I must have hit her hard."

Involuntarily, Will's fist curled into a ball. "You remember now." He wanted to accuse his father of previously lying, to punch him in the face, but that was pointless. "Why are you always so hateful?"

"It isn't hate. I only want what is best for you and your mother."

"Yeah. And what is that?"

Will waited, but his father sat slumped, his eyes closed, his hand pressed over his mouth.

"You're always hurting us." Will prodded. "And now . . ."

"I want you to grow up strong, independent. Your mother always took up for you. Not letting you do for yourself, because you're . . ." His head hanging, he pulled his hair with his one good hand. "Is she really . . . dead?"

Tears slid down Will's cheeks. He wiped them with the back of his hand. He expected his father to say, "Choctaw braves don't cry."

"She's gone, Dad. Really gone."

His father gasped and stared at Will. "I'm sorry. I'm so sorry. I didn't mean to hurt her that bad."

If Will didn't know better, he would think a tear glistened on a rim of his father's eye. "Why would you want to hurt her at all? You were always hurting her. That didn't help."

"So she would let you learn. I know you can do anything. If she did it for you, then you couldn't."

"So now you think I'm helpless?" Will said.

"If you can do, it's because of my discipline—the punishment."

"I still don't see what beating Mom did, except hurt her."

"Did it work or not? Are you helpless, or can you take care of yourself?"

"Because you beat Mom, you think that made me self-sufficient? She wanted what was best for me, too. She taught me a lot, and to be kind and considerate. Not hateful."

"If she taught you so well, then be kind and considerate . . . of me. If I taught you best, then . . ." His father began breathing extra hard. "Then, then if what you say is true, if my way was so bad, then let me die. Die from the wounds you inflicted on me. Let yourself be that murderer. How terribly then I have taught you. Father—murderer! Son—murderer!"

His father's words stabbed Will to the core.

"How I wish I was not," his father said. "Velma, please forgive me. Velma . . ." His eyes sought Will's. "I know how much you loved her. I loved her. Will, forgive me." He looked to the ceiling. "Forgive me."

There were tears. Will was sure of it. Tears from a Choctaw warrior—a weapon.

"It's too late for that," Will said. "That won't bring her back."

"Not for you to forgive me. I don't blame you for trying to . . . to kill me. That is what you were trying to do, wasn't it? I almost wish you would have."

"If you don't blame me, why should I forgive you? Then I'm doing what you deserve, what you want. Do you even forgive yourself?" Will sneered. "Are you willing to change? You still had to take a nip, even after all of this. I hate you! How do I know you wouldn't do it all over again? You don't think I remember the time in Haskell County, when you knocked Mom out, and then, when the police came, you begged forgiveness? And she forgave you. Do you think I was too little to remember that?"

"The whiskey is for my arm, to relieve the pain. And this time will be different. As rotten as you say I am, I forgive you for trying to kill me. Can't you forgive me, then?"

"What for? I didn't ask you to forgive me. You deserved to die, but are still alive. I should leave you here alone, throw this wood back outside. You couldn't take care of yourself now, couldn't get wood. You'd starve. Or freeze to death. In your condition, you could never walk through the snow."

Will squinted and thought aloud. "I could go for help now and be really slow about it. By the time I got back, you would be dead. Nobody is going to blame me. They'll think I tried to help."

"Will, I didn't think you were like that."

"I'm not. I'm just so mad, Dad. Mom—you killed her. Even if I help you now, you are going to jail."

"Okay, Will, one last time. Forgive me. Let me know that you do before I die. Be like your mother. Forgive me. And I'll be like her; I forgive you. If I die, and you don't forgive me, you'll regret it. I know. If I live, I'll never tell what you did, if that is what is worrying you."

"I don't care. Nobody would believe you. Everybody knows that old barn was falling down. You can't make me forgive you. Even if I said the words and didn't mean it, what is that?"

Will stared coldly at his father. "I'll cook us some grits. I'm starving and can't do anything more. Then I'll cut some wood to make sure you keep warm while I'm gone for help. You aren't going to die. I'll make sure of that. You can be miserable the rest of your life.

"Here's your bottle. I'll leave a pan on the stove. You can decide whether to drink your whiskey or pour it into the pan and allow it to cook out. Let me get you some willow bark from off of the shelf. Use that for your pain."

* * *

Will stood at the front of his house and looked across the unbroken snow toward Mr. Sutter's house. The snow was deeper than before, much deeper, and he didn't want to face going across that field again, although now he had a coat and boots. Besides, that old car could not make it through high unplowed snow, chains on or not. He looked down the drive at the tractor's tracks leading to Chestnut Avenue and let out a deep breath. The drive led in the direction he needed to go—and also the reason he wanted to head that way.

Chapter 25

The reality of what he was about to do slapped Will in the face—hard. He trembled, but not from the cold. He mentally turned and stared at the door behind him, but found nothing behind it—no warmth, no love, no mother. The north wind whipped at his back. He searched the big Oklahoma sky for a sign. The clear blue that everybody loved was dimming now, with a tinge of crimson to the west. Up high, the wind blasted the clouds into long wisps. It would probably snow in a day or two. His father had taught him to read the sky.

He swung on his crutches, following the furrows in his drive left by the farmer's tractor. In places, he dragged himself through drifts above his knees. He paused to pull his hat down and sighed.

Compared to crossing the open fields, using the streets doubled the length of his walk to the railway. But the snow and drifts in the open were more than he could have managed. The farmers, with their tractors, had plowed the streets. Besides, heading down his drive placed him on Randolph Avenue, Irene's street. He had to see her. Perhaps she would be outside, savoring the snow. If not, he would knock on her door.

Each crutch handle had tied to it a bundle of clothes wrapped in a square cut from his door curtain. His backpack, with its heavier provisions of grits and a pan, weighed him down. The heft and feel of the hatchet under his belt at his left hip annoyed him, but he considered it indispensable. For practice, he had spent a few minutes drawing the hatchet quickly from beneath his coat with his right hand. Hopefully, he would only need it for chopping wood. One of their kitchen knives rested in a homemade sheath tied to the outside of his calf beneath his pants. His amulet bobbed against his chest, reminding him of the precious contents of his shirt pocket. Through his coat he patted the pocket, making sure the carefully folded paper was there. He had labored over it during numerous evenings without knowing when the time for giving it would arrive.

He must get it to her house. He must place it directly into her hand or else her father would destroy it. Even thoughts of his own father and mother, or of the train he hoped would take him to Haskell County and his relatives, was replaced by Irene's face. His breathing came more quickly at the thought of his arrival at her house. His very life, his reason for existence, lived there. How could he have entertained the thought of not seeing her before he left? His heart ached with yearning.

He reached then lingered at the spot next to the sidewalk where, during their walk, he had bid Irene a bittersweet goodbye. He finally moved on, but then stopped where they had fallen with her on top of him. The memory of her so deliciously close embraced him. Their laughter had resounded up the street. He recalled how, before that, he had relished the warmth from her body as they sat together on her sofa and she looked into his eyes, feeding him wonderfully delicious cookies. Then they presented "Duet" to her mother, the poem they had read to each other breathlessly in Mrs. Johnson's class. In spite of a room full of students, it had been as if no one else had been present.

Looking down at his feet, he realized he had been in the same place for uncounted minutes. The poem welled once more into his mind. Hurrying, he swung his legs between his crutches.

He was here, in front of her house, standing in the plowed street. He looked up her shoveled sidewalk at her front door. He would, at least, tell her goodbye and gaze once more into her black dancing eyes. And at her lips, begging him to kiss them. He would hand her the paper in his shirt pocket, the poem he had written for her at home while everyone slept.

Never mind Mr. North. Will would push him aside. Will did not care what he thought, not any more.

Or would telling her goodbye be too hurtful for her? Would it not be best to disappear, not evoking memories and creating new ones? Or would she say, "He did not even say goodbye?"

Will stood long, longing. The vapor of his breath rose, betraying that he was indeed alive and not a statue, and not hewn from ice and cloaked in clothes. A bus, coming from behind him, revealed its approach by the snow-muffled sound of its clanking chains. He turned to look. The bus slowed, then stopped across from him. The driver slid open his side window. "Want a ride?"

Will started. Perhaps this was the answer, but he had very little money, only a few cents, not enough for a fare.

"Free!" the driver said.

A lone passenger midway down the bus stared at him, the window fogged by the passenger's breath.

Will shook his head. "No thanks."

The driver slid his window shut. The bus moved on, finalizing Will's decision.

With his crutches he struggled to step over the piled snow that the plows had heaped along the side of the road—and then he was on Irene's shoveled walk. Only a small snowdrift stood between Irene and him. He moved swiftly.

He rang the doorbell. Silence answered, and then footsteps, but not Irene's hurried dancing ones. The door opened a bit. Who would visit on a cold snow-filled, late afternoon? Mrs. North's face appeared at the crack in the door. It then swung wide.

"Will! Do come in! Get yourself warm. I'll call Irene."

Will set his crutches over the threshold and swung inside the doorway.

"Like the devil! Let her be," Mr. North said from his easy chair. He shook the newspaper he had been reading to add emphasis.

"Please, Mr. North, I only need to see Irene for a few minutes." Will reached inside his coat and pulled the poem from his shirt pocket.

North stood and threw his paper aside. "She's confined to her room. And you . . ." His forefinger stabbed the air. "I told you to never set foot on my property again, and to leave my family alone. Now, git!"

"Don't pay any attention to him, Will. I'll call Irene for you."

Before Mrs. North finished speaking Will heard the clatter of footsteps skimming down the stairs. It sounded like the same happy patter he had heard on her porch steps that first icy morning.

Irene rounded the landing. Shining eyes met his. She flew at him. In spite of her sturdy build, her feet skimmed over the floor.

Will braced himself. He saw only Irene, her arms outstretched toward him. He saw not her mother, not her father, not the room.

"Will!" she said.

His heart exploded in his chest. That she cared so that she ran at him, he could hardly fathom.

A shadow slid between them and blotted her out. Mr. North's body took form as Irene's momentum carried her into her father's back and rocked him into Will. Mr. North snarled as his nose banged into Will's. "You—and that good luck charm of yours—keep away from Irene."

Will rubbed his nose and leaned to one side to look at Irene. "Irene, I'm leaving town. I need to talk to you."

"Like the Devil you'll talk to her." North moved to keep his position between Will and Irene.

"Oh, Will. Please. You can't go!" Irene said.

"Irene, I'm going to—"

"Shut up! And you get yourself back to your room, young lady," North yelled. He turned to face his daughter. "You are not to talk to him—ever." He took her by the arm and turned her around.

"I didn't do anything to deserve locking up."

"Please, Mr. North, let her go," Will said through gritted teeth. Sam's advice to use his crutch on bullies popped into mind.

"Let her go, or what?" North, his face red, turned to Will. "She's *my* daughter."

"Let her go, or—or—I'll explain what you did at the mining company. I bet they don't know the danger you left the miners in."

"*You* don't know anything, you lying Injun." North increased his grip on Irene's arm. "You weren't there. Get out!"

"No! Not until I talk with her—privately."

"Daddy, please let go, you're hurting me." Irene struggled to pull her arm away. North released her arm but entwined his fingers into her sweater.

Will stepped within inches of North's face. "Let go of her!"

North retreated a step. He released Irene's sweater. "You're nothing but a lying Injun."

Mrs. North frowned at her husband. "Just let him talk, Ira. We know you didn't do anything wrong. I'm sure it's nothing."

"You're right. It'll be nothing but a tale."

Irene and her mother looked at Will.

"Tell us, Will," Irene said.

"You heard about the mine explosion, right?" Will asked.

Mrs. North nodded 'yes.'

"I knew Daddy worked there. Oh, Daddy! Were you almost killed?" Irene said.

North cast his eyes aside. "Nothing like that. You wouldn't understand. My job didn't require me to go into the mine. Nothing I did made that explosion. Don't listen to that Injun."

"See?" Irene said. "Daddy didn't have anything to do with it."

"Maybe if he would have gone into the mine, it could have been prevented," Will said.

"You know how bad it was? Seventy-two men were killed. One was my Uncle Lee."

Words tumbled from Will. "But my father did go down into the mine—the Number 6. He was mine foreman. The morning of the disaster, before it happened, he ran to your father's office—the Number 6 manager's office."

Will pressed between Irene and her mother and glowered at North. "My father ran to your office. He told you to get the men out immediately, close the mine. There was gas in the mine. You refused, wouldn't order the miners out. My father was so mad, he knocked you off your office chair."

North looked at his wife, his eyes wide. "That's an obvious lie. Nobody would ignore a legitimate warning. Why wouldn't I order the men out? In fact, with the slightest hint of something wrong, that was the standing procedure. As foreman, Charlie Coleman, Will's father, was supposed to evacuate the mine—and he didn't. That's why I fired him. He was responsible for all those men's deaths. He should have been jailed—hung."

"I'll never forget your reply to my father, Mr. North. You said, 'What happened? Did the little birdie die?' And it had. Then you said, 'Go back to work.'"

"Ira, you didn't!" Mrs. North said.

North blanched and looked at his wife's feet. "You believe him? How . . ." The words caught and he cleared his throat. "How could that boy know all this? He wasn't even born yet." North glanced at the women. "He thinks up lies faster than a fox chasing a jackrabbit."

"Not long ago my father told me all about the mine disaster. Also, I heard him many times, when I was too little to understand, saying things to my mother. Sometimes she cried because of my Uncle Lee."

Irene stared intently at Will, coming closer to him. "What's that mean about a 'little birdie,' Will?"

"Miners carry caged canaries into a mine. The gas kills them even when the miners don't notice the gas. The reason your father had said what he did was because a canary had died weeks before in this mine, and the miners had run out. But there was no fire or explosion."

Will turned to North. "Mr. North, without inspecting the mine, you ordered the men back to work—or be fired. Irene, the men didn't smell the gas, but a canary died again, and they came out. Your father said no fires, no explosion, it was safe, go back. My father tried to stop them. They were afraid they would be fired, so they went back down."

"Your father made up that lie about the canary to cover up. You think he would tell you the truth about himself?"

Irene and her mother looked expectantly at Will. Irene's eyes narrowed. "Will, did you ever wonder why your father wasn't with them?"

"Why wasn't my father in the mine at that time? Like I told you he was—"

"Because he was afraid." North scowled, his lips were at a half smile. "I could see it in Charlie's eyes when he came into my office."

"Afraid of what, Mr. North?"

"To be in the mine, of course." North sniggered.

"He'd been a miner before he became foreman. And he still worked down in the mine. He knew he had to keep the men out, but they didn't listen to him, so he came to you—again. This time it was urgent. If he thought everything was okay, he would have been with them. You fired him because you didn't like what he kept telling you. And he was so persistent this time. Like I said, he even fought you. You fired him minutes *before* the explosion."

"He was lazy, trying to get out of work."

"If you had admitted the problems, mining operations would have had to stop until the mine was fixed. But it was producing so much coal, making the company lots of money, that it looked good for you. That mine needed more ways to control the air so it wouldn't mix with explosive gas. That took time and—"

"You think you're some kind of mining engineer?"

"—and money. No, my father explained this. The roof supports were too far apart. It was cheaper and faster to mine that way. Even getting safety lamps—Mr. North, you balked at that. My father didn't tell me this, but maybe you don't even believe canaries die from mine gas.

"Then the mine exploded, killing all those men. You blamed it on my father and said he didn't report any problems with the mine—he showed me the newspaper clipping."

North stuck out his finger. "There's the proof of his incompetency—it was in the paper."

"Because that's what you told the reporter. The men that knew my father, what happened, were dead."

"I told the truth then, and I'm telling it now."

"Even if true that my father was afraid, which he wasn't, you in effect admitted my father told you earlier there were problems in the mine, things miners should be afraid of. But they went in any way. Did you ever go down into the mine, Mr. North?"

"Oh, Ira." Mrs. North shook her head. "After that disaster—that's why we rushed off to Enid so fast," Her eyes, wide in recognition, glued themselves to her husband. "You could have remained with the mine, you said, but we left for the 'opportunities in *Enid*.' I can hardly believe it. You didn't want to face Charlie Coleman and what you had done—or not done. Were *you* fired, Ira?"

North shrunk back; his voice caught in his throat. "Of course not. Why would you think such a thing? Enid Bank belongs to San Bois. What else would Coleman tell his family, but lies about how it wasn't his fault?"

"The truth—we don't lie!" Will said. "Even when I was little—the same bits and pieces. Then recently he told me all about it, and it made sense."

Will glowered at North. "What have you been telling your family? Nothing. If you want to show yourself to be a decent man, admit the truth. Also, you could get help for my father now. He's at home—injured, dying. The barn collapsed on him."

"Another lie. You have no proof. Your father had none. You just want to get me out of here so you can get with my daughter. You are one slick SOB, just like your father. Irene has a lot better fellow than you after her. She doesn't like you. There's the door, use it!"

"Will, you don't have to go," Irene said. She slipped next to him to put her hand on his arm.

Will glared at North. "Proof or no proof, we know what happened. And so does Mr. Mattison. He probably won't admit it either."

North looked at his wife.

"Don't look to me. I think we know what happened, now."

"You believe that rotten Injun! How could you?"

Will turned to Irene. "Here, Irene." He handed her the poem. "I wrote this for you." North opened his mouth to object, but said nothing. He looked at Irene, then stared toward the far wall.

"Irene, I'm going to Haskell County, where I used to live," Will said. "I'm leaving here. I'll let them know at the hospital about my father." Will directed his voice at North. "And I'll tell them that I told you, just in case that's helpful. Mr. North, this is your chance to show yourself to be somebody. You can get there faster than I can, maybe even drive him to the hospital. Goodbye, Irene. I'll never forget you. I'll be back for you. You can count on it."

"Will, you are welcome here, any time," Mrs. North said. She threw a defiant stare at North.

Irene's eyes, red around their rims, met his. Tears spilled down her cheeks. She turned and ran up the steps.

Will's heart felt squeezed as if in a vice. He turned and hurried his way through the still open door. It slammed behind him. He swung down the walk and turned to look up at Irene's empty bedroom window. He kept walking, albeit slowly.

It occurred to him that even at this very moment—perhaps, she was reading his poem. He had attached a note that read:

"Dear Irene, I wrote this just for you. I hope you like it. Love, Will."

It had been hard for him to write "Love." Even now, his breath came in short gasps. Would she understand? Did she feel the same way? Would she laugh at him? Would he ever know?

Maybe Mr. North was right. LeRoy was the one for her.

No! LeRoy Mattison would never have her! He had to make sure.

His heart pounding in his chest, Will bulled his way through snow between houses until he was on Maple Avenue, the street behind Irene's, and turned back toward her house.

Upon reaching the rear of her house, he again struggled through snow, past the North's garage, through their backyard, and up to the house. A small porch, designed primarily to protect the rear door from the weather, lay directly beneath the second-floor window. The snow on the porch's roof glistened from the light cast through the window's curtains. Whether this window looked out from Irene's bedroom, he did not know. He hoped everyone, except Irene, was downstairs.

Immediately, he saw how he could access the window. The drainpipe from the porch gutter was fastened to a supporting post. If he could climb a rope to the gym ceiling, surely, he could climb the 8 feet of pipe to that roof. The roof sloped gently, but the snow on it was deep.

Was he acting rashly, stupidly? Surely, Irene cared if he disappeared, never to be seen again. Maybe it was selfish, but he wanted her to know his plans, why he needed to leave. He had to tell her that his mother had died and more about his father. He would tell her how much he loved her. That he really meant his promise to her that he would come back for her. If she felt the same way she would wait for him. He would hold that promise in his heart wherever he went. Weakness flooded him at the thought.

If she didn't love him, he would look like a fool, lying in the snow on the roof outside her window. He smiled at the imagery. How it would hurt! She was worth that chance.

Moreover, if Mr. North caught him, what could North do?

Chapter 26

Will left his belongings on the porch below him. Climbing the spout was more difficult than he had imagined. Pulling himself up the pipe was hard, but clearing the snow in front of him from the roof while finding enough traction to pull himself up the slippery slope took every ounce of strength in his fingers and arms.

He lay on the roof, gripped the windowsill, and tapped the window, hoping only Irene heard. Cold from the roof penetrated his very core. His hand clutching the sill stiffened into a claw. He rapped harder and waited. Finally, footsteps approached. The curtains parted. In the dim light, he saw his beautiful Irene. Her face was drawn. His own, benumbed with cold, could not break into the grin it felt.

Unable to see past her own reflection in the glass into the night, Irene put her nose to the window and peered past him. He tapped. She recoiled, clapped her hands over her heart, then looked again. She saw him and broke into a smile. With a forefinger to her lips, she signaled to him to remain quiet.

She struggled to open the window. It was stuck. She pushed around the window frame to loosen it. Will watched helplessly while the cold bored into him. Seconds were like minutes.

Finally, the window flew open. She grabbed Will by the coat and hauled him inside.

The bedroom was a narrow open attic room running from the front to the back of the house with sloping ceilings on each side. Single windows looked out the gable ends. An open stairway nearer to the front window led to the main floor.

The warmer room temperature set Will to shivering.

"Oh, Will, you're so cold. I can feel it coming off of you," she whispered. She grabbed his hands to support him. "Your hands are like ice."

Actually, he could barely move, stiff as a shirt hung out to dry in freezing cold.

"Don't you have gloves?"

"N-no. S-s-sometimes I p-pull my hands inside my s-sleeves. Usually w-w-walking on crutches works my hands and they get warm."

"Shhh!" she said, "Speak softly." She pointed at the floor. She turned on a radio atop a small table.

"Wow! You h-have your own r-r-radio."

She nodded. "It will help cover up our talking—if we whisper. Where are your crutches?"

He continued to look at the radio, and then gestured toward the ground outside. "On the porch."

She supported him by an arm. Her lips brushed his ear. "Sit on the bed while I take your coat so the room can warm you." She guided him to her bed located between the stairway and the center of the room. Her breath, warm in his ear, mesmerized him. "I read your poem. I loved it."

He felt a thud in his chest. She began unbuttoning his coat. The thuds came faster.

Again, she whispered into his ear, "You said you'd be back." She stifled a giggle. "I didn't know it would be so soon."

He loved her closeness. Her warm breath caressed his neck.

With difficulty, she pulled his coat from his rigid body, sat next to him, and then put her arms around him. "I have to warm you up. I wouldn't do this if you weren't so cold."

She read the hurt flitting through his eyes.

"Oh, I want to, but it's not right. I mean, well . . . we're not . . ."

Downstairs, the doorbell rang, from its distance, softly cut into their conversation. They sat quietly; their ears trained on the stairway.

"Come on in, LeRoy." The words floated up the steps. "Make yourself at home and get warm." Will could scarcely hear Mrs. North. He held his breath while Irene involuntarily squeezed his hand.

"I came to see Irene. With the snow and all, I just haven't been able to get out. And looking for a place to park, and then it was so far away, I might as well have walked from home."

Mr. North said something about walking.

"I'll get her from upstairs, Mrs. North said. "She'll be happy to see you."

"Thank you, Mrs. North."

"Good to see you, LeRoy," North's voice carried up the stairs. He must have arisen from his chair. "Take off your coat. Your father let you drive his Studebaker in this snow?"

"Yes, sir. He says I'm a better driver than he is."

And then louder, "Don't trouble yourself, Mrs. North. I can go on up."

"We don't usually permit young men to visit in our daughter's bedroom." It was North's voice. "But since it's you, go on up and bring her down."

"Ira, are you going to start breaking the rules now?"

"Well, she is sixteen. Go ahead, LeRoy."

"I should take off my galoshes."

"Oh, excuse me. Let me have your coat, too, LeRoy."

Will panicked. How could he explain his presence to LeRoy? There would be chaos in the bedroom, and then downstairs. And for what? It would not end well. Or should he try to hide? Hide first. And then if caught . . .

Irene pulled Will to the side of the bed, pointed beneath it and shoved him to the floor. Will struggled to crawl under the bed. Only a leg, arm and shoulder would fit.

Irene looked at the room's light switch near the head of the stairway. Footsteps sounded on the step—too late to turn out the light.

"Don't you dare come up here, LeRoy Mattison," Irene called, and tip-toed quickly toward her chifforobe. "I don't let boys into my bedroom. Besides, I'm getting ready for bed." She opened the closet's door, grabbed her nightgown and frantically struggled to get it over her clothes.

"So early?" The footsteps neared the middle of the stairway.

Will pressed himself harder against the side of the bed.

Irene, still struggling with the nightgown, hid behind one side of her chifforobe and its open door. "You come up here and you will never see me again, LeRoy Mattison."

The footsteps paused, then continued. Will, looking under the bed, could see LeRoy's head, and then shoulders, appear above the floor. They disappeared from view above the bottom of the bed, were replaced by his body, and then his legs.

"I told you to stay out," she said

Will could see Irene's bare feet—even in this situation he noticed how beautiful her feet were—below the hem of her night gown. They flitted toward the stairway, then opened in a wide stance.

"Not one step farther," she said.

LeRoy's shoes, shiny and new, stepped toward Irene's bare feet.

"You know you wanted me to come up. Come here."

The shoes stopped next to her bare feet.

There was the sound of a loud slap.

"Oww!"

"I told you to stay out."

The shoes turned toward the stairway. Will saw LeRoy's legs, then body, then shoulders and finally head, all accompanied by the sound of footsteps descending the stairs.

Irene let out a breath. It reminded Will he could breathe again.

There were voices from downstairs, but he gave them scant heed. He smiled. He loved watching Irene's feet approach and make their way toward him. Then she was there, standing in front of him, looking fat with her nightgown over her dress. None the less, after what transpired, she looked more beautiful than ever. She reached to help him up, but he waved her off. He pushed off from the bed and stood. He was more than warm now. She removed her nightgown and returned it to the chifforobe. He could watch her night and day.

She turned the volume up on the radio a little. At the head of the steps, she pushed the off button for the overhead light. The light from downstairs floated up, soft and dim. She came back toward the bed.

The front door slammed.

From the bottom of the steps, North said, "Young lady, you should be ashamed."

Irene projected her voice toward the stairs. "I'm not feeling well. Please leave me alone. I don't want to see anyone."

Will heard Mrs. North speak softly, evidently to Mr. North.

"And all because of that dirty Indian," Mr. North replied. "She'll have to get over him."

"He's a very nice young man. You are jealous because he's smart and she likes him—and you should be ashamed of yourself."

That was the last that Will heard from the first floor.

Irene sat on the bed, patted the space beside her and whispered, "Come, Will, tell me your plans." He sat and took her hand, something he thought he would never do. Her hand was soft and smooth in his rough and sinewy ones. He had never been this bold. He blushed. She leaned against his shoulder, her head resting on his. They sat silently. He took a deep breath and let the air out slowly.

"Will?"

At that moment, the things he wanted to tell her deserted him, save the one that had chased the others away.

"I love you, Irene." There, he had said it. "I love you; I love you." He didn't want to stop. "I want you in my plans." She didn't reply, but she didn't pull away, either. She laid her head on his chest and put an arm around him. He was sure she could hear the hard pounding of his heart.

"Will, then why are you leaving? Is your whole family moving?"

How could he tell her in a brief amount of time? "My mother died." Could he tell her the rest; should he? "My father killed her. The old barn fell on him because I . . ." She would reject him if he told her. However, without her knowing, he would never know if she could really love him anyway—and for who he was. His throat seemed to close. His voice was a whisper among their whispers. "I made it fall."

Why did he tell her that? This was the end. His whole world had been hers for the taking.

Now he had thrown it away. His face sagged; tears forced their way to his eyes. He felt himself trembling, out of control, anything but a man. She would run from him.

"Oh, Will." She raised her head to look into his eyes and took both his hands in hers. "I'm so sorry. And I understand. That evening I visited—I saw what was going on." She wrapped both her arms around him, hugged him and kissed him on the cheek.

Did she only feel sorry for him? Was this a goodbye kiss?

"That's why I love you," she said. "Your courage, your honesty, and I know you are true. You are not just strong on the outside, but on the inside, too, where it really counts. I love you, too, Will." She leaned back to look at him. "And good-looking, too." She laughed, then clamped a hand over her mouth.

Heat rose in his neck and face. He felt as if he couldn't breathe. She must have misunderstood him. Really love him? The darkened room blurred. He wondered if he might be dreaming. He had never fainted in his life; he must not now. "You love me, too?" His mouth was agape. "After what I've done?"

"Yes. Can't you see, Silly? I just told you. I told you why."

Will shook his head, his eyes wide.

"You don't believe me—I'll tell you again." She pulled his head to her lips and whispered into his ear, "I . . . love . . . you!"

He pulled back to look into her eyes. "Oh, Irene, Irene!" She put a finger across his lips. He glanced to the radio, wondering if he had shouted over the radio. He remembered to whisper. "In school I watched your every move, listened to everything you said. How I hated it when you were with LeRoy, if you even looked at him."

Irene's face darkened. "Don't even mention him."

He wrapped his arms around her and pulled her to him. "Okay." His heart pounded with hers. "Believe me, I love you more than I can say. And you love me? You really love me. But I have to go back to Haskell County. I hate to leave you."

"Oh, Will. You can't. Not now. Just when we—"

"What else can I do to live? Working for Mr. Whiz isn't nearly enough. I know people in Haskell who might help me find a job. I can learn to do anything."

"How are you going to get there?"

"By train. By freight train. My father told me lots of hobos ride the train. Even boys, like my age, whose families couldn't afford to feed them, and are looking for a place to live."

She suddenly straightened up, her eyes bright and laughing. "That's so exciting. I'm going with you! I always want to be with you. My father tries to control everything I do, who I talk to, when I go to bed, what job I can get, who I'll marry. But I wouldn't leave with anyone but you. So, on the way you can tell me all about what happened in your family."

"No, you can't go. It's dangerous. Besides, you're a g—" His mother's voice rang in his head—"*He's only a cripple,*" and then his father's—"*Never say that again*," and then the beating. "Look, I brought this." He twisted to show her the hatchet hung at his side. "It's handy for lots of things—even as a tomahawk."

"Yes, I noticed it when you took off your coat."

"And this," he pulled up his pant leg to reveal the knife at his calf. "That's how dangerous it is. People get desperate, even good people, and steal—or worse."

"It will be safer with two of us. Never mind that I'm a girl. Girls can be strong and tough and all that other stuff, too."

"Irene, I couldn't stand it if something happened to you."

He paused. This was sudden. His future raced in front of him. "We would have to get married. Now. After I get established, I'll come back for you, I promise."

"Sometimes it's hard for me to make up my mind, but once I do, that's it. You try to leave now without me, and I'll be right behind you. On the other hand, you can wait a few minutes while I pack some stuff in my bag and we'll go out that window together. I'll even let you be a gentleman and get that ladder lying on its side next to the garage to help me climb down."

Will nearly laughed aloud at the thought of the ladder waiting there while he had struggled up the slippery downspout.

He rose and held himself up with the bedpost. With his other hand, he helped Irene to her feet. "I'll be more of a gentleman than that. We'll walk down that stairway and leave together by the front door. You can bid your parents goodbye."

"But my father, he'll stand in our way."

"If he can't be polite, tell you goodbye and move aside, then he won't be standing for long." Will smiled at the image of North lying unconscious on the floor.

With one arm he encircled her waist and pulled her to him. He stared at the lips that for so long had invited him to kiss them . . . and did it.

EPILOGUE

Will's Poem to Irene:

THROUGHOUT ETERNITY

For whom have I a love so rare?
Irene, the maid who is so fair.
For when I saw her standing there
I knew I would forever be
In love, throughout eternity.

But wind blew cold; snow swept away
My chances for her love that day.
She did not see my longing way.
I'd thought I would forever be
In love, throughout eternity.

A storm had never been so bold.
My love thought lost, my heart went cold.
No caress, that eve, would unfold.
I'd thought I would forever be
In love, throughout eternity.

On this the day when snow did blow
My soul within then let her know
I was the youth who loved her so.
I knew I would forever be
In love, throughout eternity.

Then hurried she to take my hand,
Our love, to share, throughout the land
For cold but brings a tighter band.
We knew we would, forever, be
In love, throughout eternity.

Made in the
USA
Middletown, DE